The Second Chance Fixer Upper

A SWEET ROMANTIC COMEDY

GRACE WORTHINGTON

The Second Chance Fixer Upper by Grace Worthington

Copyright © 2023 by Grace Worthington

Published by Poets & Saints Publishing

ISBN: 979-8-9887709-0-9

Cover Design by Alt 19 Creative

This novel is a work of fiction. Characters are the product of the author's imagination or are used fictitiously.

Get a free romcom! *The Dating Hypothesis* is available at graceworthington.com

The Dating Hypothesis

A FREE ROMCOM NOVELLA

What happens when you're forced to team up with the MOST infuriating man alive for a research experiment on dating?

You make sure you don't fall for him. Easy, right?
Not when it's the guy known as Dr. Romeo.

The Dating Hypothesis is a free prequel novella when you join Grace Worthington's newsletter at graceworthington.com.

ONE

Maeve

P eople who say children are perfectly sweet creatures have never been awakened at three in the morning by a small finger poking them in the arm.

"Mommy!" a tiny voice whispers. *Jab, jab.*

I hold my breath, hoping that if I *look* like I'm asleep, she'll give up her mission to wake me.

"Mommyyyy!" she says louder, like the long whistle of a freight train.

Lately, Violet's been waking at night with the usual complaints: *I had a scary dream. I'm itchy. I need a glass of water. My sheets are wet.* And the occasional oddball question from nowhere: *Why don't worms have bones?*

Ninety-nine percent of the time, I make a conscious effort to be a good mom: rubbing her back, offering water (except if she wet the bed), changing the sheets (because she had too much water), and explaining why worms are squishy invertebrates. But after one potty break, two back rubs, and three explanations of why worms have no eyes, bones, or hands, I've had enough. I hustle her back to bed, then collapse onto my mattress, because my five-thirty alarm will have no mercy.

But tonight, I can't seem to drag my heavy limbs out of bed.

And this time, there's no one to pinch hit. Not since Dex left. It's just one more thing I miss now that I'm single again.

The bedside light clicks on, then a tiny fist lightly taps my forehead. "Mommy, I know you're in there. Wake up."

My daughter has resorted to knocking on my face.

"Stop, Violet," I mumble, yanking off my sleep mask.

"Mommy, can I ask you a question?"

Here it comes. *Another random question about worms.*

"What is it?" I frown.

"Why do you have hair there?" She points to my face.

"Where?" I touch my cheek.

"On your chin."

"What?" I cover my chin with my hand.

"It's just one long hair."

As if that makes it better.

Now that I'm a mom, I barely have time to shower, let alone pluck every stray hair that randomly sprouts on my body.

Nobody warns you about the many ways your body turns against you as you age.

"Can I sleep with you tonight?"

I open one eye and squint at her. "Did you wet your bed again?"

"No."

"Bad dream?"

She shakes her head.

"Then what is the problem?" I ask, exasperated. Surely she didn't get up to tell me I have a rogue hair on my chin.

"There's something in the attic."

I prop myself on one elbow and give her a pointed look. "I told you before. There is no such thing as the bogeyman. Or monsters."

"Or zombies?"

I shake my head. "Especially zombies. And they do not live in closets, under beds, or in attics. They are a figment of your imagination."

"But this time I heard it!" she exclaims while playing with my tangled hair.

"You can't make up stories as an excuse to come sleep with me."

"It's not an excuse. And why is your hair so messy?" She pulls my long hair over my eyes so I can't see her.

This is the fifth time she's asked to sleep with me since we moved a few weeks ago. I'm guessing the transition of moving, along with a new school and my new job, have majorly disrupted her sleep. Which is very bad for me, since I have to act perky and engaging for my eight a.m. chemistry class at the high school.

"Violet, go to bed. *Now,*" I moan, rolling over.

"You say there are no monsters in the attic, but I hear its nails digging into the ceiling."

That's a very specific thing to say about an imaginary creature. But Violet also has a vivid imagination. That's why she thinks her dad is going to propose to me again, which is just as much of a fairy tale right now. Unbeknownst to my daughter, I stopped believing in happily ever after a long time ago.

"There is nothing in the attic," I tell her. "And we both have school tomorrow. And if I don't get some sleep, I'm going to be Miss Grumpy Pants tomorrow."

"That's okay, Mommy." Her fingers twirl my hair into two long twists. "Daddy said you were grumpy *a lot.*"

I clamp my lips to keep from saying something that I will regret about Dex. Because even though he cheated on me, I still want Violet to have a good relationship with him. "Well, Daddy's not here. The only thing that can help is sleep. And you're keeping us both from getting any of that."

She folds her hands together, begging me. "Can I sleep with you? Please?" Her high-pitched request is adorable, like she knows how to pluck my weak, vulnerable heartstrings.

"Okay."

"Yay!" she cries, crawling over my body, her knee digging into my stomach.

No one told me how easily I'd crumble when I'd have kids. As much as I don't want to make this a habit, I really hate sleeping alone since Dex left.

She settles next to my side, sinking into the warm space in the middle of the bed.

"Mommy, could you protect me from the monsters in the attic while I sleep?"

I roll over and wrap my arm around her, nuzzling her hair while breathing in the scent of strawberry toothpaste and kids' shampoo. "Violet, I'll always protect you from the monsters."

"One last thing. The hair on your chin isn't *that* noticeable. Just when the lights are on."

Thanks, kid.

When my alarm goes off a few hours later, it's like being kicked in the head. I slowly open my eyes and blink a few times. That's when I realize something *is* kicking my head.

My daughter's foot bumps against my forehead.

She's sleeping with her head at the wrong end of the bed and has stolen all the blankets.

I move her foot and gently shake her shoulder. "We need to get up."

Violet doesn't move, so I ruffle her hair. "Hey, sweetie. Time to put on your clothes for school. We can't be late again."

I used to think I was a prompt person until I had a child who took fifteen minutes to put on a pair of unicorn tights. Now I'm just lucky if I'm on time.

As Violet slowly rolls out of bed, I grab my bathrobe and head to the shower, thinking over my lesson plans for my high school biology and chemistry classes today. In biology we're doing worm dissection, so I need to find the tools for that. Then in chemistry . . . *what are we doing in chemistry?*

My mind is still foggy, but I'm sure I planned something for class. As I step into the steamy water, letting it soak my body and run down my back, Violet bursts into the bathroom.

"Mommy!" She throws back the shower curtain, interrupting

my five-minute break from parental responsibilities. "I heard it again."

"What are you talking about?" I say, pulling the curtain away so we don't flood the floor.

She pokes her head around the plastic. "You said it was a *pigment* of my imagination."

"Figment," I correct.

"I don't care. There's something up there."

I can already tell that my five-minute shower is now going to be reduced to a mere rinse-only cycle. Hopefully, it's enough to face six periods of high school students. I turn off the water and grab my towel, while Violet pokes a soft spot on my belly. "Mommy, why does your belly jiggle like that?"

I frown. "It does not jiggle." She pokes it again. So maybe it does *a little*.

Violet tilts her head and looks up at me. "Yes, it does. I just poked it, and it jiggled like Jell-O."

I grab her hand right before she pokes me again. "Mommy is *not* like Jell-O."

My body is not that much different, is it? I am softer, like motherhood gave me a softness I didn't have before. And to be honest, I like it that way. Because kids make the hard edges softer in all the right ways.

I slide on a robe and hurry out of the bathroom to the attic stairs, outside of Violet's bedroom. We've only been in this house for a few weeks, so it's only natural that she would have fears about the attic.

It doesn't help that the house is old, and the attic looks like something out of a horror movie. The rest of the house is livable, even though it's dated and worn, and has so much potential if you can see beyond the surface. In the end, what sold me on the property was that I imagined the house as it *could be* someday—a darling Cape Cod with a white picket fence—even though it looks nothing like that now.

I stop, my hand resting on the door to the attic stairs. Somewhere upstairs, there's a tiny *scratch, scratch, scratch.*

"Did you hear it?" she asks.

I paste on a confident smile. "Sounds like we have a cute little mouse."

Her face lights up. "A mouse? I've always wanted a pet."

"Um . . . absolutely not." I don't dare mention how I'm going to snap off its head and ruin all her princess dreams of mice who whip up gowns from fabric scraps.

"But what if he likes it here?" she says, looking concerned.

I shake my head. "The problem is, *I don't.*"

When I slowly open the attic door, something dashes across the attic. A small rodent leaps onto a rafter and freezes, curling a long, fluffy tail.

"That's not a mouse," I mutter in shock. "It's a humongous squirrel."

I glance around, looking for something to chase it away. I don't know how that rodent found its way inside, but I'm not about to let it squat in my attic.

As I grab a broom, the squirrel darts away, daring me to chase it. I lunge forward, swinging the broom, but the creature dashes from one storage box to another.

"Why, you little stinker . . ."

"Do you need help?" Violet asks from below.

"Nope! I'm totally fine!" I take another swing and miss again. It's like playing Whac-A-Mole at the arcade. As I lunge forward, I stumble over a shoebox and nearly twist my ankle.

The squirrel leaps to the far corner, like he's enjoying this game of keep-away.

"You wanna play dirty?" I mutter. "Because all I'm asking is for you to leave."

As I lunge forward, the squirrel tries to leap onto a rafter but misses and lands on my back instead.

I scream and wheel around, frantically trying to get the

squirrel off me. At some point, the creature tumbles to the floor, and I flee toward the stairs.

That's when I almost slam into him. A tall, bearded man with a familiar crooked smile has somehow found his way into my attic to witness my humiliation. His dark gaze is fixed on me in amusement, and I instantly flush with heat.

"I found help!" Violet says with pride. "He was riding by our house on a bike."

What Violet doesn't know is this man isn't a stranger. At least, not to me.

He's the last person I imagined in my house.

The last person I *want* to run into.

My former high school crush.

Jack Oliver.

TWO

Maeve

His eyes slide down to my bathrobe, and the heat prickles up my neck. Though my outfit reveals nothing inappropriate, this isn't exactly what I'd choose to greet my neighbors or old boyfriends in. Immediately, I wrap my arms around my body, yanking the collar of the robe tightly closed, like I'm cold, even though I'm sweating after that squirrel chase.

"We keep running into each other," I say stiffly, despite having only seen each other once at a party, right after I moved back. He talked to me briefly before returning to his friends, and I ended up leaving the party early that night, feeling like the new kid in town.

"Mommy, why are your cheeks so red?" Violet asks.

"I'm overheated," I say, fanning myself, which does nothing to actually cool me down. "A deranged squirrel just attacked me." All the blood in my body feels like it's pooling in my neck—whether from the squirrel or seeing Jack again, I'm not sure.

"*Attacked* is kind of a stretch," Jack says. "You were in the wrong place at the wrong time."

Almost like Jack riding by my house in time to see me humiliate myself.

"Do you know of any pest control companies in the area?" I ask.

He glances around the attic, then pins me down with his dark eyes, and my stomach twists. "I don't really recommend that."

His body is relaxed as he leans against the wall, arms crossed, one corner of his mouth curling with amusement. Although he still has the same boyish smile, chiseled jaw, and high cheekbones, he's added a beard and quite a bit of muscle since high school, and it's hard for me to pull my eyes away. How do some guys get *better* looking after high school?

"I can't let it stay here. I don't know what he's been eating, but he must be the laziest squirrel on the block."

Jack pauses in the corner. "It's a *she*, not a he. And I've found why she's here." He points at a mound of leaves and twigs. "She's a mom."

I scramble over to Jack's discovery, but he stops me before I get too close. Five baby squirrels snuggle together in a nest.

"Oh, no," I moan.

"What is it, Mommy?" Violet says, rushing over before I can hide the baby squirrels from her.

"Babies?" she squeals. "Can I keep them?"

"Absolutely not," I insist. "We are moving them."

"I don't recommend it," Jack says. "If you attempt to move the nest, the mama squirrel will abandon them, and they'll die."

I cross my arms. "I can't let a family of squirrels live in my attic. Next, they'll be in my house."

"Let me do some research on this." Jack pulls his phone from his pocket and starts typing.

"I don't need research. A squirrel tried to attack me."

"I doubt that," Jack says with a laugh.

He isn't taking my squirrel concerns seriously, and I'm getting annoyed.

Violet frowns. "But we can't kill them."

I glare at my daughter. "I'm *relocating*. It's different."

"Unfortunately, you can't relocate them until they're older,"

Jack says, showing me the state's wildlife laws on his phone. "They're protected under state law."

"The law protects baby squirrels? What about *me?*"

"Even if they can't be moved, they'll leave, eventually."

"Eventually?" *Like I have time to wait for that.* "I can't let these squatters stay that long. Isn't there someone I could call? An expert who knows about local wildlife?"

"Well, yes," he says, still searching for information.

"Who?"

He finally looks up. "Me. I'm a local volunteer for the wildlife rehabilitation and rescue organization."

"You?" I say, surprised. "I thought you worked for your dad's financial investment company."

"I do. This is what I do for fun."

"You find this *fun?*" The comment slips out before I can stop myself.

His mouth hitches up on one side. "Yes, Maeve. Some people *like* nature."

"I like nature," I say quickly. "When it's *outside.*"

One side of Jack's mouth quirks, and my body flushes in reaction. His smile *still* does something to me.

I turn and peek at the babies. They are somewhat cute, if you enjoy little brown rodents.

"So you're saying I'm stuck with them—until they grow up?" I ask.

"It won't be that long," he assures me. "You'll survive."

I shake my head. "No, Jack, I won't. Have you ever tried to sleep with squirrels living in your attic? They've been disturbing Violet at night." I glance at the baby squirrels nestled against each other. "I'm only giving them a week. Maybe less."

"But, Mommy!" Violet complains, and I take her by the shoulders and walk her toward the attic stairs. The chance of me making it to school early has already vanished, and I'll be lucky if I have time to brush my teeth.

Jack follows us, looking painfully aware that he's put me in a bad position. He might as well have labeled me a squirrel killer. "Is there anything I can do?"

I wheel around to face him. "I think you've done enough today. Thank you."

Jack shoves his hands into his pockets, and his T-shirt stretches across the hard lines of his shoulders. "The good news is I live about a block down the street. Not exactly neighbors. But close enough to call."

"I'll keep that in mind," I say vaguely. *Like I need Jack stopping by when I'm in my bathrobe looking like a drowned rat.*

"I mean it," he says, the corner of his mouth hitching up in an attempt at a peace offering.

Something flutters in my chest, a drowsy feeling from the past, slowly waking up. I shouldn't think about Jack's half-smile, his well-fitted shirt, or any of his exceptionally positive attributes right now. We're both different people since high school. And I'm sure Jack has a girlfriend who would appreciate me only remaining a distant acquaintance.

"I hope this isn't weird to ask," he says slowly. "But can I do something else to help?"

"Don't you have somewhere to go? Like work? Or helping an injured sea urchin or baby shark?"

He laughs, and I'm reminded of how joyful the sound is, like the full tenor of a struck bell.

"No injured animals right now. I still work for Oliver Financial, and my dad won't notice if I'm late."

Back in high school, Jack always wanted to work for his family's company and hoped to take over the business eventually. It appears that things have turned out *precisely* as planned for Jack, while my life looks like a train wreck.

"Wow, must be nice. I wish my principal didn't care if I was late."

"You're in school?" he asks.

"Sort of. I'm a high school science teacher."

"Ah, that makes sense." He nods, and his eyes grow distant, like he's remembering high school.

Violet comes out of her room, dressed for school in a pair of shorts with a butterfly T-shirt. "Can you make me breakfast?" she asks Jack directly.

"Violet, that's not how we treat guests," I say, embarrassed that she'd take up Jack's request to help.

"I don't mind." Jack turns to Violet. "I can pour a mean bowl of cereal."

Violet smiles. "Do you like Jell-O? Because my mom and I were talking . . ."

I immediately shove a hand over her mouth. "We don't have Jell-O," I say with a forced smile. "Cereal only."

Jack glances back at Violet. "Can you show me where the cereal is?"

She nods and runs off toward the kitchen while Jack follows.

I hurry into my bedroom and close the door, my body still prickling with uncomfortable heat. *Not from Jack,* I tell myself. *From the squirrel chase.* It would be entirely inappropriate to feel anything else after this long.

I glimpse myself in the mirror and cringe. My hair is still damp and uncombed, and my face is completely bare of makeup. No wonder the squirrel fled when she saw me coming. I'm surprised Jack didn't do the same.

I slide on a school T-shirt and dark jeans, thankful it's Friday and I can dress casually.

"Mommy, we're out of milk!" Violet yells from the kitchen.

Great. Now Jack probably thinks I'm an irresponsible parent. I'm definitely not winning at adulting right now.

After brushing my teeth and combing through my unruly waves, I swipe on some lipstick and mascara, hoping I look less frightening. Then I hurry downstairs, stopping in the front hall where Violet waits at the door with her backpack, her hair neatly combed with two tiny butterfly clips pinning the sides back.

My mouth falls open. "You're ready first?"

She smiles. "I even finished breakfast and brushed my teeth."

Apparently, Jack's charm works on more than just me.

I spin around to Jack. "Okay, what did you do with my *real* daughter? Because this is clearly an imposter."

He sinks his hands in his pockets and shrugs. "We enjoyed a healthy breakfast of Lucky Charms and had a nice chat about Jell-O." He winks at Violet.

I stare at Violet, praying she didn't say anything about my stomach.

"Sorry we have to rush off."

"Hey, wait," he says, then pulls something out of his pocket. He hands me an expensive protein bar that I definitely did *not* buy.

"What's this?"

"You didn't eat breakfast," he says. "I had an extra bar with me. Can't have the teacher's stomach growling during class."

"Oh, um . . . thanks," I say, slipping it into my bag while a tiny niggling feeling in my stomach reminds me why Jack and I got along so easily in high school. He was always watching out for me in ways I never could.

"Have a great day," he says, following me out to my old gold Taurus in the driveway with the duct-taped mirror and dented fender.

Remarkably, Jack doesn't seem to notice.

"I enjoyed meeting you, Violet," he says. "And I'm always around if you need another squirrel rescue."

He smiles, and his eyes sparkle like pennies glittering in the sun. For a moment, I'm caught in his gaze, and I force myself to look away, like I've been staring at an eclipse.

"That's an interesting way to fix a mirror." He nods toward the duct tape that's holding up my side mirror.

"I had an unfortunate incident backing out of the garage," I explain.

"I know a place that can fix that. I could drop the number by later."

"I've got it covered," I insist. By *got it covered*, I mean I'm pretending it doesn't exist because I don't have the money to fix it. Hopefully, he doesn't notice the pen I have jammed in my broken windshield wiper either.

I don't want Jack to see how much I'm struggling, especially since he comes from a family with more money than they know what to do with.

"Sorry, we have to run!" I give him a wave as my car rumbles to life.

He watches me back out, hands in pockets, clearly in no hurry to leave.

For some reason, I can't drag my gaze away from him, mesmerized by the fact that he looks *better* than he did when we dated, while I'm struggling not to look like a hot mess.

"Watch the mailbox!" he yells as my bumper clips something behind me.

I stop the car and lower my window. "I just took out my mailbox, didn't I?"

Jack slowly nods, trying to hide a smile.

He knows the truth as well as I do. I crashed into my mailbox because I was staring at *him*.

And that means one thing. After all these years, Jack is *still* highly distracting.

THREE

Maeve

After leaving my broken mailbox by the road, I drop Violet at school, then speed to the high school while calling Dad and eating Jack's protein bar. Hitting the mailbox was a wake-up call on this chaotic morning, and I don't need another reason for Jack to stop by.

"Good morning, Dad!" I try not to sound stressed even though I'm shaken from this morning.

"Aren't you supposed to be at school?"

"Yep, don't ask," I say, before getting right to the point. "Do you know anything about getting rid of a squirrel family from the attic?"

"Does Violet want a pet?" He chuckles.

"Don't encourage her. She's already convinced she gets to keep one."

My dad is a retired vet who has more stray pets than he knows what to do with. "You know, Bob Ross had pet squirrels."

"Bob Ross also painted happy trees. We are clearly *not* the same people. Are you familiar with any pest exterminators in town?"

"Hate to tell you this, Maeve, dear. They won't touch them." Which is exactly what Jack told me. This is not good news.

"Don't we have millions of squirrels? It's not like they're going extinct soon."

"That's not the issue. It's protecting their health and safety. My best advice is to wait and see if they leave."

Ugh. Just what Jack suggested. "That does not work with my schedule. I'm fixing up my home."

"I know, but it's the best option. Right, Julianne?" He's asking Mom, and I hear her mumble something in reply. I hate it when my parents are having a separate conversation while I'm on the phone, like this is a Zoom call and everyone leaves their microphone on. "Mom agrees with me."

Why does this feel like déjà vu all over again? Everyone is against my squirrel eviction plan.

"That's what Jack said," I grumble.

"Wait. You mean *Jack Oliver*?" Dad asks with a little too much interest. In the background, Mom asks, *Did you just say Jack Oliver? How did she meet him? Don't let her off the phone until you find out the details!*

Dad clears his throat. "Mom wants to know how you ran into him."

"Well, a funny thing happened," I say, pulling into the teachers' lot and gathering my bag. "Jack lives in my neighborhood and was biking past when I discovered the squirrels. And then Violet invited him in, and I completely humiliated myself."

"That's great!" Dad chirps, tuning out everything I've said, except for the part about Jack. "Maybe we could all have dinner together some night."

"He's really busy," I reply quickly, shooting down any possibility of setting up Jack and me. "I probably won't see him again . . . *ever.*"

In the background, Mom asks, *Maybe we could arrange something? Saturday dinner or a Sunday luncheon?*

Dad clears his throat. "Well, Mom says we could ask him over . . ."

"Um, sorry, I've got too many papers to grade. Gotta run!" I say. "Also, I knocked over my mailbox. Could you fix it? Okay, bye!" Then I hang up.

I feel a little bad cutting off my parents' idea of getting together, but I don't need any more reasons to prove to Jack that my life's a mess. Since the divorce, the transition moving back to Sully's Beach has been rocky, especially since I had to find a new teaching position. But I'm thankful to live close to my parents now, and Violet has her grandparents around whenever she wants.

The five-minute-warning bell dings, and I step up my pace, rushing into my classroom and throwing open the doors of the chemistry lab closet.

"Maeve, did you turn off your alarm again?" my art teacher friend, Annie, asks. She leans against the doorframe holding a matcha tea latte, her long boho skirt swishing around her sandals. Annie and I have known each other since college, and she's the one who helped me get this job after my divorce. Because she's the only friend I have in town, I'm forever grateful to her.

"I had an unexpected guest," I reply, only half focused on her question, because I need to assemble the supplies for demonstrating a fire triangle.

"A hot, single neighbor, by chance?" She smirks, then sips her tea.

I turn to her. *It's like she knew.* "Try my ex from high school."

Her mouth drops. "Do you mean the one you saw at that party a few weeks ago?"

I nod. The first week I returned to Sully's Beach, I happened to run into Jack's friend, Grant, who invited me to a barbecue at his house. I had no idea Jack would be there and ended up cornered with Jack before he wandered off, more interested in dancing with the other girls than talking to me.

"What happened between you two in high school?"

"We were good friends for years before he asked me to prom," I say, remembering what it was like to dance with him, his hands sliding around the curve of my waist, the way his breath hit my ear, sending a rush through me. "Then a month after senior prom, he broke up with me, saying we were too different. Our goals for the future weren't even remotely the same. And our families were even more different. He's probably so relieved we didn't end up together."

"You don't know that."

"If Jack's family knew I was a divorced woman living in a fixer-upper, they wouldn't allow him to even talk to me."

"He's a grown man. Who cares what they think?"

It still shouldn't matter, but I care. I'll never let his stepmother treat me or my family the way she did before. "You don't know Jack's evil stepmother. She despised me."

"You?" Annie lets out a laugh of disbelief. "You have so many wonderful qualities. It's impossible that anyone could dislike Maeve Baxter. All the students *adore* you. How could they not?"

"I'm sure Jack's stepmother could give you a list of reasons," I say, dropping a spoonful of oil in a heat-resistant bowl. Today's lesson is about how oil acts as a fuel for fire, and I'm only half paying attention while keeping up with Annie's questions.

"It doesn't matter anyway. I'm not interested in dating Jack— or anyone. Don't you remember how disastrous my single blind date went? I had a panic attack in the bathroom, and now I'm terrified of dating again. That's why I'm waiting for Dex to come to his senses."

She sighs. "I know you want to reconcile with your ex. But based on his behavior, I don't think he feels the same."

"What behavior? He only cheated on me with one woman, but it's not like he's dating anyone *now*. He's just trying to figure out what he wants in life."

"That's *exactly* why. He shouldn't question whether he wants *you*."

Her comment stings, but I refuse to let her squash my hope that maybe Dex will remember the good times we had before things went south. For some reason, I'm still hanging on to hope because I refuse to be a quitter. "People change," I add. "You said it yourself."

"Sometimes they do," she says. "But not always." She pauses and takes a sip of her tea. "Will you see Jack again?"

"Never." I ignore her implied suggestion that I should.

"It's been a year since the divorce. Aren't your ovaries protesting yet? Because mine would be."

"Um, excuse me, but my ovaries are none of your business. And you can tell yours to take a number. Jack probably has a long line of women. Not that he *wants* to be married."

"I bet if he met the right person . . ."

"Not Jack. He won't ever settle down. It's part of the reason we broke up. He always wanted to stay single, while I wanted a house full of kids."

I take out the matches and roll one between my fingers while Annie scrolls her phone.

"I'm going to look him up and check if he's in a relationship."

"Please *don't*." I shoot her a look, while attempting to lasso my thoughts for today's lesson, but it's like catching a squirming puppy. Everywhere I turn, everyone wants to talk about Jack. Can't she see that he's the last person I would want to date?

Our goals have always been completely misaligned. Jack's desire was to rise to the top of his dad's company and become CEO after his father. He was driven in ways that I wasn't, and he didn't want any obligations that might hold him back.

I strike the match against the box, and it bursts into flame. *I need a man who can be the hero for the woman he loves.* Not Jack.

"I don't want to know whether he's happily in love with someone," I say.

"That's good," Annie replies, turning her phone to show off Jack's Instagram page. "According to his profile, Jack's single."

"What?" I narrow my eyes and see that his bio says as much.

Suddenly, my finger burns, and I yell, dropping the match into the bowl of oil. It immediately flames.

"Oh, no, no, no," I say as the flame licks the edges of the container. I'm so distracted by Jack that I temporarily forgot I was playing with fire. And I wasn't even trying to be metaphorical.

"I'll get the extinguisher," Annie says, turning to go.

"I've got it," I say, scrambling for some baking soda and putting out the flame before the smoke alarm kicks in. Ever since Jack showed up today, I'm a bundle of nerves. Like he's lit something that's as highly combustible as this experiment.

Or maybe I've just been single for way too long with too big of a dating phobia to overcome.

"Are you okay?" Annie looks concerned as I snuff out the fire with the baking soda. "You seem off today. Are you sure you can keep from burning down this school?"

"I'm fine," I say, letting out an aggravated sigh. "Everything's under control."

Except for the squirrels in my attic and the fire in my heart.

Everything is definitely *not* under control.

Especially now that Jack is back.

FOUR

Jack

As I head outside for a morning run, my black Lab, George, sniffs the grass beside me. I'm waiting for my jogging partner to show up, and the street is blissfully quiet on this Saturday morning. I've always loved this quaint, old neighborhood that looks nothing like the obnoxious beach homes where my parents live. After living in their massive beach estate, I intentionally chose this modest neighborhood, lined with older, well-kept homes and small pockets of lawns. I can't see the water or walk to the beach, but every day I wake to the sound of children playing or the occasional dog bark—sounds I always missed in my gated community as a boy.

As the sun burns off a few stray clouds stretched out like cotton, I check my watch, waiting for Brendan to arrive. I don't really want to run, but it sounds better than tackling the financial reports I'm supposed to finish today. As the boss's son, I'm expected to work extra hours. It's part of the curse of being in a family business. As much as I hate it, I know I won't always be stuck with this job. If I'm chosen as CEO after Dad retires, I'll gladly hand off those tasks to my stepbrother, who tries to pass off work to me every chance he gets in the office now.

"What are you doing?" a voice says.

I glance over my shoulder and see Violet, dressed in unicorn tights and light-up tennis shoes.

"Trying to touch my toes."

"But you can barely touch the tops of your shoes."

I release the stretch and straighten my back. "Do you think you can do better?"

"Yep!" She bends over like her body is made of rubber bands.

I lift an eyebrow. "Impressive. You win."

She smiles, then looks at George, who's flopped down on the grass. "Can I pet your dog?"

"Sure, just be gentle. George is old." George gives me an offended look.

"I wish I had a pet," she says, rubbing George's belly.

"You don't have anything?" I ask, surprised Maeve doesn't even own a single goldfish won from a carnival. As a vet's daughter, she grew up with all kinds of odd animals.

"Mommy says we don't have the money, and that I can visit Grandpa's pets anytime. But we have to drive to their house, and it's a *whole* five minutes away."

"A whole five minutes, huh? Well, you're welcome to pet George anytime."

I look down the street, expecting to see Maeve at any moment. "Does your mom know you're here?"

She shrugs. "I don't know. She was on the phone when I left." I can tell by Violet's unconcerned tone that she probably snuck out.

"Don't you think you should tell her so she doesn't worry?"

"She was talking to someone about the baby squirrels. So far, everyone has told her they can't help us."

"Really?" I act concerned, but secretly I'm glad. "Why don't we make sure your mom knows where you are."

I send Brendan a text letting him know I'm going to be late for our run.

As I stop on the porch to ring the doorbell, Violet bursts through the front door without waiting.

"Guess what, Mommy? Jack's here!"

Maeve walks out from the kitchen, phone tucked under her ear, wearing a silky short pajama set. Her cheeks turn pink as she realizes I'm standing at her front door with my dog.

"Jack!" she says, then turns back to the phone call. "No, not you. Can I call you back? I have someone at my door."

She hangs up and then tucks her hair behind her ear self-consciously. "Violet, you should have warned me we had a visitor."

"Jack walked me home."

"You were gone?"

Violet nods and smiles.

Even though she just rolled out of bed, Maeve still looks good, with her long, wavy hair and wild green eyes that look mossy brown the closer you are. Memories roll to the surface—arms tangled up in each other, bodies pressed close, sand in our hair— and I tamp them back down.

I clear my throat. "I was about to head out for my morning run."

"I'm sorry Violet was bothering you."

"She's not a bother. I'm the one who should apologize for barging in without knocking." I keep my eyes leveled on her face. "Since you're not dressed." I realize my mistake too late. "I mean, you *are* dressed."

"I knew what you meant," she says, crossing her arms.

"Have you found anyone to help with the squirrel situation?" I ask, changing the subject.

"Nope," she says. "You were right. No one will move them."

"Does that mean I can have a pet squirrel?" Violet asks, her eyes wide.

"Absolutely not," Maeve says, ruffling her hair. "Why don't you head outside to play? Jack and I need to talk for a second."

"Can I take George?" Violet asks me. I nod and hand off George's leash.

Once Violet's gone, Maeve turns to me with a determined look. "I can't let them stay."

"If you leave them until they're able to survive on their own, then I'll move them."

"But how long will that take? I've got a house to fix up, Jack. I don't have time for squirrels."

"They're not going to attack you in your sleep."

"I know that. It's just creepy." She shivers. "What if I wake up and they're watching me?"

"You can call me." I take out my cell phone to text her my contact information. "I'll also send you the number for that car repair place."

She gives me a quick look. "Um, that's okay. We'll be fine."

Most women are only too happy to take my number, but Maeve seems wary. Maybe it's because we got off on the wrong foot yesterday.

"Give me your phone." I hold out my hand, and she pauses. "I promise not to sell your number or send you weird stuff."

She reluctantly passes her phone to me. As I'm texting her the contact info, her phone rings.

"Are you waiting on a call from a painting company?" I ask, noting the name on the screen.

"Oh, yes. I'll be right back." She takes her phone and heads into the kitchen.

As I glance at the living room, I notice the house is in worse shape than I realized the first time I was here. The walls have peeling paint and are covered with cracks, and the carpet is worn thin. This house is definitely a fixer-upper, but like most houses in the neighborhood, it has good bones. Despite these imperfections, the Cape Cod design has charming arched doorways and gorgeous built-in bookshelves in the living room, which Maeve has filled with children's books.

In the back, there's an overgrown yard of weeds that might be perfect for kids, if someone took a machete to that jungle.

As I sneak glances through Maeve's home, her voice rises from the kitchen. "That quote is more than I can afford. Is there a way to cut the cost?"

I shouldn't listen to her conversation, but it seems like Maeve has more problems than just squirrels. This house is going to take major time, and I wonder what happened to her husband and why they're not together.

"Okay, I understand," she says. "Well, thanks, anyway."

As I attempt to let myself out the front door, the door handle spins uselessly. I fiddle with it for a second, and then glance around for a screwdriver to tighten it.

Just then, Maeve returns, rubbing her forehead.

"I noticed your handle is loose." I twist it back and forth for proof.

"I've got it on my to-do list, which is about a mile long. Between all the repairs, I'll probably end up working on this place for the next ten years."

"Do you have a screwdriver? I could fix it for you in five minutes," I offer.

She hesitates and her brow furrows. "I wasn't asking you to do it."

"I know. I don't mind."

She bites her lip, trying to decide if she should let me help.

"Don't be stubborn, Maeve. It's one less thing on your to-do list."

"Okay, fine." She heads to a nearby closet and returns with a screwdriver. "Just so you know, I'm not usually this distracted. I think the squirrels are messing with my head."

"You have your hands full." I kneel to fix the handle. "What are your plans today?"

"Well, I was hoping to find a painter. But it looks like they're all out of my price range, which means I'm going to do it myself."

"It sounds better than doing spreadsheets," I say, tightening the handle. "Since I work on my computer all week, I'd rather do physical projects on the weekends." I turn the handle and it works perfectly. "The only problem is I already fixed up my house."

"You're welcome to help me paint."

"If it means I don't have to spend another Saturday doing reports, I'd love to help."

Her eyes widen. "Oh, no, I wasn't trying to twist your arm."

"It sounds fun. Seriously. And I don't have anything else to do." It's a slight oversimplification since I *always* have something due for work, but Maeve doesn't have to know that. "I'll go home and change into paint clothes and text Brendan that I can't run today."

"But aren't you like a big, important CEO or something?"

"Uh, not yet. Believe it or not, my dad *still* hasn't retired. Which means I'm free to help you."

She frowns. "What kind of weirdo are you?"

"Apparently, a weirdo who'd rather work for you than his real job."

She shakes her head. "You don't have to do this."

"I want to," I say. "Just once."

Even if I help Maeve out today, I need to keep my intentions clear. I'm not looking for something from her now that she's single. Taking over Dad's company—if that ever happens—is going to consume my life, but it also solves the one thing I can't solve myself. My mother's situation. Until that promotion happens, there isn't room in my life for any other goal.

She looks me over, then finally nods. "If you promise it's only once . . ."

"I'm not making promises," I say, giving her a look. "We know how those turn out."

If there's one lesson I learned from dating Maeve before, there's no way I'm making promises I can't keep.

FIVE

Maeve

"Why can't I help?" Violet asks, crossing her arms. "I don't want to go to Grandma and Grandpa's house."

"Because it's too messy, and I can't watch you and paint at the same time."

I slip a light jacket on her, trying to hurry her along so she leaves before Jack returns to paint

If Mom and Dad run into Jack, they'll ask too many questions, and Mom will preemptively organize a dinner party for five.

For which I can only give a resounding *No, thanks.*

Because someday Dex will come to his senses.

At least, I hope he will. And maybe I'll have it in me to trust someone again.

"I promise not to get in the way," Violet promises.

My daughter doesn't know how to *not* get in the way. And if I'm going to make whirlwind progress today, I need a kid-free environment. "It's just for today."

"But why can't I go to Daddy's house instead?" she asks.

"Because Daddy had to cancel," I say, trying to hide my disappointment. "Go brush your teeth."

Even though I love having Violet around, I worry she'll feel bad when Dex cancels on her like he did this weekend. He didn't even give an excuse. Which means I have to cover for him. *Again.*

It's something I didn't expect when I met Dex in college and then fell into a whirlwind romance with him. He said he wanted all the things I did—three kids and a house with a white picket fence close to family. But when we had Violet, things changed. He started spending more time at work and less time at home and grew distant from me. Only later did I find out he was cheating on me with someone from work.

Even then, I kept holding on to the dream that I could be married to the same person my entire life. I thought that waiting on someone to take you back was what a good wife and mom would do.

But Annie tells me I'm crazy for waiting. And my parents are still angry at Dex.

If I'm being honest, I'm still devastated. I'm just not sure I can try again with someone else.

Because once you've been hurt, it's twice as hard to open your heart again.

The doorbell rings, and I rush to the door, hoping my parents will sweep Violet off her feet with promises of a fun-filled day.

When I open it, Jack stands on the other side, wearing a smile and another fitted T-shirt that looks just as good as the last. He said he was changing into his paint clothes, even though they appear brand new. Seriously, that man could look good in a paint tarp and nothing else.

I'm wearing an oversized yellow T-shirt and ripped jeans that have clearly seen better days.

"Are those your paint clothes?" I ask as he steps inside. "Because you're going to get dirty."

"I expect to," he says, like it's no big deal.

He probably has piles of money to buy clothes, while I can barely afford new shoes for Violet.

Just then, the door opens, and my parents' astonished faces flick from Jack to me.

"This is a pleasant surprise," Mom says, a smile growing on her lips.

There's no way to avoid this unplanned meeting. "You remember Jack Oliver?"

"Couldn't forget him," Dad blurts out. "Didn't you guys date in high school?"

"Um, we were *friends*, too," I say, trying not to make a big deal out of it.

"Haven't seen you in years!" Dad holds out his hand to Jack.

"I work a lot," Jack says, shaking Dad's hand.

"Still as ambitious as ever," he says. "I always liked your drive."

Jack and Dad always got along well, and my parents were disappointed when we broke up, unlike Jack's stepmother who never thought I was good enough for their family and made no attempt to hide it.

"Jack, what are you doing here today?" Mom asks, looking Jack over.

"It's good to see you, Julianne." He gives her a hug which pleases my mother, who'll never turn a hug down. "I live down the street from Maeve, and I offered to help her paint."

"You live in *this* neighborhood? Isn't it a little *small*?" She doesn't have to say what she's really thinking. That it's too small for an Oliver. She's shocked he doesn't live in a gated community near his family.

"I wanted a smaller place," he says. "Less upkeep. And I like the history here, with the old homes and full-grown trees."

The neighborhood is about fifteen minutes from the beach and was built before the millionaires swooped in and bought all the premium beach properties, like Jack's parents.

"Are you . . ." Mom glances at Jack's hand. "Seeing someone special?"

"Mom!" I say, between clenched teeth.

Jack's face goes blank. "I'm not with anyone, no. Don't have time with my job."

"Really?" Mom's lips curl into a satisfied grin.

I step forward and open the door before she says anything else to embarrass me. "We should probably get started, don't you think?" I say, waving my parents out the door with Violet. "Jack, could you get the paintbrushes? They're in the garage."

"It was good to see you, Mr. and Mrs. Baxter." He waves before leaving, and I breathe a sigh of relief.

Mom leans toward me. "Don't pick up Violet until close to her bedtime." Then she winks at me.

That gives me plenty of time to spend on the house and with Jack. *Too much time.* "You don't need to . . ."

"You have a lot to get done." Mom shoots a knowing grin at Dad. It's clear she finds this scenario extremely amusing. Jack and I, together. All day long. *How convenient.*

"I'm not looking for a date. In case you forgot."

"I didn't forget," she says. "But have fun." She takes Violet's hand and heads to the car while Dad follows.

"Hey, Dad, thanks for fixing my mailbox."

Dad frowns. "What mailbox?" He glances over at my repaired mailbox, now on its wooden post, then shrugs. "It wasn't me."

I turn around, and Jack is holding a stepladder, smiling at me. For a moment, seeing that crooked grin sends my heart into free fall and I scramble to think of something to say. "Have you painted before?"

"I painted my house after I bought it, even though my parents couldn't comprehend why I didn't hire someone. My dad doesn't even know how to work the vacuum cleaner."

"You vacuum?" I ask, shocked. "You should *definitely* put that on your resume."

He lets out a bellow of laughter. "Does having a robot vacuum count? And don't tell anyone, but I secretly love washing the dishes."

"A man who loves to wash dishes?" I clutch my heart. "Be still my beating heart. I bet women *love* that."

"Most women assume I hire a housecleaner," he says, setting up the ladder.

Even though I'm dying of curiosity, I skip the subject of Jack's dating life. I can't let him deflate my self-esteem by knowing the number of women he's dated over the years.

"Isn't your dad paying you enough?"

"That's not the issue," he says. "Believe it or not, we're different people."

I don't say anything for a few seconds as I pry open the paint lid. "How are things going at Oliver Financial?"

"Another record-setting year," he says without enthusiasm. For someone who wants to be CEO, he doesn't sound excited.

Jack climbs the ladder and starts peeling flecks of paint. I follow his lead and grab a scraper, attacking the lower part of the wall.

"Does that mean your dad has announced his retirement?" It's all Jack has dreamed of. Becoming CEO. Making his father proud. Which is why I can't understand his lack of enthusiasm now.

"Not yet. It's up in the air who will take over since my stepbrother, Craig, wants the position too."

"Craig?" I say aghast. His stepbrother was only two years behind Jack in school, but never seemed interested in the family business. "He didn't seem like the type who'd enjoy running a business." Craig was always more interested in girls and partying, unlike Jack who was always responsible and an outstanding student.

"Elizabeth thinks he's perfect for it. And she's trying to convince my dad the same thing." Jack keeps scraping away, avoiding my gaze. "For my stepmother, it's a power play. She wants to win."

"But if Craig takes over, what happens to you?"

"It means Craig becomes my boss," he says flatly. Even though he's trying to act like it doesn't bother him, this would be a tough blow. Jack has wanted nothing more than to take over the family business after his father. No wonder he's not excited about it.

"Why would he choose Craig over you?" I ask incredulously.

"Elizabeth wants the power, and the only way she can get that is through her son. Basically, she sees me as a threat to her future."

"Wow, Jack. That's terrible."

Jack's parents split when he was in middle school, and then his dad remarried soon after. Even back then, I knew things were bad when his stepmother and brother entered his life. At least his biological mother was more grounded and made sure Jack had some sense of normalcy. She came from nothing, and had never fit into the lifestyle that his dad wanted. So when Donald Oliver remarried, he chose someone as driven as him, and Elizabeth Oliver has never stopped spending his money since.

"When I left for college, things really changed at home. Elizabeth turned my bedroom into a guest room, like I didn't even belong there. And then Mom had a stroke, and I became responsible for her care since I'm her only son. It all was so devastating at the time, but I've figured out how to work with my dad without causing family tension. It's like I have two separate parts of my life. And as long as I keep them apart, then everyone is happy."

I stop scraping and turn to look at Jack. "I'm so sorry. You shouldn't have to be the one making everyone happy, while you're miserable. That just seems wrong." I feel so insensitive complaining about my life when Jack has had the burden of pleasing his dad while taking care of his mother.

"College was rough, but I'm less unhappy than I used to be. That's why I bought a home here. It feels like I finally have a place where I can build the life I want, separate from my father and stepmother. And now that my mom lives in a long-term care facility, I visit her most days after work. Unfortunately, her insurance is fighting over her care, and we're trying to appeal. So if I don't get the CEO job, that's a big unknown."

He doesn't say it, but I'm starting to understand why Jack

moved to this neighborhood and fixed it up himself. He's using all his resources to pay for his mother's care.

"How could your dad *not* choose you? I can't imagine anyone more committed," I insist. "You're taking care of your mom. You even do your own housework. How could he need more proof?"

"It doesn't help that my stepmother makes comments about my lack of discipline."

"Undisciplined?" I almost shriek. "When you look like that?" I point to his body, as if he needs more evidence of how hardworking he is. You don't get a body like that by bingeing Netflix.

"Like what?" He stops and smirks, clearly amused by what I've just admitted. That his body is noticeably ripped.

"Like you should be on the cover of a men's fitness magazine," I say.

"According to my father, self-discipline involves two things: making money and settling down. Which is why Craig gets all the bonus points, since he's married."

I crinkle my nose in disgust. "Why would that help?"

"He thinks marriage is a sign of maturity. And hopefully, they'll give him a grandson who can take over the company."

"Seriously?" I gasp. "It's about the heir? I thought only royal families cared about that."

"My stepmother *thinks* she's royalty, and she's drilled it into Dad."

"So it's all about loyalty and power?"

"Pretty much," Jack says, a subtle pained look flashing across his face. From the outside, Jack's life looks perfect. But I can already see it's making him miserable. "Maybe you could show your dad that you've settled down, just in a different way. Has he seen your home?"

"Why would that matter?"

"To show him you're a responsible adult."

"How do you know I'm responsible?" he says, shooting me a wry grin. "I could live in a messy bachelor pad."

"Nice try, but your shoes prove my point." I nod toward his

pristine Chuck Taylor sneakers. "At least let me buy you a sandwich later as payment for helping me."

"I won't let you buy me anything." He climbs down the ladder, his dark gaze level with mine, and my heart bucks against my ribs.

He pauses, then wipes a fleck of chipped paint off my forehead, the heat pulsing where he touched me. "But I'd still love to eat with you."

He grins, and it makes me feel light as air, like I could float away.

I turn back to the wall, hiding my face, buckling down every emotion that's fighting to break free. "Good." I scrape at the wall.

Maybe it's because I've been alone for over a year—and even longer since I've been kissed. But something strange is happening as panic and excitement swell up inside me, fighting to win.

I try to tamp it down, telling myself, *We're just two friends who made plans to go out to eat, right? No big deal.*

Except it is a big deal. Because the only time I've been out with a man since my divorce, it went disastrously, and I had a panic attack in the bathroom.

I can't let that happen this time. And maybe Jack's just the person to help me get over my fears, once and for all.

SIX

Jack

"Do you want to take my car or yours?" I ask, washing the last paintbrush.

It's late for dinner, but we finished painting the living room, and it looks incredible compared to earlier today.

"If we take yours, I'll need to clean up," Maeve says. "You probably have a Porsche, and I don't want to get it dirty."

"I sold my Porsche," I say.

Her eyes widen. "Oh, well, I was kidding about the Porsche. Except you *actually* had one."

I'm not going to tell her that I sold it to provide for my mom. That will just bring up more questions I don't want to talk about. And I still have a really nice black Volvo. "Don't clean up for me."

"Well, maybe we should drive separately. I need to pick up Violet later."

"I can pick up Violet." It seems wrong to take two cars if we're headed to the same place, and I like spending time with Maeve. "It wouldn't be a problem to swing by your parents' house."

"What about those spreadsheets you're supposed to get done for work? You've got to beat Craig out for the job."

I grin, pleased that she's rooting for me, even though it's the reason we broke up. "I'm not worried about them."

In order to finish them, I'll need to pull an all-night session, but I won't tell Maeve that.

As she opens the front door, she stops and turns the handle again. "I didn't know what a pain it was to jiggle the door handle every time. But now that it works, it's such a luxury."

I shove my hands in my pockets. "If I can make your life easier with a five-minute fix, call me anytime."

She smiles. "You might regret saying that when I've asked you for a few hundred favors."

I shake my head. "You're wrong. I get weird pleasure out of helping people. Probably because I was never allowed to help anyone growing up. My stepmother considered that a form of indentured servanthood."

She tilts her head. "How did you *not* become an entitled slob?"

I burst out laughing, which makes her smile even wider. "If anyone's an entitled slob, it's Craig. He still mooches off my parents and rarely does any work other than flirting with the women in the office."

As I reach to open her car door, she rushes to open it first, intent on making it clear we're not on a date.

"What are you hungry for?" I ask.

"Something big and meaty," she says. "Like a pig slow roasted over a spit."

I lift an eyebrow. "I thought you'd ask for a salad."

She crinkles her nose. "Why would I want a salad?"

I grin as we pull onto the main road. "And if I can't find any Hawaiian luaus, then what?"

"Then Frank's would be the next best spot."

Frank's Sub Shop is where we frequently hung out in high school after basketball games. It's fast and cheap, and their sandwiches are messy, loaded with so much meat and melted cheese, half of it spills out before you eat it. Plus, Frank is the kind of owner you don't forget. His few strands of graying, thin hair stick straight up, and he has one lazy eye that wanders when he talks to you.

When we arrive at Frank's, Maeve chooses the corner booth where we always sat in high school. I don't bring up our many nights here, but it's shimmering between us, a memory of late nights and hand-holding under the table that neither of us wants to mention. Because before hand-holding and beach kisses, we were just friends. And it was everything.

"What are you getting?" she asks, searching the menu, tucking one stray wisp of hair behind her ear.

"Steak and cheese," I say, clapping my menu shut. "Let me guess. You'll order the Italian sub."

She stares at me, dumbfounded. "You have a great memory. My ex could hardly remember my birthday, let alone what I ordered."

Then your ex is a moron. How could a guy not make the effort to mark his wife's birthday on the calendar? I know it's not my place to ask, but I'm dying to know what happened.

"I just remember weird stuff about people."

She puts down her menu and rests her chin on her hand. "What do you remember about me?"

I pause, wondering if I should really say or pretend I've forgotten all about her, even though there's no way I could.

"Let me think," I say, although I don't really have to. This feels as natural as remembering my own favorites. "When you're frustrated or overwhelmed, you run your hand across your forehead, like this." I imitate her movement, the way her wrist tilts almost imperceptibly.

She frowns. "I do?"

"You also furrow your brow in this cute way," I add. "You like peach pie with ice cream. Thanksgiving is your favorite holiday after Christmas, and you can't stand the sound of people eating crunchy things." I could go on, but I don't want to creep her out.

"You remembered all that?"

"It's not like I've kept a list." Except that I have—because I'm a data head, which means I remember details that other people don't, and I keep it in a spreadsheet in my mind. Maybe it's because she was the first girl I felt something for, but I've remembered more about her than anyone I've ever dated.

Frank interrupts by taking our order on an old-fashioned notepad with a blue Bic pen that he plucks from his shirt pocket, his lazy eye drifting toward another booth.

Maeve gives me a knowing smile before ordering her usual, and then Frank shuffles away to prepare our food in the kitchen.

"I can't believe you're not dating anyone, especially as the future CEO of Oliver Financial. Aren't all the rich, single women in town begging to go out with you?"

I laugh. "I've already dated most of them, and none of them are really my type."

"The rich part or the single part?"

"All the above," I say. "They're like miniature versions of my stepmother."

"Okay, so no mini-Elizabeths," she says, studying me carefully. "What characteristics should the right girl have?"

"Someone genuine and caring."

"You sound like a Hallmark commercial," she says.

"Is it better if I say I want a lying, emotionless hag?"

"So much better," she says with a straight face. "That's at least good enough for a country love song."

"She has to drive a pickup for a country song. And I don't know if I can date a woman with bigger tires than mine."

She bursts out laughing. "Because you'll have tire envy?"

"And jacked-up-wheels envy. But at least she's a lying, emotionless hag, so there's still that," I add, grinning.

For a minute, we both stare at each other and smile, like it's a private joke only we get. The restaurant is empty except for Frank, and it feels like we're slipping right back into the same roles we had in high school.

"How about you?" I ask. "I mean, is there a male equivalent to the hag?"

"Oh, no. I'm actually terrified of the whole dating thing," she says, waving my question away.

"Maeve, you're not getting out of this. I told you my answer, and you said it sounded like a Hallmark commercial. The least you could offer is the same."

She scrunches up her lips, like she's trying to summon her courage. "Jack, I'm thirty years old, and let me tell you, it's so much harder to start dating again at thirty than it ever was in high school." She pauses, taking a sip of the tap water that Frank just dropped off. "After my divorce, my friend Annie told me I had to get back in the saddle. So I took her suggestion and tried to go out on a date with a stranger she set me up with. *He's a nice guy,* she promised. *You'll hit it off so well.* We were supposed to meet at this country karaoke place where the honky-tonk sounds like crying guitars and the line dancing is filled with hooting and hollering. Not my kind of jam, but I thought I should go, just to get that terrible first date out of the way. I was so nervous when I arrived, I could hardly breathe. My heart was hammering in my chest, and I thought I was going to die. So I ran to the bathroom and threw up before meeting him. But the problem was, I couldn't face him, I was so scared. So I stayed in the bathroom for two hours until I knew he'd returned home. Later, I learned I was having a panic attack, but the fear of having another one kept me from trying again. I couldn't take that risk."

"So you're not dating *ever* again?" I ask.

"I realized I was rushing into things. I wasn't ready to date yet. And I thought maybe this was a sign that I need to give Dex more time."

"Your ex-husband?" I try not to sound surprised, but I assumed she didn't want him back.

"Yeah, I know." She rolls her eyes. "Everyone thinks it's weird that I'd wait around for someone who cheated on me. But he isn't seeing *that woman* anymore, which gives me hope that maybe . . ." Her voice drops off, and her eyes skate out the window, hazy and distant. "I've realized that forgiving him for a single affair is the right thing to do," she says, like she's trying to convince herself it's true.

Even though I know Maeve wants to be a good person and do the right thing, I wonder if she's holding out for something that might not ever happen.

"Who was she?" I ask carefully, unsure if I'm treading into territory that's off-limits. Even though we're slipping into our old roles easily, there's still so much between us.

"Someone from Dex's office. That's the reason he wanted the divorce. He thought he was going to marry her. But now that it's over with her, I think he just needs some time."

"You think he's coming back?"

"He's Violet's father. Doesn't that count for something? At some point, he's going to see how much he misses having a family."

For her sake, I hope so. But if he doesn't, I can't stand how much this is going to hurt her and Violet.

She shrugs. "I thought if I did this for him—let him go—he would eventually come around, and realize how much he misses me. But he doesn't even look at me the same way." She shakes her head. "I just don't know how to get his attention."

"You want his attention?"

"Yeah. Why?"

"Have you considered doing something crazy? Like showing up at a party with another man?"

She looks at me like I'm the one who's crazy. "Why would I do that? Do I look like I want to have another panic attack?"

"Not a *real* date. To make him jealous. There's nothing like envy to spur a man to action."

She frowns. "But I'm not interested in anyone."

"I didn't say you had to be. You just need someone who's in on the plan."

"Who would be stupid enough to do that?"

"You'd be surprised," I say. "When there's no commitment, no expectations—no one gets hurt."

"I don't know any guy who would agree to that."

I lean back, eyeing her carefully. "I would." The words spill out before I can think them through. "As your friend, of course."

She laughs in disbelief. "You? But why?"

"Seeing your ex's expression would be priceless."

"That's a terrible idea," she says shaking her head. "I don't want to use you to make my ex jealous. That seems . . . wrong."

"Why not? I'm your ex-boyfriend. The perfect person to make him believe that you've moved on."

She runs her hand across her forehead. "I don't know. Violet might get her hopes up. And then when we call it off, she'll be devastated. Dex leaving was so hard on her."

"Then we make it clear there's zero chance of me being her new dad."

"What will our friends and family think? I can't deceive all these people. I'm a terrible liar."

"We can't tell anyone, Maeve. That's the key. Our plan would fail otherwise."

"We keep it a secret from everyone?"

I nod. "For one night."

She bites her lip. "I'm not sure. What if it drives him away even more?"

"How would it do that? He already cheated on you."

Her face flinches for a second, and I realize my comment was thoughtless. "I'm sorry, I didn't mean it like that."

She looks down at the table, thinking this over. "You're right. He's not even remotely interested in me. I need to do something drastic. Maybe dating someone else would shake him up. And if it doesn't work . . ."

"We can stop at any time," I reassure her. "This isn't an arranged marriage."

She runs her finger across her lips, thinking. "I still don't understand. You're attractive, single, and potentially about to take over a very lucrative position in your company. Why would you pretend to date me? It doesn't sound remotely believable."

"We can make it believable. You just need to be convincing. And I've done the dating scene. I'm not interested in any long-term commitments if I'm chosen as CEO. This job is going to take everything from me. It wouldn't be fair to pursue someone right now." I pause, unsure whether I should say this. "And my motives aren't entirely pure. If Dad believes I'm dating someone, it might actually work in my favor. Make him believe I'm ready to take over this company."

"Just because you're dating me?" She shakes her head. "That's the dumbest reason ever."

"I agree, but it's not dumb for Dad. He still equates settling down with maturity and leadership. I think my hard work and loyalty to the company should prove my skills, but Dad favors Craig, thanks to my stepmother's influence, because she harps on the fact he's *settled*. If I can prove I'm ready for the job, then I won't have to worry about my mom's care again because I'll have the means to pay for everything."

"So basically, I'm helping you, and you're helping me, so we're even?"

"Exactly."

She swirls the ice in her water. "I'm still not sure because . . ." She pauses, and I don't understand why she's holding back.

"Is it the logistics?"

She makes a face. "Logistics sounds like the military. Could we at least have a code name?"

"You mean cool initials only we know about?"

Frank carries over two subs and places them in front of us without a word.

"Does SOS sound too desperate?" she asks.

"Unless you're a sinking ship in need of rescue, yes."

"When it comes to dating, I *am* a sinking ship, Jack. I don't even remember how to date, let alone all the other stuff."

"What other stuff?" I ask.

"The art of . . . flirting. You know, *seduction,*" she says in a low voice. "Honestly, Jack, I've become a bore."

I laugh. "So you want to become a bimbo? That's not really how a science teacher should behave."

She smacks me on the arm. "Not a bimbo or a flirt, like you're thinking," she corrects. "I need to learn the science of attraction."

"Excuse me?" I nearly choke. I put my sandwich down and fold my hands. Because whether she realizes it, Maeve was always good at attracting the opposite sex.

"You know how in chemistry there's a formula for everything? I wonder if there's a formula for love," she says. "Some women have mastered the formula of how to attract a guy, but not me. I'm not good at flirting or knowing how to catch a guy's attention. And now that I panic on dates, it's even worse." She almost looks embarrassed.

"I'm not sure how I can help with that." *Or that I should.* "And I don't think there's a formula."

She leans her head on one hand. "I just feel out of practice. I only know how to be a mom and science teacher."

"So embrace *that*. It's beautiful how you do all these important things for others."

"I did before, and it wasn't enough. At least not for Dex." She glances at her sandwich, and I suddenly realize this is about more than dating. It's about her feeling like she's worthy of someone's unconditional love.

"Just so you know, a mom and science teacher can be attractive. You don't have to change to get him back."

I want her to believe it. Because she deserves someone who will not hurt her again.

Her eyes meet mine and there's a determination under that gaze. "I know I don't have to change, but I need to try to win him back. Figure out the formula. For Violet's sake. And you're the perfect person to help me do that."

I shake my head. "I think you have the wrong guy. I don't know any formulas."

"Jack, that's not true. I'm sure there are some universal dating rules you know. You've probably dated some experts."

She's not wrong. I've dated some professional-level flirts, and they were all wrong for me.

I don't want someone who's only trying to entice me into a temporary relationship. I want someone who will still be flirting with me when I'm eighty.

"Are you sure you want to do this? I might ruin you forever." I smirk. Perhaps if I get her comfortable with the idea of dating, she'll be able to pull this off and feel more confident.

"I'll take my chances," she says. "We're trying to figure out what works. Like an experiment."

I take out my phone and open a new note that I title: *The Attraction Formula.*

Something sparks beneath my fingers, like touching the edge of a hot pan.

What happens if the experiment goes off the rails? What if I help her crack the formula and it works *too well*? What if I'm the one who gets caught up in this game?

My own dysfunctional family has taught me that love is dangerous. Love can break you and use you and destroy you if you let people get too close.

Every loaded argument in my mind is telling me to back out now. Abandon ship. Stay in my own safe world of working harder and avoiding people who can hurt you—that it's imperative for my survival. I should let this experiment go. *Your safety depends on it, Jack.*

But I don't want to listen.

Because the other side of me—the side who plays the good guy in this drama—tells me we can both have what we want. We can both win at this game. I can pretend to have Maeve back in my life. Even if it means losing her again.

SEVEN

Maeve

When Jack pulls into my driveway for our first group date, I'm practicing my breathing exercises, letting out a slow hiss of breath, like a bicycle tire with a hole.

So far, I'm failing miserably at controlling my anxiety over this date. My heart is nervously bumping against my ribs like a Mexican jumping bean. I'm a logical person, so the fact that I agreed to participate in this experiment where I can't control the variables is highly unlike me.

As a science teacher, I should know better: Never get involved in an experiment with so many random variables. But as a person with a weird phobia, I'm desperate for help. And Jack is the only man I feel comfortable enough to try this with.

I glance down at my vintage NASA T-shirt, paired with a long bohemian skirt on loan from Annie. I hope it passes as casual boho and not a random pairing of something old with something borrowed. Annie talked me into wearing a swimsuit under my clothes—a lovely bright floral suit I bought pre-pregnancy and never wore.

Since I have no idea how adults dress for a beach party that includes swimming and games, this seems like a safe choice, somewhere between breezy cover-up and cute date wear. Because I'm pretty sure my normal Friday evening attire—pajamas with sleeping kittens on them—won't work for a nighttime beach party.

Let's be honest: I'm ignorant at knowing what people do without a small human interrupting them every second. My social life has been on hiatus for at least a decade, so I can still spend the evening in my pajamas. Even though I'm about to embark on my first adults-only party in ages, I'm feeling oddly lonely without Violet, like I'm missing an appendage. They say people who experience limb amputations still feel their missing body parts even after surgery. That's how it is when you're away from your children. Like they're still there, even when they're not. That's the weird thing about parenthood. Instead of feeling excitement, I just feel out of sorts, like I don't know what world I belong to.

Plus, the idea of curling up in bed and bingeing Netflix sounds amazing compared to parading around in a Spanx-like swimsuit I hope I don't pop out of. I haven't worn a torture device like this since before Violet was born, and it feels like a Victorian corset, reining in all my unmentionables.

Just have fun! Annie texts me. *Don't worry about a thing!*

But my idea of fun is not skipping around half-naked on the beach with body parts jiggling like Jell-O (thank you, Violet).

Maybe someday I'll have that kind of confidence, but right now, I'm just hoping I won't throw up.

As Jack's car pulls into my drive, my heart rate accelerates, and I forget all about taking long, deep, slow breaths, despite my incessant repeating *just breathe, just breathe, just breathe.*

His black Volvo is clean and shiny, like a pair of new patent leather shoes, a stark contrast to my clunker in the driveway, which looks like the doors are about to fall off.

I adjust my swimsuit under my T-shirt and vow not to get in the water. Maybe I'll make some excuse about the temperature and then eat celery all night.

I open the door before Jack reaches the house, eager to get tonight over with, and his gaze slips down to my shirt.

"Hey, is that the same shirt from high school?"

I run a hand across my stomach, trying to quell the raucous waves inside. "You remember it?"

"Of course I do. It was your favorite." He smiles, and my heart tilts precariously. "I can't believe you still have it."

The print is worn, the color faded, but it's still softly oversized, the way I like it. "I should change, then. I don't want your friends to think I haven't bought new clothes since high school."

"No, you should wear it," he insists. "My favorite shirts are from my college frat days, and I only wish they looked as good as yours. I like it on you. Reminds me of old times."

Old times? Like I'm *old*? This is not helping my confidence level. I prop my hands on my hips.

"Why do you remember everything, and I can't even remember whether my daughter put on underwear this morning?"

He laughs, then leans against the doorframe. "I wish I could forget certain things," he says, his body propped up by the frame, like the weight of these details are bearing down on him so he can't stand straight. "People remember the things they like."

Something prickles through my body, little shocks of pleasure running through my corded veins. *What does he mean by that?*

His eyes rove over me for a brief second as my heart leaps, then he looks at the ground. "You ready for this?"

"Don't be offended, but no," I say. "And in case you're wondering, *it's not you, it's me.*"

"You're already giving me the breakup speech? We haven't even gone out on one date."

"My heart doesn't know that. My stupid nerves are freaking out."

"Maeve, we're not going to a karaoke bar where ten-gallon hats are required. I won't even make you ride a mechanical bull."

"That's too bad. Because the way my stomach feels, I might as well be riding a mechanical bull."

He pulls a plastic bag out of his pocket and holds it up. "That's what this is for."

"You brought a barf bag for me?"

"In case of emergency only. Please use the bathroom if you can make it." He grins at me, and I'm falling to pieces inside. Because Jack has always been like this—the friend who remembers to take care of me when I don't even remember how.

"Please bring that barf bag on all our dates. You never know when I might need it."

He places both hands on my shoulders, pinning me in place with his gaze, and I'm suddenly highly aware of his touch shooting tingly sparks through my body. "Maeve, this isn't a date. Tell yourself that. I'm your friend, trying to help you get over your *issue*."

"I know," I say. But my body doesn't. *Just breathe. Just breathe. Just breathe.*

When I step outside, the chilly breeze hits my arms, and I cross them around me to keep warm. Without asking, he removes his jacket and drapes it over my shoulders.

"You don't have to give up your clothes," I say. "You're the one who just reminded me this isn't really a date."

"This has nothing to do with dating. You're cold. The wind is supposed to die down later. But until then, I insist you wear it."

I don't fight him on it. Because Jack just gave me a reason not to swim.

I'd forgotten this side of Jack. If you refuse to let him help, he'll force it on you.

On more than one occasion in high school, he forced me to eat when I was stressed out over a test. Even now, he makes sure I have what I need before I realize it, which feels oddly refreshing since I'm always the one making sure everyone has what they need.

While Jack backs out of the driveway, I nod toward my mailbox. "Did you see it's fixed? I still need to figure out which of my neighbors did this random act of kindness." I turn and stare at him. "Unless you want to confess to me."

His lips curl on one side. "I was wondering how long it'd take for you to figure it out."

He drapes one arm over the wheel and steers, the same way he drove in high school. Back then, it freed up his hand for holding mine, but somehow the habit stuck.

"You think I'm helpless, don't you?" I ask. "Like in the silent film where the woman is tied to the railroad tracks, crying for help."

"You are *not* helpless. You juggle parenthood with a full-time teaching job, and few people could do that."

"Well, I don't juggle it well. Have you seen my messy house? I'm completely in over my head. But even on the hard days, I remind myself that I get to do what I love."

Jack thinks about this for a second, and I wonder if he gets to do what he loves, too. He never had a choice, not the way I did. Because of his dad's expectations, Jack has been destined to work at Oliver Financial since the beginning.

"So . . . do all the boys have crushes on you?" Jack asks with a smirk.

"No . . . and gross."

"I bet they do, just like when we were in high school."

"For the record, no one had a crush on me in high school. I wasn't the popular girl."

"I think they were intimidated by you," he admits. "I was."

I frown, hardly believing this. "You were my friend. How could I intimidate you?"

"You always knew the right answers in class and didn't care if people accepted you. Your parents were these science geniuses. And that meant you didn't fit the mold of what most boys expected. You weren't the beach babe. You were the smart girl with killer wit. All the guys were scared of looking dumb around you."

I study him. "Did you feel that way?"

He shakes his head. "You weren't that way with me. You never made me feel stupid. Neither were your parents—they never let me feel inferior."

I play with my bracelet, spinning it around my wrist. "That's funny, because I felt anything *but* normal with two brainy parents. My mom is a botany professor. That isn't exactly cool when you're sixteen. I always warned my friends, *don't ask Mom about any plants unless you want a lengthy botany lecture.*"

"So you're saying I shouldn't ask your mom about the lilies I can't keep alive?"

"Unless you want to be cornered for an hour, no," I warn him. I love my mom, but she won't shut up about plants.

"At least your parents seemed happy together," Jack comments as he parks in front of Grant and Ella's house.

"They made it look easy," I say, trying to hide that slow trickle of sadness behind my words. "When I got married, I thought it would mirror theirs. Nothing prepares you for what marriage is really like."

Jack pauses, staring at Grant and Ella's restored beach home, the tangerine clouds painting the backdrop behind it. "But the right person makes the hard parts of marriage a little bit easier."

"But what if there isn't one right person?" I say. "Or maybe I'm just not that naive anymore."

I believed in happily ever after before I met Dex. But now I'm not so sure. Maybe love is about making the best of what you've got, even if it's not perfect. Maybe happily ever afters do exist, just not the way we believed or how we once thought. Aren't most people's happy endings tinged with sadness?

"You were never naive, Maeve. You're just wiser." He says it softly, like he's talking me off a cliff. "And that's why we're doing this tonight. Because you want to overcome your fears."

"But I'm actually happily single and would rather live in denial," I reply.

"You're not backing out now," Jack warns with a look. "Just be yourself."

"That's exactly the problem. I've forgotten how to be myself."

That's probably why I picked out this shirt. It reminds me of who I was before I became a mom. I want to find that girl again—naive or not—the one who was so sure about who she was and what she wanted.

Jack opens my car door and studies me. "You're overthinking things," he says, leaning on the door.

"I am not."

He raises an eyebrow.

"Okay, so I am. I haven't gone to a party since . . ."

"Since Grant invited you to the last one?" he finishes.

He has a point. "But I left early because I don't go to parties anymore. My only friend is Annie from school. And that's because she feels sorry for me." I'm rethinking this whole idea of conquering my phobia, afraid I'm going to make it worse instead of better.

"Annie isn't your friend because she feels sorry for you. She's your friend because she likes you. Which is the same reason I'm your friend." Jack gives me a lopsided smile, and the warmth of it fills me up. "Violet's in great hands with your parents, and you deserve a night away."

Maybe he's right. If I actually try to have fun, perhaps I'll forget my lack of social skills.

As I step out from the car, his arm brushes mine. It's been so long since a man has treated me like this. I step back and nearly trip on the curb.

Jack grabs my arm so I don't fall, and electricity jolts through my body where he touches me.

"Easy, now." He steadies me with his hand, and my heart pinwheels in my chest.

In this same scenario, Dex would have laughed at me for my clumsiness, made me feel smaller—foolish, even.

But Jack has always been like a steady wind, propping me up instead of tearing me down. Perhaps because in his own life, he's had to brace himself to weather the storms in his own family. I was a starry-eyed dreamer when I met Jack in ninth grade, zipping through the sky like a falling star, while he was fighting a battle to survive a demanding father and a tumultuous family breakup that even I didn't understand. What we learn about love is always shaped by our experiences—who stays with you, the people you can trust and won't let you fall when you stumble.

"One more thing," I say as Jack and I cross the lawn, my hand looping through his arm, my fingers splayed across the crook of his elbow. "If I forget to tell you later, I had a good time tonight."

He tilts his head curiously. "What if there's a surprise mechanical bull waiting for us? Or karaoke that requires wearing a ten-gallon hat?"

"I'll be okay, because you brought the barf bag, Jack. Greater love hath no man than this."

"Than to lay down a barf bag for his friend?" Jack asks with his usual smirk.

"You know me so well," I say, my fingers spread into the warmth of his skin, like he's all I can hold on to right now. Like we're slipping into an unknown future that's both familiar and entirely new.

EIGHT

Jack

Behind Grant's house, we head down a grassy beach path toward the distant hum of voices. A few beach chairs, gathered into a circle, sit just beyond where the waves lick the shoreline. Somebody turns on music—an Afropop mix with a bouncing bass line—as Jaz and Mia wave from their brightly striped chairs, their feet dangling in the foamy waves.

"Jack, my man." Grant slaps my shoulder, and his lips curl when he sees Maeve. Since I gave him a lot of grief when he first dated Ella, I know he's biting his tongue.

"Hi, Maeve," he says. "Do you remember my wife, Ella?" Grant turns to find Ella as she jogs over to him in a lemon meringue swimsuit that's as bright as sunshine.

"Maeve, I've heard so much about you!" Ella reaches out to hug Maeve, despite the hesitancy on her face. Maeve steps shyly forward, enduring the overzealous bear hug that's part of Ella's greeting.

Then Ella turns to me and squeezes my neck hard before pulling away. "You good?" she asks. "Need a drink or anything?"

"You got a mechanical bull, by chance?" I say with a straight face. Maeve shoots me a look.

"Um . . . no?" Ella says with a confused frown. "But I'll keep that in mind for next time. Maeve, come over and meet Mia and Jaz." She links arms with Maeve and pulls her away before she can even protest.

Given Grant and Ella's easy relationship, it will be easy to convince them we're dating. Ever since they got married, they've dropped multiple hints that I should stop spending weekends alone and *find* someone, like I'm shopping for leather dress shoes.

Just pick someone, Jack, Ella would remind me. But the problem isn't picking a date, it's sticking with one. I've always been a one-and-done kind of guy. *If the shoe doesn't fit . . .*

Brendan wanders over, his eyes dancing with amused delight.

"Were you going to tell me about this?" Brendan flicks his chin toward Maeve.

"Tell you about what?" I ask, playing dumb.

He drops his voice. "You *brought* someone. You *never* bring a date. I bet that's why you canceled our Saturday run."

"I can't bring a friend to a party?"

Brendan laughs in disbelief. "*Friend.* We both know what that's code for."

"It's not code for anything." Then I remember what Maeve and I agreed to—to make this look like more than a friendship. And that means not telling anyone, especially Brendan or Grant. "So, what if it is a date?"

"I called it," he announces to Grant, like they were placing bets on my dating life. Brendan reaches into a cooler of ice, fishing for a cold can from the bottom, then cracks the top open with a *pop.* "So have you kissed her yet?"

I roll my eyes. "I'm not like you."

"Well, you should be," he says with a smug smile.

"That wasn't a compliment." Because even if I tried to kiss Maeve, it would probably set off her panic, and she'd go sprinting for the bathroom. She's like a skittish wild animal, too terrified to trust anyone yet.

"It's none of our business," Grant says to Brendan. Then he hands me a drink from the cooler, the ice still dripping from the top. "This is a good step for you, Jack. You've dated a lot of girls, but you don't bring them to our gatherings."

It's true that I've kept my dating life separate from this group, because these people are special to me—my garage bandmates, the ones I tell everything to. I'm not going to share this world with someone on a first date. "She doesn't know a lot of people since she moved back. I'm just trying to introduce her to some friends."

I glance over at Maeve as her wavy hair blows around her face, like she's sitting in front of a box fan at a photo shoot. As her wild green-brown eyes dart toward mine, her lips curl at the edges, like she's trying to tell me she's okay. *No reason to panic.*

Her look spears my heart. *Beautiful.*

If I were going to date someone, it would be someone *like* her. Because it could never *be* her. She's already made it clear who she wants, and it's not me.

"I hope this isn't another injured animal," Grant says.

I frown. "What's that supposed to mean?"

"You're good at saving the day," he says. "For animals. And people."

Grant knows me better than anyone, and has told me I need to stop my hero complex. But this isn't a situation I can fix.

"She's not injured." At least, not once we fix things between her and Dex. That's why this situation is safe for both of us, because there's no chance she'll get dragged through the mess of my past. I can't disappoint someone who doesn't love me.

"Isn't this the place where you first kissed her?" Grant asks. "Back in high school?"

My gaze flicks to Grant's knowing smile. Back then, Grant's grandparents owned this house, and I asked them if I could bring Maeve here to look at the stars, which turned into more than just stargazing.

"Maybe. Why does that matter?" I say, trying to pretend these memories aren't snapping like Pop Rocks through my veins.

"Perfect night to recreate it," Brendan says, taking a swig of his drink.

"Speaking of fun, any requests for our first game?" Grant asks.

"Let's do something as a group," Ella suggests, wandering over as the rest of the girls follow.

"What games do you like, Maeve?" Jaz asks.

"I usually play games with my five-year-old, so unless you're into Go Fish or Twister, I'm probably not a good person to ask."

"I haven't played Twister in ages!" Ella chirps, clapping her hands together. "I've always thought it would be fun with adults. I'll grab it, and we'll play on the beach." Ella runs back to the house with the other girls before Maeve can respond.

"I was kidding!" she says weakly, then turns to me with a panicked look.

"First thing to know about my friends," I tell her. "Never mention any game you don't want to play. Because they play to win."

"I don't want your friends to think I'm incompetent based on my Twister ability."

"You said you play this with Violet."

"I do, but she always wins." Maeve sinks onto the sand like she's already given up. "I'm not ready to humiliate myself with your friends yet."

"They're normal people. Just pretend you're a five-year-old. Ask yourself, what would Violet do?" I sit next to her, watching the waves swell in the distance.

"Violet would play to win."

"Okay, so play to beat me. Where's that competitive streak you had in high school? You were always making things a game between us. Like that time I lost a bet to you over the science competition?"

"Are you still upset over that?" she asks, her eyes widening.

"Yes, I am," I say, studying her. "The bet was that whoever lost the science fair had to make dinner for the winner. *Whatever* they asked for."

"Oh, stop. You knew what you were getting into," she says

with a mischievous smile. "It could have been so much worse. I could have posted your naked baby pictures online."

"I burned those a long time ago. Kind of like the dish I made for you. I didn't even know the first thing about cooking. Dad hired someone to do that after he divorced Mom. But I burned the pan and set off the smoke alarm in my house." The gulls circle overhead, waiting for us to look away so they can fight over our crumbs.

"Technically, I never did get that meal. It was so badly burned, we couldn't get beyond the stench and ended up at Frank's instead."

I tilt my head. "Which is why I'm asking for a rematch."

"I don't know, Jack," she says with a grin. "You haven't tried my cooking. It could be awful."

I think for a second. "You're right. How about whoever wins can make any request of the loser? It doesn't have to be cooking."

"Okay, fair enough," she says. "I have a long list of repairs I would gladly pass on to you." Then she gives me a look. "Wait. Did you just figure out a way to trick me into playing Twister?"

"I don't know what you mean," I say with a wicked grin.

When Ella returns, she unfolds the Twister mat and hands the spinner to Mia, who's agreed to be the official referee for our adult Twister match. Maeve and I stand at the opposite end of the mat from Ella and Grant, while Jaz and Brendan stand to our right. Most everyone in the group is wearing only a swimsuit, except for Maeve, who still has on her clothes over her suit. I keep my T-shirt on too, just so she doesn't feel left out.

"Are you ready?" Mia announces and everyone nods, then she spins the spinner. "Left foot, blue."

"I always hated this game as a kid," Brendan mutters to me as he reaches for his first circle.

"That means you're more likely to lose," Grant says, as we all scramble for circles nearby.

Mia flicks the spinner again. "Right hand, yellow."

Jaz reaches for a yellow circle, stretching her body awkwardly across mine. "This is supposed to be fun, guys. Not an opportunity to prove you're men."

"Everything's an opportunity to prove something to Grant," Brendan says, elbowing Grant in their downward dog positions. It's clear these two alphas can't even play a game of Twister without trash-talking.

I could join in, but I'm staying out of their little competitive match. The only person to beat here is Maeve, even though I haven't decided what I'd use my win for.

"Right foot, green."

As I reposition my body to reach a green circle, I glance at Maeve, who moves into her position by crossing her leg over mine, since Jaz took the green circle nearest her.

She gives me an easy smile, and so far she seems comfortable, so maybe I've misjudged how easy it will be to beat her.

"Left hand, red."

At the command, Grant stretches toward the same circle as Brendan and claims it first, intentionally bumping his friend in the ribs so that Brendan loses his balance and falls into Jaz. As they both topple, Brendan reaches for Grant at the last second and pulls him down, causing the three of them to knock Ella off-balance.

"Hey, no fair!" Ella cries. "I don't think I should be disqualified for that."

Mia adjusts her glasses as she glances at the rules. "It doesn't define disqualification other than taking your hands and feet off the colors. So technically, you're out."

Ella frowns as Grant helps her up. Brendan and Jaz clear the mat.

"I call a do-over," Jaz says.

"The judge has ruled," Mia announces. "It's down to Maeve and Jack."

"Jack looks too comfortable," Brendan says.

"I'm not, really." A muscle in my leg twinges painfully.

"You could just quit," Maeve says.

"Oh, I'm not quitting," I say, grinning.

"Can I make one request, ref?" Maeve asks.

"Which is?"

"I'd like to remove my skirt for the rest of the game."

"Permission granted," Mia says. "As long as Jack gets a break too."

As she slips off her skirt, her T-shirt falls over her hips, covering her swimsuit. It's an obvious advantage for playing this game. *And a distraction.*

The wind has died down, replaced by a sticky heat that's making sweat prick the back of my neck. I slip off my T-shirt, throwing it on the sand, and Maeve's gaze catches mine, then flicks away. It's not like she hasn't seen a guy without his shirt on before, but I get the feeling we're both trying not to look at the other.

"Ready?" Mia says. We both stretch into place as Mia flicks the spinner. "Right foot, red."

I stretch to reach the closest red, right next to Maeve. I get there first, which leaves her no option but to stretch her leg over me. As her bare leg brushes mine, I'm suddenly distracted by her closeness, and distraction is *exactly* how you lose this game.

"Comfortable?" I ask, trying not to stare at her leg, which is next to impossible.

"Totally. How about you?"

"Not bad," I say, even though everything hurts.

Mia spins again. "Right hand, blue."

Maeve grabs the one closest to me, leaving me with no option other than bending over her in an extremely awkward position.

Brendan snickers from the sidelines.

Focus, Jack, I tell myself, even though she's so close I can breathe in her scent. I'm surrounded by lavender fields with a hint of vanilla, and all the blood rushes to my head.

Until now, I've been able to keep my mind on winning the game. But now her fragrance is throwing me off in the worst way.

It's the same sweet floral fragrance from years ago when we

kissed in this spot, the dizzying scent left on my skin after holding her, the one on the collar of her shirt, the delicate skin of her wrist.

If her memory was sealed with a scent, it would be lavender and vanilla.

"You sure you don't want to give up?" she asks, her leg pressing against mine, her body glistening with the soft sheen of sweat.

"Left foot, yellow," Mia announces.

I glance at the yellow circle and inwardly groan. This is going to hurt. As we both scramble toward yellow, I barely edge out Maeve, who quickly sidesteps toward another circle. Her T-shirt is gaping so that I can just make out the strap of her floral swimsuit. She notices I'm looking and quickly glances down at her neckline, the heat rising in her cheeks.

"Right hand, red."

We both reach for the same red circle, elbows bumping first, shoulders jostling, heat pressing at every place our bodies meet, trying to push each other down. I knew Maeve was competitive, but the game seems to have ignited in her a fierce desire to win.

I reach the circle first, but her hand lands on mine, and there's a brief moment where we're holding hands without meaning to, the heat running like a circuit from her hand to mine. She pulls her hand away as if she's been burned and tries to catch herself before she falls, but it's too late. She collapses on the mat.

"Looks like Jack won," Mia announces.

Maeve sits up, avoiding my gaze. "Okay, Jack Oliver, what are you going to use your bet on? No mechanical bulls, okay?"

"You guys were betting on Twister?" Jaz asks.

I stand, putting out my hand to help Maeve up. "Maeve won't tell you she has a fierce competitive streak when it involves me."

She ignores my hand and rises on her own. "You didn't answer my question."

"I'm going to hold on to this until I have the perfect opportunity." Whatever I ask her to do, it has to be the right thing. But one thing's for sure—I won't forget.

"Hey, Maeve," Jaz says, heading toward the water. "We're all going for a swim. You in?"

She glances at the others, who are already running into the waves, falling forward, plunging in headfirst.

"I don't think so," she says. "But thanks, anyway." Then she sinks into a blue-and-white-striped beach chair. "You can join them."

"I'm not letting you sit alone."

"I don't want you to miss out." She's playing with her swimsuit strap under her shirt like it's cutting into her skin.

"You can't leave without swimming. House rules."

She shrugs. "I don't know. It's been so long since I swam in the ocean."

But I wonder if it's something else, the same underlying fear she's been dealing with all along. It's not just a fear of dating, it's a different fear—resulting from when you've been knocked down too many times.

"We're supposed to be a couple, right?" I say. "It would be weird for us not to hang out."

"You go ahead," she says, still hesitating.

I start toward the water, but when I look back, she's standing there, frozen.

I stop and wait for her, waving her toward me.

She shifts her feet, like she's wrestling with whether to follow. With one swift stroke, she pulls her shirt off and drops it on the ground next to her feet, the soft curves of her body outlined by the lovely floral suit.

"Make me do it, Jack," she says. "Otherwise, I'm never going to get in the water."

"You want me to *make you*? Like, pick you up?"

"I know it's better to jump in than take it slow. But I can't get my feet to move." I watch the muscles in her throat constrict as she swallows. "I need you to throw me in."

I frown. "Are you sure? What about . . ." I move closer so I don't embarrass her. "Are you going to throw up on me?"

She closes her eyes. "Just make it fast so I don't have time to think. And whatever happens, don't let me chicken out. Promise?"

"Okay." I pause, afraid to touch her and set off her panic button. I'm not sure if this is part of her fear, but if it is, I need to guide her through it. "Listen, it's okay if you throw up on me. I was only kidding. I'll even hold your hair back."

For a second, her mouth flinches. "I know you would."

Then I slowly scoop her up. Her body stiffens for a few seconds in my arms, before her muscles slowly relax. She closes her eyes as I carry her, like she's trying to imagine something other than her churning stomach or the anticipation of the cold water.

Her body heats every place where our skin meets, the scent of lavender and vanilla burning into my mind.

As I slowly wade into the water, her eyes flick open. "I want to go back."

I keep going, refusing to let go, going deeper into the water as the waves crash into us. "If we're going to get wet, it's better if we do it together."

"This isn't necessary," she protests. "And you're probably tired from carrying me."

I laugh. "Hardly. You're like a dainty feather."

"Seriously, Jack," she protests. "I think I'll stay on the shore."

"That's not an option, Maeve. We'll do it together. Together, we'll chase down the fear."

As the water soaks her swimsuit, her breath hitches. We're both shivering slightly, but with her body against my chest, the heat between us is enough to keep from feeling the shock.

"On the count of three, we go under together."

"Jack, I changed my mind," she says. But I remember what she made me promise earlier. That I wouldn't let her chicken out.

"One."

She wiggles in my arms. "Jack, did you hear me?"

"Two."

"Jack!"

"Maeve, I'm a man who keeps my promises. And I'm doing this for you. *Three.*"

Then we plunge underneath the water together, her legs kicking, our bodies tangled like seaweed, before we both surface. Her face lights up with exhilaration, and she gasps for breath, like she's been holding it for so long, she forgot how to breathe.

NINE

Maeve

I wrap a towel around my shoulders to stop my shivering. As much as I didn't want to get in the water, once Jack threw me in, I got over my fear of being in a swimsuit in front of Jack's friends. For the last few hours, as the sun drifted lazily to where sea meets sky, the girls chatted while the guys threw a football. Nearly every time I turned around, Jack would look my way, checking to see if everything was okay, making sure I was having a good time.

"Do you want to stay longer?" Jack asks as we make our way along the dark path back to the house. Now that the sun has set, everything has turned to shadowy outlines, and I only hope I don't stumble over something.

"Don't be shocked," I say. "But I'm having fun."

To my surprise, I don't want to leave. For once, I don't have to watch Violet, or get home before bedtime, or worry about anyone except myself. Maybe I'll even remember who I used to be before I became a mom. Even though I'm the same person, there's a part of me that feels like a stranger to myself. I want to get to know *her* again—that girl who used to dream big, the one who believed I could find someone who loved me without reservations.

Jack's mouth hitches into a grin. "You enjoy hanging out with my friends?"

"I do. And I like not being Mom for one night. As much as I love Violet, I've hardly thought of her for the last hour."

"Look at you, staying out late with new friends. I'm proud of you." He smiles like I'm a kid who just learned to tie my shoes.

I laugh. "Proud? I think this means I'm pretty pathetic."

"The way you care for Violet—it's beautiful."

I glance through the window, the warm light crowning everyone in a golden glow as they pour grapefruit spritzers and scoop chips into fresh salsa, the heavy scent of cilantro wafting through the open window. "But do you think they're convinced we're dating?"

"My friends know something's up. I don't bring girlfriends to our get-togethers. For company parties, yes, but only because it's expected. But not these friends. This group is special. I don't let in just anyone."

I smile, honored Jack would invite me even if he's only doing me a favor.

"I feel totally out of practice at this dating thing." I wrap my towel tighter, suddenly feeling exposed since I'm still only in my suit.

"What do you want me to do?" Even in the dark, his eyes spark, sending a warm feeling soaring in my chest, the same way it did the first time he kissed me here.

"I'm not sure," I say, still feeling like that girl in high school, the one who didn't know if we should stay friends or if there could be something more between us.

Jack and I had been close ever since we met in high school biology class. The teacher assigned us as lab partners, and we hit it off as friends during our first experiment—a rat dissection. The biology lab reeked of formaldehyde, and Jack made jokes about the poor rodent we were mutilating while he handed me the scalpel and invited me to make the first cut. He didn't know that I'd seen more than my fair share of animal surgeries in my dad's office. But he also didn't have anything to prove. Of course he'd let me go first. From that day on, I was always first to him. That was how we functioned as friends. Jack always saving the seat next to him, always eating with me in the cafeteria, always making me feel like I wasn't the weird smart one.

In our senior year of high school, something shifted, a growing push-pull chemistry between us, something we were both too afraid to talk about but could sense just the same. A member of the golf team asked me to prom, someone I didn't really want to go with, but since Jack hadn't asked anyone to prom, I figured this was my only chance. I'd never been to prom, and it felt like I was missing a rite of passage, even if it really was nothing more than a chance to dress up. When the golfer dumped me the night of prom, I called Jack, raining tears all over my peacock-blue gown, and he immediately came over.

Even then, I had no idea why Jack raced to my side, knowing what I needed as soon as he saw me, sinking down on both knees so that he could cup my cheek and wipe every tear before it splashed across the silk fabric of my dress. That's when Jack asked, "What do you want me to do? If there's something I can do to make it better, I will. If you need a date to the prom, if you need *anything*, just tell me." He'd said it slowly, measuring my reaction. Then he reached up and placed his hands on the sides of my face, cupping my cheeks featherlight, afraid to break me any more than I already was. "Because I could never say no to you."

It was all he had to say to send my heart spinning in dizzy circles. *I could never say no to you.*

Only later, he confessed he'd been too scared to ask me to prom, worried that the growing attraction between us would ruin our friendship for good. And it did, eventually.

So why am I surprised that over a decade later, Jack is asking me what I want him to do? And why is it that all I want is the same answer now as he gave me then? *I could never say no to you.*

"Tell me how you'd treat a real date," I say in the dark before we head in. "I need to know, in case tonight is the first test."

Jack's amber gaze flicks over me, and I can see the muscle in his jaw leap. "You really want to know?"

I barely nod.

"I'd probably hold your hand. Maybe wrap my arm around your waist."

My hands clam up, but I'm also flushed with heat, like my body is having a physical reaction to his description.

"But what will your friends think?" I feel like this is my first test. If I fail it, then how will I make it through any more dates?

"I guess we're about to find out."

Before I can respond, he grabs my hand, all the heat and energy pulsing through the hot, sludgy blood in my veins. When Jack touches me, it's like something combusts inside, pumping liquid energy through me.

"If it gets to be too much," he says, his eyes tracing the outline of my face, "tell me. I'll stop. Promise."

As we step inside, Jaz turns, and her gaze drops to our laced fingers. She elbows Ella, and my face heats like a torch. I know it's just because I'm out of practice, but I'm instantly taken back to feeling like an awkward high schooler, showing off her boyfriend for the first time, both embarrassed and elated.

Grant is leaning on the island, smirking. "You really took your time coming in."

The warmth prickles across my chest. This shouldn't be as difficult as I'm making it. Maybe it's because it's not real, even though my body thinks it is. Or maybe it's because Jack's not my ex-husband. Either way, I wish my body would stop freaking out.

"I was enjoying the view," Jack says, and then looks at me. Is this just part of the dating charade, or did he mean something by it?

I try to let go of Jack's hand, but he keeps his grip firm, like he's trying to remind me why we're doing this. Even though I need to get comfortable with him so I can get over my dating fear, I can hardly stand everyone smiling and staring at us, like we're a spectacle at the zoo.

Ella glances at my swimsuit. "Do you need a place to change? You can use the guest room." Jack finally lets me go, and I hurry upstairs, only too happy to take off my suit and change back into my other outfit. When I return, Jack is waiting at the bottom of the stairs while everyone else has disappeared to play games in the renovated garage.

Even though, without an audience, we don't have to pretend like we're a couple, Jack brushes a strand of hair from my cheek, his touch an electrical wire against my skin. He picks up a red bubbly drink from the kitchen counter. "Thirsty?"

"What's this?" I take the glass, spinning it to admire the bright color.

"I'm not sure. But there's no alcohol. We'll call it red fizzy bliss."

"Great," I say. "Because alcohol is like an evil stepsister who once tricked me into believing she was nice before kicking me in the head. I'm one of those people who has a weak tolerance for the stuff, so I avoid it."

"We need to make sure that doesn't happen again," he says. "Do you want something different?" I adore the way Jack wants to make me happy and spoil me with drinks and affection. If this is how he treats a friend, I can't imagine how much more atten-tion he would lavish on someone he loves.

"This is perfect." I give Jack a reassuring smile, then take a sip. "It makes me think there might be more magical nights ahead. Silly me, I used to think *fun* was a night of binge-watching old *Fixer Upper* episodes."

"What's wrong with that?" he says, grabbing the fizzy bliss for himself, the red bubbles shooting toward the surface like lit sparklers.

"Because that's the *only* fun thing I do, other than working on my own fixer-upper. Which isn't nearly as fun as watching someone else fix up a house. Clearly, I was insane when I bought my place."

"Not insane. Ambitious, maybe, but not crazy."

"Well, this ambitious house project is quickly drowning me. I've watched home shows for the last ten years, and I thought I knew what I was getting into. Turns out, it's way harder to actually renovate your own home than it appears on TV."

Jack smirks. "Imagine that."

I shake my head. "I'm afraid it's turning me into a bad mom, and my daughter is going to need therapy because I worked on our house constantly and missed all her school events." I slide onto a barstool. "What have I gotten myself into?"

Jack straddles the barstool next to me. "First off, you're not a bad mom." He slides a hand across my shoulder blade, his fingers splayed light, following the curve. "I've seen you with Violet. You're always putting her needs first, even with the house projects. Second, if you need a sitter, you can always call me. I like hanging out with you and Violet."

I nearly drop my drink. "You're volunteering to babysit?"

He runs a hand through his hair. "Why do you look so shocked?"

"I don't understand. You're a single guy who wants to babysit, instead of taking selfies with beautiful women on expensive yachts?"

"You want to know the truth?"

I nod.

"I already am hanging out with a beautiful woman."

Although I know he's just being kind, heat rushes over my body. "You don't have to say that."

"I know. I like you and Violet. I didn't have a normal childhood. We didn't do fun stuff at my house. My dad only cared about my achievements and pressured me to focus on racking up the awards and accolades. Only later did I realize that earning those accolades was my way of trying to fix everything wrong in my family. To make our family look normal."

"So are you trying to tell me it's therapeutic for you to hang out with Violet and me?"

"Yes, because it is."

"But you're already helping me get over my dating phobia."

"I enjoy spending time with you. That's all I want."

As he says it, my heart flutters, like the soft wings of a moth caught inside a lamp. I know Jack doesn't want anything more than friendship, but part of me wishes he did. Part of me wonders what would happen if he were less ambitious and didn't have the pressure of trying to provide for his mom's care. In every way, he'd make up for his father's lack of affection. In every way, he'd be the man his father never was.

"I enjoy spending time with you, too, except when you cheat at Twister," I say, digging an elbow in his side.

"Cheat? How? You fell down."

"You didn't follow your own rule when we fought for the last circle. *Ladies first.*"

"Do you want a re-do right now?" Jack asks.

"I can't. Thanks to you, I pulled a muscle in my butt, and now need to use muscle cream, which is the equivalent of rubbing hot wing sauce on your bum."

Jack laughs while he swallows, and the red drink spurts out his nose.

"Did you just spray the counter?" I ask incredulously.

"You could have warned me before the hot wing sauce visual," he says, still grinning.

I smile, feeling thoroughly vindicated for losing Twister. Tonight feels so perfect as we ease back into a friendship that's as soft as an old sweater. Because Jack makes me feel lovely, and funny, and worth listening to. Over the last few years, I forgot what it felt like to be that kind of person to someone. To be someone worth listening to. To laugh at the same jokes, snorting carbonated beverages through your nose and not caring if the other person witnesses it.

If my own fear of loving someone new didn't consume me, maybe I could imagine the slow unfolding of this friendship into something more. Even now, Jack makes something flutter, featherlight, under my skin, something I'd thought I'd long since lost.

But even if I could, even if we hadn't already tried this before and failed spectacularly, we've already agreed to keep things in the "friend zone."

There is no gray area. There is no *what if.* At least, not for me.

In my mind, every single woman should be falling all over themselves to snatch up a guy like Jack. But even imagining it gives me an odd twinge of jealousy.

"So why aren't you dating anyone?" I ask, trying to sound breezy and noncommittal. "You said you're busy, but you clearly have time for Twister and hanging out with five-year-olds. So I think that's just an excuse."

He shrugs. "You mean, besides the fact I might take a job that will consume my entire life? That is reason enough. I refuse to become my father." His words are laced with hurt as his mouth tightens into a line. And suddenly, I imagine Jack as a boy, sitting on his massive steps, waiting for his dad to play ball, waiting for his dad to come home, always waiting for something, and learning to lessen his expectations, until there were none at all.

"Jack, you are not your father," I say, laying one hand on his wrist, feeling the corded tendons, like rope beneath his skin. "You're the kindest man I've ever met."

His mouth softens, all the hard edges blurred like a soft filter. "I have my mom to thank for that. Before her stroke, she was always there for me. I'm not sure why she ever married my father." He drains the rest of his glass, then sets it on the island. "Which is why I'm uncertain about dating anyone. If my mom couldn't see my dad for who he was, how can any of us see each other clearly?" He runs his finger around the lip of his empty cup, studying it. "One time, I went out with a woman Craig set me up with. She was more interested in getting a good selfie on our date for her Instagram account than talking to me."

"But you post dog pictures on Instagram. You know, George is very vain with his selfies."

He shoots me a surprised look. "You checked my Instagram account?"

I suddenly realize my mistake. "My teacher friend, Annie, looked you up."

"And why would she do that?" His eyes dance, like he enjoys finding out why I was spying on him.

"Because Annie is always scoping out men. I told her you weren't looking."

"So your friend is interested?"

"She's not your type." Annie is *so* going to kill me for this.

"Then who is my type, other than the emotionless hag we talked about the other day?" He levels his gaze, and my stomach does this weird flip.

"I don't know," I say. "Maybe George?"

Jack laughs. "I do like him better than most women."

"Personally, I think Violet and I are quickly becoming George's favorite people."

"He's not the only one who feels that way," Jack says, grinning, and I nearly fall off my barstool smiling back.

"One confession," Jack adds. "Annie isn't the only one who's a silent lurker. I scoped out your Instagram account before you moved back."

I turn to him. "You did?"

"I wanted to know what happened to you," he says. "That's when I saw you were married with a daughter, and I was happy for you. You always wanted to become a mom and teacher."

"Well, we can't all be George, lazing around on a dog bed, getting our bellies rubbed."

My phone vibrates on the counter, and Dex's name appears on the screen.

I give Jack an apologetic look. "I should take this." Even though I'm not his wife, I know it's the right thing to do, so I answer, just like when we were married. It's a habit I'm still struggling to break.

I sneak into the back hall for privacy and gaze at Grant and Ella's wedding photos on the wall. I'm not trying to hide that I'm at a party with Jack, but I'm also not ready to answer questions.

"Hey, Dex. What's up?"

"Do you think your parents can babysit Violet next Thursday instead of me?"

"What happened to *Hello, how are you?*" It annoys me he doesn't even bother with a greeting and cuts straight to the demand.

"Um, how are you?" he says. "And can you ask them?"

"I'm fine, thanks," I say, pretending not to let my frustrations seep through. "Why can't you help that night?" Even though I'm hoping Dex will see the light regarding our relationship, this is not the conversation to make that happen. I can feel where this discussion is headed, and it's steamrolling toward an argument.

"I had something come up," he says vaguely. It's probably work-related, but I don't ask.

"I told you about this weeks ago," I say. "It's not like I can skip parent-teacher conferences."

"That's why I thought your parents could handle it."

I prop a hand on my hip. "My mom has a big lecture on bonsai plants she's giving for the Master Garden Club. And my dad has to go with her because they're bringing her bonsai plant collection, and she can't haul them herself."

"She can't reschedule?" he asks.

"They only meet once a month. And no, I'm not asking her to reschedule. She's been looking forward to this all year. What's Violet going to think when you cancel again?"

"Tell her I can make it up to her over the weekend," he says. "I'm still planning on seeing her then."

"Yes, but what about me? I have to work, Dex. It's not like I can tell my principal I'm not attending parent-teacher conferences. It's a requirement for my job." Not that Dex understands what it means to compromise. He never recognized my job as a valid scheduling concern. It was always just an add-on to our lives, a thing of convenience to fit in and around his schedule of events.

"Can't you find anyone else?" he asks, putting me in an awkward situation.

I glance toward the kitchen and see Jack pouring me another red fizzy bliss. I know he offered to babysit Violet, but I don't want to take advantage of him every time Dex cancels. On the other hand, I'm left with few options because I can't skip this event.

"I'll see what I can do," I say, hiding my exasperation.

"Tell Violet I'll take her to the zoo next weekend."

I don't hide my sigh. "I'll let you surprise her." Because if I tell her, and he fails again, she'll end up even more disappointed. That's the problem with Dex. He doesn't uphold his side of the bargain. "If things change with your schedule, let me know."

I hang up and paste on what I hope passes for a calm face.

"Everything okay?" Jack asks, studying me.

"Yeah, fine," I say, sliding onto the stool. "Co-parenting is a barrel of laughs, in case you're wondering."

"You look like you need some more of this." He slides over my cup filled with red fizzy bliss.

"Was that Dex?" Then he shakes his head. "You don't have to tell me. It's none of my business."

"I don't mind you asking, and yes, it was. How could you tell?"

"You sound different," he says.

"Annoyed? This is the second time he's canceled on me. I'm supposed to work at parent-teacher conferences."

"I can help with Violet," Jack says, without me even asking him.

I frown. "You don't even know what night it is."

"I'm free all next week. Just tell me when, and I'll be there." Jack brings up his calendar on his phone.

"Seriously? It should only be for a few hours on Thursday evening."

He types in the date. "What does she like to eat? I'll bring her dinner too, if you're okay with it."

"Okay with it?" I want to kiss his face, I'm so thrilled, but I hold back. "I'm more than okay with it."

"When I come over, I'll check on the squirrels, too. I started on an idea that will keep them out of the rest of the house, and I need to finish it."

"So it doesn't involve permanently rehousing those freeloaders?"

"I'm sorry to say it will not." Then he smiles. "But it will protect you and Violet."

I'm so relieved, I wrap my arms around his neck. For a moment, his body tenses, before leaning into mine and finally softening. His arms circle my waist as his shoulders relax, and his hand finds the space between my shoulder blades, that tender, soft spot where his fingertips dance lightly on my skin, sending fireworks up my spine. I let my hands fall to the hard, muscular lines of his chest and I think about what it would be like to nestle my head there. Because hugging Jack is like an instant antianxiety pill. The stress just disappears, and I can breathe again.

Just then, the door from the garage opens, and the girls interrupt our moment.

I quickly leap back, feeling like I've broken some unspoken rule about hugging a friend too long.

Logically, I know this doesn't make sense. There's nothing wrong with hugging Jack in public.

But it's the hope in their expression that leaves me unsettled. They're smiling and glancing at us, like there's a hidden promise in this hug.

Their looks ratchet up everything, causing my anxiety to roll in like a giant wave.

Never mind that my body says *this is right*, that Jack is the missing puzzle piece and everything in my world could crumble because of him. It has before.

Our relationship is impossible for many logical reasons, including that I'm too scared to risk my heart again.

But all it takes from Jack is one intense gaze, and everything in me ignites, burning down all my reservations.

Just breathe. Just breathe. Just breathe.

TEN

Jack

"That's not the way you drink tea for a princess party," Violet says to me, lifting her cup with an exaggerated pinky curl.

I try to make my pinky bend like hers, but mine looks more like a monster claw.

When I agreed to babysit Violet, I never imagined I'd be persuaded to wear a pink princess tiara while squatting at a munchkin-sized table drinking from a miniature teacup. Violet sits across from me in a fluffy pink and purple princess gown that looks like a sparkly unicorn vomited on her.

"You're supposed to do it gracefully," she instructs before clinking cups with me.

"I'm pretty sure my pinky doesn't do that. And what's wrong with my way? It's not like the queen is here."

"In case you've forgotten, I *am* the queen." She points to herself. "Mr. Jack, can I ask you something?"

"You don't have to call me Mr. Jack," I say. "That's reserved for important people. I'm just Jack."

"I don't like *just Jack*." She pauses. "Oh, I know. I'll call you Uncle Jack."

"I like that, but I'm not your real uncle," I clarify. I don't want her to get our relationship mixed up.

"I know that. And I'm not a queen either. We'll just pretend."

"I'll drink to that." I lift my cup, and we clink again. "Well done, Queen Violet."

"Let's celebrate with animal crackers!" She runs to the kitchen and searches through the pantry.

"Are you sure you're supposed to have animal crackers before bed?" I ask Violet as George follows us, hoping for a dropped crumb.

"I'm the queen, so yes," she says, getting out the box. She carries it back to our table and dumps a small mountain of crackers on her plate.

"You probably shouldn't eat all those."

"It's okay. I won't get sick," she says, munching on a hippo. "Dad lets me have whatever I want."

"How many does your mom normally allow?"

She shrugs.

"You don't know?" I ask. "Or don't want to tell me?"

"I don't know," she says, biting a camel's head off.

I make a mental note that I should ask Maeve about these things later. I've never been a dad or taken care of kids before, so I don't know if I should set more limits or let her have fun. I lean toward fun, because my dad was just the opposite. Mostly, he treated me like I was a nuisance.

Just then, I hear a small cough behind me. I turn quickly, knocking the plastic tiara off my head.

"Fabulous costume," Maeve says, smirking.

"You're home already?" Violet asks, running over to Maeve. "Uncle Jack makes a great princess, doesn't he?"

"Yes, he does." Maeve doesn't hide her amusement.

"I aim to please." I wink at Violet. "Care to join us? We have gourmet animal crackers."

"Tempting," Maeve says, setting down her laptop bag and sinking into one of the small chairs. She bites into an elephant and slips off her shoes as Violet climbs onto her lap. "It looks like you two had fun."

"Uncle Jack and I played Old Maid, and I beat him twice!" Violet giggles. "Which meant he had to play princess tea party with me."

"So you're an honorary uncle now?" Maeve lifts an eyebrow. "Your status has gone up a few notches."

"I'm trying not to be a sore loser about becoming an old crone who's forced to attend a princess party."

"Can you come over tomorrow, too?" Violet asks.

"Honey, tomorrow you're going to Dad's place."

"I'd rather play with Uncle Jack."

Maeve glances uneasily between us. "It's your weekend with him. I'm sure he has fun things planned."

"Like watching TV all day and as many cookies as I want?" she asks.

Maeve's smile falls. "Probably." It's obvious she doesn't approve, but she's trying not to say anything. She glances at her watch. "Why don't you get ready for bed? I'll be up in a few minutes."

"I can't wait for cookies!" Violet says as she skips off to her room.

Maeve props her elbows on the small table and looks at me. "It's been hard going back and forth. We have different house rules."

"But TV *and* cookies? It's every kid's dream."

"That's the problem. That's all he gives her. I thought Dex would be an involved dad, playing with her when he was home. But he just didn't know how to. That's why Violet wants to hang out with you. She's never had a dad who would wear a tiara."

"I'm sure most dads wouldn't wear a tiara," I tell her. Given that my dad was never around, maybe I'm just making up for what I feel like I lost. And Dex is the one missing out because Violet is a great kid.

"You're setting the bar high." Her gaze flicks to me, and her eyes glitter in the soft light. "You're such a natural at making people feel comfortable."

"You mean because of my costume?"

"Definitely the costume," she says, eyeing my plastic crown. "Actually, I meant winning people over with your charm. You've got Violet wrapped around your finger. Can you teach me how to do that? I mean, if I'm getting back into the dating game, I need to learn your secrets."

"Maeve, charm is just an act . . . it's nothing, really. There is no secret to winning someone over, other than being yourself."

"That's easy for you to say. My whole life, I've been trying to be myself, and now I'm a divorced single mom who's too scared to try again. I'm obviously doing something wrong, because some women are just naturals at being . . ." She pauses, searching for the right word.

"Naturals at what?"

"Being *that girl.* The one men go for. They know what they like. How to catch a man's attention."

"Maeve, you don't want to be *that girl.* Believe me. They attract the wrong type."

"I don't mean that I need to change, *exactly.* But if I'm going to win over Dex—or anyone—I need to overcome my fear and build up my confidence. I passed our first test at Grant and Ella's house, and everyone believed us. I'm ready for the next step of the formula."

I shake my head. "There's no formula for attraction. If there is, it's highly individualized. I'm not the person to teach you that." Something heats in my chest, like I want to run from danger and play with fire at the same time.

"But you're the *only* one who can." The conviction in her face is almost too much. Being her pretend date was one thing, but this is venturing into more dangerous territory. It's not just fake dating now. It's role-playing, and I have the feeling this experiment to fix her up for Dex is like she's trying me on for size until she gets the real guy.

"There should be some boundaries to our arrangement." I shoot her a concerned look. "For both of us."

"Yes, of course," she says, studying me. "Boundaries are essential. And I don't want to freak out like I did before."

"If I do *anything* that makes you uncomfortable, just say the word, and we'll stop. If you start to panic—even if it's mild—you need to tell me."

"I will." She nods, like she's thinking over our rules. Something passes over her face that I can't read, a tiny flicker of doubt. "And you won't make fun of me if I'm a failure?"

"I promise I won't make fun of you. Cross my heart," I say, drawing an X over my heart.

Her face relaxes. "Oh, good. Because I need all the practice I can get. Last time a guy tried to flirt with me at the grocery store, I dropped the melon I was carrying and was chasing it through the produce section as it rolled across the floor. I was such an idiot. We're talking Three Stooges material."

"Maeve, you know some guys find that endearing."

"Chasing a cantaloupe?"

"No, being imperfect. Laughing at yourself over a runaway melon."

She shakes her head. "Only you, Jack. Everyone else looks at me like I'm insane."

"You're saying a nice guy flirted with you, and you didn't flirt back?"

"I was too busy crawling under a table of grapefruit."

"That was your first mistake. First rule of dating: *Let the melon go.*"

"See? I failed and didn't even know it."

"There's no failure. There's only learning from your mistakes and moving on."

"But if I only get one shot with someone, how am I supposed to get it right the first try without practice?"

"Then let's try it, right now," I suggest. "Let's replay your traumatic melon experience."

"Now?" she asks, looking at me like I'm crazy.

"Yes. Go across the room and pretend you're shopping for melons," I instruct.

She lifts an eyebrow as if she's questioning my sanity, then moves away from me, tucking one of Violet's balls under her arm. "This will be the melon."

"Now, pretend you're shopping, and I'm a guy staring at you from over the onions."

"It wasn't onions, Jack. It was watermelon."

"Okay, so I'm gazing at you over a massive pile of watermelon. What would you do?"

"You need to say to me, *Nice melon.*"

"The guy actually complimented you on your melon?" I say incredulously.

She nods, and I burst out laughing. "What'd you say to him?"

"*Thank you.*" She pauses, then looks at me. "Wait, was he *not* complimenting me on my melon?"

"I don't know, Maeve. There's so much subtext that happens in flirting. It depends on his body language. He could have been joking. It could have been innuendo. Or maybe, he *really* did like your cantaloupe."

She throws up her hands in the air, frustrated. "I give up. I obviously don't know the rules to this game."

"You're not giving up. Let's try again. I'm the melon guy. And you're going to read my subtext. I make eye contact with you over the watermelon, and what do you do in response? Before I've even complimented your melon?"

I've never coached a woman on how to flirt. Now that I think about it, the women I've been around have made it look easy.

"Um, stare at you, like this?" She gives me a hard, unfeeling gaze.

I frown. "You look deranged right now."

She throws up her arms, exasperated. "I'm doing what you said!"

"Just look at me more naturally and smile." I stand across from her, helping her get into the role-play.

She blinks, fiddles with the rubber ball, and then stares at me with a forced grin. "How am I doing? Do I look any better?" she asks through gritted teeth, like a ventriloquist.

"Like a serial killer," I say, trying not to laugh.

Her face falls, her body slumping. "I can't even smile at you without failing."

"You're not failing," I tell her. "You're trying too hard to flirt with me. Attraction is an art, not a science."

"Which is problematic, since I *am* a scientist."

"I think you need to trick your brain by *not* thinking about flirting."

"Easy for you to say. I'm all about thinking, rationalizing, logic. It's what makes me a good scientist, but terrible at love."

"Who said you're terrible at love? Whoever told you that was wrong." I level my gaze at her. "The art of attraction isn't about luring a man like bait on a hook. It's more about figuring out what you like about someone. When you feel that connection with another person, you explore it, like an adventurer in an unexplored land. Then you let your curiosity lead you, and you don't stop exploring what makes that person tick, because the connection . . . is sacred."

Her mouth drops open. "That's beautiful, Jack." She pauses. "But it's also intimidating and impossible. Therefore, I quit. I'm going to accept my lot in life as an old maid. Goodbye, Jack."

She spins on her heel, and I race over to block her.

"You can't leave. You live here," I remind her. "And I'm not letting you give up because you missed an opportunity over a melon."

Her mouth curls at the edges, like she's trying to suppress a smile. "But you waxed on about sacred connections and the art of attraction. All I want to know is how to stop freaking out over flirting with a guy in the produce section."

"Okay, I'm sorry," I say, thinking of how I can make this less difficult for her. "I need you to understand that this isn't a bait and switch. You're not trying to trick Dex, or anyone, into liking you."

"I know that." She almost looks hurt by my accusation.

"You wouldn't do it on purpose. But flirting can be unpredictable. And I don't want anyone to be misled." *Especially you.* I can't tell her that because I don't want to make her even more scared of trying. But that's the problem with teaching her *any* part of this game. It's a dangerous tool when used the wrong way.

She rubs her forehead, and I can see how tired she is after working all day.

"Maybe we should continue this another day," I suggest.

"No," she insists firmly. "I'm just getting in my own way. It can't be *that* hard."

"Why don't we forget the melon scenario and just pretend you're introducing yourself to me at a party."

Maeve drops the rubber ball and moves toward me, stiffly holding out her palm for a handshake.

"Hi, I'm Maeve."

I clamp my lips shut.

"What?" she asks, frowning.

"You just introduced yourself like you're at a political rally."

"Well, it's harder than it looks." She props her hands on her hips. "I'd like to see you try."

I move inches from her and brush a strand of hair out of her eye with a light touch. "Hey," I murmur.

"Why are you smiling at me like that?" she asks, totally oblivious to the fact that I'm showing her what to do.

Finally, her expression shifts, like a curtain opening on a sunny day. "Ah, I see what you're doing." She points at me. "Are you going to use some cheesy pickup line on me, too?"

"Maybe." I grin. "See how I'm holding your gaze, trying to get you to smile? It worked, didn't it?"

She bites her bottom lip, her teeth snagging her smile as her eyes soften, like she's melting under my gaze. "I don't know what I'm doing."

"What do you feel?" I take a step closer to her. "Let your eyes say it."

I'm now only inches from her, and my heart bucks in my chest, like it's finally waking.

Her eyes drop to my lips, and she swallows. "Then what do I do?" she murmurs hesitantly.

"Is this yours?" I ask, bending over to pick up Violet's tiara on the floor.

She frowns. "Is this part of the role-play?"

"It's improvisation, Maeve. Just go with my lead." I hold out the tiara to her. "Lose your crown, princess?"

She cracks a smile. "So, you *were* saving a cheesy pickup line for me."

I laugh. "I'll always save a pickup line for you. Flirting is about spontaneity. You make it up on the spot, based on the person's reaction. I wanted to make you smile."

She's trying to hold back her joy, but it's like pushing back the ocean. It just spills out from her. "You are way better at this than I am."

"Not better. Just different." I place the small glitter-encrusted crown on her head, lightly brushing a few silky hairs into place. "But you have ways of making people smile, and I don't." I tip her chin toward me so she can't look anywhere else. "Do you believe me?"

"I *almost* believe you."

I can see how hard this is for her. Letting her guard down for me. Trusting me. We're so close, I can see the green-copper flecks in her eyes, like flames dancing in the light.

"What are you doing?" a small voice interrupts.

I spin around. Violet stands on the stairs. I don't know how long she's been there, but Maeve steps back, putting space between us, trying not to send the wrong message.

"It's late, and you should be in bed." Then she brushes by me to take Violet upstairs.

"I think I'll head out too," I say, gathering my things.

Maeve gives me a quick glance before hurrying away.

As I put on George's leash and head to the front door, Violet asks, "Mommy, what *were* you doing with Uncle Jack?"

As much as I'd like to stay to hear the answer, I duck out into the night and ask myself the same question. *What are you doing, Jack?*

ELEVEN

Maeve

"What's happening with your dating life?" Annie stands at my desk, eating her strawberry spinach salad during our school lunch break. "Any interesting conversations or flirtatious advances you'd like to tell me about?"

I frown. She couldn't know about the flirting practice with Jack the other night. The only person who witnessed it was Violet, and I told her no matter what it looked like, Jack and I weren't about to kiss, hug, or do anything that involved PDA.

Never mind that my body was a dumpster fire of hormones. I'm a thirty-year-old woman who hasn't been kissed in over a year, so I can't really help what happens when a guy like Jack pays attention to me.

"Nothing's happened," I say, taking a bite of chicken. "Why do you ask?"

Based on the way her lips press together into a mischievous grin, Annie *knows* something. "I heard that Heather's dad asked you out at parent-teacher conferences."

I nearly drop my kung pao chicken as my mouth falls open. "Who told you that?" I had totally forgotten that brief incident. At the time, I was caught off guard and trying not to read into things.

"Does it matter who told me?" She takes a bite of her salad and leans toward me like we're about to discuss her favorite true crime documentary. "Is it true?"

"Even if he did, I'd be the last person to know. I wouldn't recognize it unless someone plastered their lips to mine."

"Wow, really? Then tell me everything. I want to live through you vicariously."

"He just hinted that we should watch his daughter play volleyball sometime." Compared to what happened with Jack, it really was a non-event. But Jack's flirting? That was *hot*.

She stops mid-chew and stares at me. "What did you tell him?"

"I said no."

Annie looks at me like I've lost my mind. "You know he's the hottest single dad in school, right? And according to you, your life is lame."

"I didn't say that." I stop. "Oh, wait. I did say that. But it's *less* lame now."

"Less lame is not a life goal. You need to have more fun."

I put down my kung pao chicken so I can level with Annie. "He's the dad to one of my high school students. I can't date a parent."

She waves her hand. "He probably doesn't care about that."

"Well, I do. It's unprofessional. And his daughter was mortified. She can't even look me in the eye in class."

Annie shrugs a shoulder. "She'll get over it."

"Well, I might not. I didn't even know he was interested. Am I that oblivious?"

"Yes," Annie says, nodding. "You are *that* oblivious."

I frown. "You could have at least hesitated for a second before answering."

"You want me to lie? I'm your friend who speaks the truth. When he picks up Heather from school, he always walks by your room, trying to strike up the nerve to talk to you."

"He does? Maybe he wants to talk about his daughter's grade."

"Unlikely." She shakes her head. "She's too good of a student."

"So you're saying he chose to make his move at a parent-teacher conference? That's just tacky."

"He was probably desperate to talk to you, and then you stomped on his heart and rejected him. Is a volleyball game that much of a risk?"

"It gives him false hope. And just for the record, I did not stomp on his heart. I let him down gently." I hesitate for a second. "I told him I was dating someone."

Annie almost chokes on a strawberry. "Why do I not know this? I thought we were friends. I'm the one who got you this job."

"We are friends. It's just complicated." When Annie found out about my divorce, she told me about this job opening since she knew I wanted to move closer to my parents. I begged Annie to put in a good word for me, and she delivered a raving letter of recommendation. Until I met Jack and his friends, Annie was my only friend in town.

Annie frowns. "Are you back with Dex? I thought he said he needed time to think about things."

"I'm not back with Dex. But that is part of the plan," I add, hopefully.

She shakes her head. "I'm so confused right now."

I lower my voice, even though we're alone in my classroom. "I'm dating Jack."

"*The* Jack?! The guy you wanted to marry in high school, who tried to help with your squirrel invasion?"

"Yes, that Jack."

She frowns, like she's trying to put together a very difficult math equation. "I thought he was your *no way*."

"My what?"

"Your *no way, never, ever getting back together* man."

"Um, he is. But we're pretending to date . . . so it's all good." I stop and look at her in panic. "I wasn't supposed to tell you that."

She crosses her arms, studying me. "First off, I can read you like a book. We're practically the same brain, so it's no use hiding secrets from me. Second, why in the world would you agree to this terrible idea?"

"To help me get back into the dating scene, since I'm terrified of trying again. And . . . to make Dex jealous." Never mind that Dex has given me zero indication that he would even consider dating again. He broke up with his girlfriend, but it's not like that was for me. For all I know, she dumped him.

Annie tilts her head like I've officially gone crazy. "That is the worst plan *ever*."

"Why? Dex is a very jealous person. I'm tired of waiting on him to get his act together. When he sees us together, he'll realize how much he misses me and come crawling back."

Annie doesn't have to remind me I'm an eternal optimist who might never give up, even when all hope is lost. If I think it's the right thing to do, I do it, even when everyone else tells me to give up.

She shakes her head, like she's not buying it. "I'm sorry, but Dex is a loser who doesn't deserve you. And why would Jack do this? Are you sure he doesn't have feelings for you?"

Now I'm the one shaking my head. "Jack is a good friend. He wouldn't agree to this otherwise."

She blinks and studies me. "He wants you."

My mouth drops open. "He does *not*. We can date and be friends. It's possible."

"Have you seen *When Harry Met Sally*? They've already answered that question."

"We're not like them. We're *actual* friends who are dating."

She holds up her hand to stop me, like we're in court and she's objecting to my argument. "Um, I disagree. Maybe you're in denial, but he's definitely not. That would require sainthood on his part."

I give her a look. "I won't argue about it. But when I get Dex back, I'll say *I told you so.*"

She pauses. "So, let's say it does work, and Dex comes groveling at your feet. What's in it for Jack? I mean, other than free dates with you."

I put my fork down. "His mom had a stroke years ago and is now in a long-term care facility. Her insurance doesn't want to pay anymore, and Jack is her only son. The only way Jack can afford her care is if he becomes the CEO of his dad's company. That's the whole reason he wants the job. But he's afraid his dad is going to choose his stepbrother, because he's married and his stepmother is lobbying for it. The promise of keeping the company in the family for generations gives his stepbrother an edge. It's like *The Crown,* Annie. It's all about power, control, and family dysfunction."

"What is this, the Middle Ages?" She grimaces. "And you're *okay* with this?"

"Well, technically I'm using him to get Dex back. And he's using me for a promotion. It's a mutual agreement to get what we want."

Annie blinks slowly, letting it sink in. "That is *so* messed up."

"Once it all works out, it won't seem as bad," I say.

"And if it doesn't?"

I stare at her. "It has to." As I say it, something twists inside me. Failure is not an option. But if Annie thinks this is a terrible idea, why don't I? More than anything, I want to be a good person who does the right thing for Violet. Trying to get Dex back *is* a good thing, right? Isn't this what a good wife and mother would do?

She sighs. "To think you gave up an actual relationship with Jack for *this?*"

"What? I'm doing this for Dex."

Annie sets her food down and sits on my desk, and I feel a

lecture coming on. "Honey, in case you didn't notice, Dex isn't married to you anymore. I think he made it clear what he wants."

I blink, trying to make sense of her conclusion. Because even if it's true, I don't believe it. "But what if he changes his mind?"

"If you wait around for that to happen, you might wait forever. And then you'll miss out on a great guy who might actually make you happier than Dex ever could."

"That's not true," I say. "And I'm not dating Heather's dad."

"Not Heather's dad. I'm talking about Jack."

I shake my head. "Jack's wonderful, but he's not interested in me that way."

"Are you sure?" she says. "You think a guy would go through all that trouble just to be your friend?"

"Jack would not agree to this if he had feelings," I say confidently.

"Did you forget that he *once* had feelings? He's giving up dating other women *for you*."

"He can date other women."

"But will he?"

I feel hurt by what Annie is insinuating—that it's not fair that I've asked Jack to do this. That it's too much.

"What happens if you start having feelings for him?" She looks at me, concerned. "This could do a lot of damage, Maeve. The last thing you need is more hurt."

The bell interrupts our conversation as students spill into the classroom, cutting off our conversation.

There's nothing to her accusation. I refuse to let myself fall for Jack, even if he's just as kind and charming as before. Men and women can be friends, despite what the movies tell us. And since I've been hurt before, I know better than to fall for someone who's off-limits.

But what if the other part is true? What if I'm keeping Jack from missing out on the woman of his dreams? At the end of this, what if I'm the one who ends up hurt?

"There's nothing going on with me and Jack," I tell Annie.

"He's free to date whomever he wants." I'm not sure if I said that for her benefit or mine, but either way, I sound like I'm trying to convince myself that it's true. And right now, I'm not even sure it is.

———

On Saturday while Violet is at Dex's, I finally gather my paintbrushes, rollers, and ladder to paint the kitchen cabinets. When I bought the fixer-upper, I knew it needed extensive cosmetic work. Nearly the entire house was painted in various shades of dreary beige that begged for a fresh coat of color. The kitchen cabinets in all their knotty pine glory look like something out of a seventies sitcom—not retro in a cool way, but like the cabinets your great-aunt Henrietta might still have, alongside her faded rooster decor and peeling avocado linoleum. Even the backyard was an overgrown, tangled Amazonian jungle where small children might disappear.

All those home renovation shows featuring homes with "good bones" that just need "a little TLC" are nothing compared to this. The house was dated and ugly, and most buyers couldn't get past that.

Beyond the cosmetic fixes, I knew I could live with the imperfections. And since I had little money, it seemed like the perfect match. I was in love with the *idea* of redoing a house, like on the renovation shows (Cheery new paint! Modern home decor! Tiny bushes and bright pink flowers in adorable yellow containers!), but I was clueless how long these home improvements would *actually* take. On top of that, I totally miscalculated how hard it would be to find long stretches of time to tackle these projects. Which means the only time I have is on the weekends when Violet is with Dex.

Today, I'm painting cabinets, and I need some motivational music for the arduous task. I scroll through my phone and find a Taylor Swift playlist, then I pry open a paint can.

"Your musical choice is *interesting*." Jack leans against the entrance to the kitchen, his usual dark hair swept off his face, looking freshly showered in a bright white T-shirt and dark joggers. It's unfair that he looks like a model without even trying, whereas my graphic T-shirt is noticeably rumpled from the laundry basket.

"Your hatred of Taylor Swift still stands?" I ask, remembering how Jack railed about her in high school whenever I blasted her songs in his car.

"Still. Yes. *Always.* That one will never change." He glances at the front door, the sunshine dancing across the screen door. "The door was open, so . . ."

"You walked in. Just like at my parents' house," I add, remembering how Jack would never call before coming over. I like the fact that Jack and I are finally at a new level in our friendship, where there's no need to text ahead with a *Could I stop by?* "As long as you can put up with my musical selections, you're welcome anytime."

"I'm not sure I can," he says, rubbing the back of his neck. "Maybe there's a compromise, as friends?"

I wish Annie could hear Jack admit we're friends. It would be proof that my instincts are correct.

"Only if it doesn't involve eliminating Taylor Swift," I say.

"What if we put together a mutually agreeable playlist containing songs we both like?"

"That's fair," I say. "With one minor addition. I'll endure your unknown indie rock bands, if you'll bite your tongue when 'Love Story' plays."

"That might be impossible."

"Take it or leave it," I say with a shrug.

"You don't want to hear my top reasons you should expand your musical taste beyond the Billboard Hot 100 from our youth?"

"You make me feel ancient, Jack. And no, I don't."

He follows me around the kitchen as I drape a drop cloth

across the counter. "First reason: There are dozens of better musicians with just as much creative talent."

I start to object, but Jack holds up his hand, letting me know he's not done. "Second, I bet your students don't even know Taylor Swift's music from our high school days."

"You're killing me," I say, pretending to pull a knife out of my heart. "Don't tell me you came here to critique my musical choices."

"I'm here to check on your attic squatters." He points toward the attic. "I started on something for them when I was babysitting."

"Eliminating the problem?"

"Not eliminating," he corrects. "Managing. Keeping them safe."

"That's very admirable of you, caring for all the baby squirrels in the world. Here I thought you cared for my safety."

"If I thought it was unsafe, I would tell you," he says. "They're harmless."

"Like Taylor Swift's music," I shoot back.

Jack's lips quirk, like he's given up on making me see the light. "I'll be up in the attic, so you can blast her songs all you want. But when we're together, that's when I'll introduce you to *real* music."

As Jack disappears upstairs, I apply the first coat of paint, and can already see a massive improvement in how the kitchen looks. After a few hours of painting, I take a break and head upstairs to the attic, where Jack has set up an elaborate chicken wire contraption around the nest, while rearranging my attic so that it actually appears organized.

"What is that, MacGyver?" I ask, using his old nickname from high school. Where there was a problem, Jack had a solution.

His mouth curls into a grin. "I'm creating a wall of wire around the nest, like a huge cage so they can't get into the rest of the house. Then I went crazy reorganizing your attic. I hope you don't mind."

"Jack, I would never say no to extra help. But you continue to amaze me with how you MacGyver everything."

"You know, you can't take someone's name and use it as a verb," he says.

"Well, it should be. Because that guy could do everything, and so can you."

He shrugs. "I like to fix things. My dad was never home, so I was always figuring out things for Mom." Then he pauses, like he's thinking about something. "Are you planning on painting all night?"

"Unless you can think of a better way to spend a Saturday? Because as fun as they make painting look on TV, it's a ton of work, and I'm starving."

He shifts, then looks around. "Do you want to grab some food and plan another practice date?"

At first, the slow rise of panic churns inside me before I remember what Annie said about having more fun. I could reject Jack's offer and paint cabinets until I pass out in bed, which is what the old Maeve would have done. Or I can hang out with Jack, and see if we can continue our plan for helping me get over my dating phobia.

"Don't you have complex financial projections to decipher? Considering you have a big, important office job, you've been spending a lot of time with me and Violet."

"First, it's not big or important. Second, I'd rather spend the evening with you than work."

"Even if it involves listening to Taylor Swift?"

"I have my limits, Maeve." Jack gives me a look, sparking my nerves.

I'm flattered that I win out over boring spreadsheets, but I also wonder why I'm so nervous when this is just pretend. Shouldn't I be more excited about dating Dex again? Why would Jack make me nervous when we're just friends and he's helping me out?

"Then I'm going to take a shower, because I'm gross," I say, turning to go.

"You're not gross," he says, shaking his head. "I like that you're comfortable with me seeing you this way."

"I'm not sure what way you mean, unless it's seeing me in all my filthy, stinky glory."

Jack smiles at my comment, and I nod toward the giant squirrel cage. "The whole squirrel family owes you big-time."

"I was doing you a favor. I wasn't looking for payment."

"I know. But why are you being so helpful? Are you going to cash in these favors and ask me to do something truly awful?"

"Except for our Twister bet, you don't owe me anything. And I'm saving that one for the right moment."

"I was hoping you'd forget that bet."

"That's the thing," Jack says, eyes flashing. "When it comes to you, I don't forget."

His crooked smile sends my stomach catapulting, shooting a quick hit of dopamine through my veins. It's hard for me not to read anything into what Jack is saying. But I also know that I'm too scared of responding to any kind of flirtatious advances since I know this isn't real.

"Something to look forward to," I say flatly, trying not to dread when Jack decides how to cash in on his unfair win.

I head to the shower and turn on the water, stripping off my clothes, hoping that the warmth will calm my nerves. I test the temperature, and the water is icy cold. It shouldn't take this long to warm up, so I let it run longer, testing again, but it's still freezing.

Since I know Jack is in the attic, I slide on my bathrobe and dash down to the basement where the water heater is. I check the appliance sticker, but the instructions are too faded to read, so I run upstairs to call a repairman. As I round the corner, I nearly slam into Jack.

"I didn't know you had a shower in the basement." His eyes flick down my robe, then back up, like he's self-correcting.

"I don't. I was checking the water heater since my shower is the same temperature as Antarctica."

Jack keeps his eyes on my face. "I can look at the water heater. How old is it?" he asks as we head into the dark dungeon of the home.

"About twenty-five."

"Years?" he asks.

"Is that bad?"

"It's not good. Before you call someone, let me check a few things."

I point toward a tank that looks like it's from the prehistoric era.

"Did you have this dinosaur checked when you moved in?" He bends to inspect the bottom and turns a knob to *Off* and then messes with what I assume is the gas line.

"Um, was I supposed to? I basically know nothing about home maintenance except how to call a repairman." The few bare bulbs dangling from the ceiling barely shed any light, and Jack squints at the sticker.

"This is unreadable. What you need is home maintenance 101," he says.

"Isn't that why you call a professional?"

"Sometimes, but there are some basic things that can save you from having to pay for a house call. Like this right here . . ." He points at a small window on the water heater. "This is your pilot light. Can you tell if this is normal?"

I squint in the dank basement, holding my robe closed so I don't accidentally embarrass myself. "Um, no. It's just dark."

"It's dark because it's not lit," he says. "Which is why your shower was cold. So the good news is I can fix this. The bad news is this water heater is really old, and you'll probably want to replace it soon."

"Maybe I could learn to like cold showers." I don't really have the money for a new water heater, but at least Jack is giving me some warning so I have time to save for it.

"And maybe you could learn to like the sound of nails on chalkboards, too. But why would you want to?" He grins, then crouches on the floor next to the water heater, and I sit next to him so I can see what he's doing. My leg brushes his, sending little sparks across the surface of my bare skin, even though he doesn't seem to notice.

"First thing is to turn off the gas line here, and then wait a few minutes for the gas to clear. I already did that, so we're good to go." He messes with a knob. "See this red knob? It needs to be in the *Pilot* position."

"That's easy enough."

"And then turn on the gas, hold down this button, and hit this striker button." He holds one button while I hit the striker button. Like magic, something flames.

"There it goes," he says, pointing to the pilot light, which is now burning.

"I did it?" I'm thoroughly shocked that I could fix something.

"Congratulations, you passed your first test." He smiles and his eyes crinkle around the edges, making my stomach squeeze in the same funny way as before.

"Couldn't you just always be around? Like my own personal handyman?" I know that's not possible. Things won't always be this way between us. We won't always have this open-door policy if things change between Dex and me.

"My goal is to teach *you* to do it." He levels his gaze at me. "Why don't you shower? I'm going to run home and grab a few things for our meal tonight."

"I thought we were going out," I say, even though the thought of staying in sounds strangely comforting. "And last time you cooked for me, you nearly burned down the house," I remind him, thinking of our high school bet.

"That's what I didn't tell you. After that happened, I decided to learn to cook because I never wanted to be *that* person who couldn't even make rice. Surprisingly, I enjoy it. I rarely have someone to cook for, so this sounds fun."

"Wow. My idea of fun is *not* cooking."

He smiles. "It's my treat. I also thought it might help with your phobia if we ease into things and stick to what's comfortable for you. At least that's what the experts recommend."

He takes his phone out and scrolls through a list. Then he turns his phone to show me a note labeled *Dating Phobia Research.*

"You researched this?"

"When you told me you were struggling with dating again, I looked up techniques to help you through it."

"Really?" I say, suddenly humbled that he cared so much to research my personal issues. "What did you discover?"

"There are several things we can try. First we need to deal with your fear of dating again, and that means testing some things to help you relax. Role-playing is one thing we've already tried, but there are other techniques."

"That sounds so clinical. I thought you were going to teach me about body language and subtext."

"That's all part of it. If you're too scared to date anyone—or even practice with me—then you're not going to send the right signals either. Your fears are all tied together. Probably made worse by the trauma you went through with Dex."

I never thought about Dex's infidelity as being traumatic, but looking back, it definitely crushed me, especially my confidence. It very well could have triggered my panic around finding someone new. "Well, Mr. Dating Expert, what do I have to do? Because I'm willing to try anything to get my groove back."

"Anything?" Jack lifts an eyebrow. "Is that a promise?"

I hold up my right hand. "I solemnly swear that I'll do anything Jack Oliver suggests to get over this fear." Then I put my hand down. "Within reason, of course. And no mechanical bulls."

"Even if it makes you slightly uncomfortable and involves me getting into your personal space?"

"Sure," I say as excitement and panic creep up my spine. "I can handle it."

Jack getting into my personal space sounds like a recipe for the best—or most humiliating—night ever. And I'm about to find out which it is.

TWELVE

Jack

It's not hard to figure what to make for tonight's meal. I want something fragrant and mouthwatering—gourmet comfort food that's not boring. So I grab a box of arborio rice, chopped leeks, a block of parmesan, chicken stock, fresh basil, heirloom tomatoes, and a few other things before heading back to Maeve's.

Cooking always calms me down whenever I'm wound tight, and I'm hoping that the sensory experience will have that same effect on Maeve.

Because if she's going to learn to get over her fear, the first step is turning off the fear instinct. I'm hoping a delicious meal in the safety of her home will help her relax in ways I can't.

When I return, she's still getting ready, so I clean up the last of the paint supplies and make sure not to touch the paint drying on the cabinets.

I grab a skillet hanging on a rack over the island and the bottle of olive oil next to the stove, drizzling it into the pan to sauté the leeks.

As the oil heats, I grab the tomatoes, carefully slicing the shiny red globes and then arranging them on a plate before adding a splash of balsamic glaze and chopped basil.

Then I stir the rice into the pan with the leeks, adding wine and broth to the mixture. The kitchen fills with the rich scent of sautéed leeks and fragrant basil, and Maeve immediately lights up when she sees I'm making risotto.

"My favorite," she murmurs, looking over my shoulder.

"I know," I say. "Remember the spreadsheet in my brain?"

"I want a spreadsheet like that."

"I thought you didn't like cooking."

"I don't like being the head chef," she says, sitting on a stool. "But I'll be your assistant. That sounds more fun."

"Chef Maeve, would you care to shred the cheese?" She nods, and I hand her the block of parmesan and a grater before stirring the risotto again.

As finely shredded cheese rains down on the counter, her hand slips across the sharp surface of the grater.

"Are you okay?" I ask, taking her hand.

"I'm fine," she says, pulling her bloodied fingertip away and wrapping it in a dishtowel.

"Let me see."

She pauses, then reluctantly holds it out for me. It instantly starts bleeding again.

I pull her over to the faucet. "I won't let you pretend it doesn't hurt."

"It's not that bad."

"Do you have bandages?"

"I'm really okay," she says.

"I didn't ask you whether you were okay. I don't want you bleeding all over our food. Tell me where they are." I give her a look, not understanding why she's being so stubborn about a bandage.

"Promise you won't laugh?"

I frown. "Why would I laugh?"

"They're superhero bandages. Violet picked them out. They're in the bathroom cabinet."

"Okay, so which superhero do you prefer?" I ask.

"Surprise me."

I dash upstairs to the bathroom, picking out a Catwoman bandage for Maeve.

When I return, she glances at the bandage I've chosen.

"Seriously? You picked her? I don't even like cats."

"It's not about the cats. Remember when you dressed up like her in high school for the Halloween party? No one guessed it was you in that costume."

"That's because everyone thought I was a geeky science student."

"You *were* a geeky science student," I say, wrapping the bandage around her finger. "I always thought you were special. You didn't care what other people thought."

"I did care about what some people thought," she says, her eyes flicking toward me. "And you're wrong about no one guessing. You guessed. And then you made sure none of the guys hit on me the rest of the night."

I tilt my head, staring at her. "You probably could have kicked their butts without me."

"Probably," she says with a grin. "But I liked you being there anyway. You cracked jokes about everyone else's lame costumes. Then we went out for pizza afterward, which was so much better than that party."

"Speaking of food," I say, turning to the risotto and taking it off the heat. "I think we're ready for the cheese."

Maeve heads over to the grater again, but I can tell that she's going to end up slicing off her knuckles.

"Let me help," I say, trying to take the grater from her.

"No, show me the right way to do it," she says, her eyes suddenly serious.

I move behind her and place my hand over hers on the handle. Her fingers flinch for a second when I touch her, like something's sparking between us. "You need to anchor the grater on the counter, otherwise it will slip." Then I reposition the cheese block in her other hand. "Hold it by the widest end for the best grip, but keep your fingers away from the edges. Now, slowly slide the cheese over the grater, keeping your hand back, so it slides right off, like this."

I move her hand slowly over the grater with mine, and my body instantly floods with heat where my waist hits her hip. It's like my body still remembers how it reacts to hers, how every touch incites a chemical reaction that I can't control. I step away, even though she felt so good next to me.

"Is that enough?" she asks.

I nod, then scoop up the cheese and sprinkle it into the risotto, slowly stirring until it melts.

"Try it," I say, holding a spoonful out for her.

She takes a bite and closes her eyes. "That's *so* good, Jack. From now on, can you please be my personal chef? Because I don't think I can go back to my cooking now that I've tried yours."

I laugh, and she smiles before grabbing two plates. We fill them with piles of risotto and melted parmesan and stack balsamic tomatoes on the side.

Maeve holds up her hand. "I've forgotten something."

Then she runs upstairs and returns with a candle in a jar and a lighter.

"If you're preparing me to date again, we should make it feel like a date." Then she lights the candle and sets it between us before dimming the overhead lights.

As we dig into our meals, she glances over at me. "What else did you discover about my phobia?"

I pause between bites. "One thing I learned is that it's important you stay as relaxed as possible. I thought food would help with that, as well as staying home, since you're comfortable here. But other things are also important, like laughter, touch, and not avoiding situations that might make you nervous."

"You mean, like meeting strange men at country karaoke restaurants?" she asks.

"Hiding out in the bathroom won't help. But I won't force

you into pointy boots and honkey-tonk line dances either. It's about balance."

She looks visibly relieved.

"But that means we need to go out together," I say. "Take things slow. Because if we see Dex, we'll have to be at a place where all three of us are gathered—like at a party."

"Right," she says, then looks down at her plate, like she's thinking something over. "What if we practice getting comfortable right now? We can role-play a dinner conversation so I can relax . . . and not avoid you."

"Okay," I say, putting down my fork, the candlelight dancing between us, the high ridges of her cheekbones dusted in golden light. "So if I were Dex, what would you say to me right now?"

She stiffens, then shifts in her chair. "I don't know. Maybe I'd tell him it was nice to see him again."

"*Nice* is what grandmothers tell their grandchildren," I say.

"In that case, I'd pinch his cheeks too. That really gives people the grandma vibe."

At least I know she's not nervous. Because she only jokes when she's relaxed.

I scoot my chair closer to hers, and for a moment, our legs brush. "I'd start by moving closer to you," I say. "Close the distance, so your body language doesn't send the wrong signal."

"Let me guess," she says, setting her fork down. "Next, you're going to tell me to loosen up. Which is impossible, since—"

"Do you know CPR?" I ask.

"Why?" She frowns in concern.

"I hope you do, because you just took my breath away."

She shakes her head, a smile curling around the edges of her lips. "That is the *worst*."

"I was trying to loosen you up, and it worked. My goal was to get you to laugh." I slide my hand to the back of her chair. "To not think about trying too hard."

"What else should I not think about?" she asks. "Because I feel like I need to relearn everything. I don't even know if I remember what to do if someone tries to kiss me."

I lift an eyebrow. "Seriously? It's not that hard. Almost like riding a bike. Except *not*."

She turns, and something dawns across her face. "It couldn't be that hard to teach me again."

"Maeve," I say, shaking my head. "I don't think . . ."

"Hear me out," she says. "This is a role-play, right?"

"I'm not into that kind of role-playing . . ."

"I wish someone would just do it so I could get it over with. Because then it will give me confidence for . . . whenever it *really* happens again."

A strange feeling stirs behind my rib cage. The reason why she's suggesting this. Because the first time we kissed, it was an experiment too.

It was our senior year, and we'd been to the prom together a few weeks before, her lavender, vanilla scent still burned into my mind. One night I took her to the beach at nightfall, and we lay down in the sand, a beach blanket smelling of suntan lotion, the sand molding to our bodies. We stared up at the starry night, a mess of spilled glitter on a black tablecloth, tracing constellations while talking about the future.

That was when I told her about my father, about how I was worried I would never measure up to his expectations. And she confessed she thought something was wrong with her, because no guy had ever tried to kiss her.

Then she turned to me and asked, "Is there something wrong with me, Jack? Just be honest."

"Oh my word, Maeve, *no*."

"Then why does it keep happening? I've dated a few guys, but they always broke up with me before trying anything. Now I wish someone would just do it, so I could get it over with."

"Why would you want to get it over with? It's not a bad thing."

"Because the longer I wait, the more nervous I am. And I know we just started dating, but we've been friends forever . . ."

I rolled to my side and studied her face, the moonlight casting light across her hair. "What do you want me to do? You want me to kiss you *now*?"

"Would you?" she asked, her eyes searching mine.

I scooted closer, our bodies barely touching as we lay in the sand. I stroked her cheek, dipping my head to hers, and our lips brushed, sending an electric shockwave through my body. She followed my movement, responding to every tilt of my lips, every sweep of my mouth, every brush of my fingers dancing lightly across the hollow of her cheek. When she wrapped her arms around me, splaying her fingers through my hair, my hands swept across her back, gentle and soft, before tangling in her hair. The liquid copper in her eyes glinted in the moonlight, and as my palms skated down her neck, our breath grew heavy and thick and warm.

"Maeve," I groaned, dragging my lips from hers. "I can't do this . . ."

Not because I didn't want to. Because if she knew how I felt, how I wanted her as more than a friend but could never be with her, I wouldn't be able to look her in the eyes again. I knew how our story ended. How my family would never accept her. How being with me would mean living with the brokenness of a family I couldn't fix. Because I can't even fix myself. I'm the son who could never measure up. From a marriage that was a mistake. The one not chosen. And I couldn't let Maeve go through that.

Even now, there's something familiar in her eyes, the same questions rippling under her dark gaze.

"What would you do if this were real?" she asks slowly. "If it wasn't some arrangement to help me overcome my fear?" The candlelight dances in her eyes, making them glow like hot metal. "And we were really dating?"

Is she thinking of that first kiss like I am? How every touch set me on fire?

I pause and swallow hard. "I'd be thinking of how I'd like to kiss you. I mean, if this were real."

"And would you?" she asks, her voice low.

"It would depend on if you wanted the same," I murmur, my voice thick. I pause, my eyes dropping to her lips again, and I feel torn about whether I should even think about this. "But probably not this soon. I'm not that kind of man."

"The kind who initiates?"

"No, the kind who thinks he can read your mind and knows I'm not breaking a promise."

"But what if we thought this was the right thing?" she asks, more urgently.

I pause, tortured by her request. "*Maeve.*"

I'm not even thinking straight now. I want to kiss her again, and not for the right reasons. But the way she's looking at me, I know she won't stop me.

"I trust you more than anyone," she murmurs.

As she closes her eyes and tips her chin toward mine, her phone suddenly beeps loudly, startling both of us.

"It's yours," I say.

"What?" she asks, looking around in confusion as the phone buzzes again.

She blinks quickly, as if the real world is snapping her back to reality, leaving us both with whiplash.

I grab her phone off the counter. "Dex is texting you."

When I hand her the phone, her face seals off, like a door slammed shut.

Silently, I want to yell at Dex for interrupting this moment, even though I think he just kept me from making a horrible mistake. Not that kissing Maeve would be horrible. In fact, I'm pretty sure I'd love every second. But I can't let my feelings get involved with a woman who can never be mine.

I gather my things and clean up the dishes from our meal.

Maeve looks up from her phone. "Where are you going?" she asks, frowning.

"Home," I say. I'm incredibly ashamed of how I almost jeopardized everything because I got caught up in remembering how it felt to kiss Maeve. I made a promise to keep myself under control. And that means reminding myself I can never have her.

"I'm sorry, Jack," she says. "I hope you don't think . . ."

"No, it's okay," I say, trying not to look at her. "You're doing great at your lessons," I add, so she knows it's not her. The problem is me.

The problem has *always* been me.

"You don't have to leave so soon."

"I really do." Because I'm clearly not making good decisions right now. "I need a shower tonight. A *cold* one."

She frowns. "But I thought you don't understand people who like cold showers."

I don't look back, just stride out the door, not stopping. "For once, I do."

THIRTEEN

Maeve

Violet runs into the house with Dex behind her, dragging her pink unicorn suitcase. He hates the pink suitcase I bought for her last year and proclaims it "too girly" to carry. So I feel a certain sort of satisfaction over the fact that he's being forced to lug it around now.

"Good weekend?" I ask Violet while giving her a hug.

"Too long of a car ride," Violet says before running off to her room without stopping to talk.

I call after her, "I missed you, too!"

Then I turn to Dex, plunging my hands into the pockets of my cutoff jean shorts. "How was she?"

"Pretty good," he says. "Except for the drive, when she talked incessantly."

In the past when we exchanged Violet, I'd say as little as possible. But now that he's single again, I need to start dropping hints, trying to lower the walls of communication and see if he responds.

His eyes flick over my paint-splattered T-shirt and the wisps falling out of my messy bun.

"Did you take her to the zoo?" I ask.

"Too crowded. We just hung out at my place. She complained about being bored."

"That's because there's nothing to do at your place." Dex still doesn't understand that his brand-new condominium isn't exactly the best place for a child. There's no backyard to play in and no toys for Violet. He's so worried about keeping his condo pristine that he constantly nags Violet not to touch anything.

"She spilled her milk on my new leather couch and left cracker crumbs on the floor of my truck."

"What do you expect? She's five."

He glances at the stacked dishes in my sink, since I've been painting all weekend. "I guess the apple doesn't fall far from the tree . . ."

I bite my lip, trying to keep from saying something snarky. This is definitely not going at all like I'd hoped.

"In case it's not very clear, I've been painting kitchen cupboards all weekend." Paintbrushes and trays are scattered across the counter. I'm finished with the cupboards, and the new gray paint gleams in the sunlight. "What do you think of the color?"

His nostrils flick. "Not my style. Why not tear them out? Or better yet, find a new place like I did."

"For one, I can't afford new cabinets. And two, why would I throw them out? They're still in great shape."

Dex still doesn't understand how out of reach that would be for me financially. He's always made more money working as a lawyer, while I'm existing on a teacher's salary. It's not even comparable.

He looks around at the walls and ceilings. "This place is definitely . . . in need of some work."

His personal commentary on my house is not what I need right now. For Dex, trading up is his standard. It's exactly what he did when he cheated on me. He traded up for a prettier and younger model from his office.

"Just because it's not new doesn't mean it can't look good."

Even though I'm talking about the house, I want him to see that this conversation is about more than that. I'm talking about me, *the girl he used to love.*

He shrugs. "No offense, But I would never live here."

I bite my lip and taste the salty sting of blood.

When I'd dreamed about getting back together, I'd hoped that we could start over here, fixing up this place together, making it something beautiful over time. But Dex just shot down that dream.

"What's wrong with it?"

"Everything. This is way over your head."

He's not wrong. I *am* in over my head. But that doesn't mean it's not worth the effort.

"Once I get it fixed up, you'll see how good it looks." I pick up a paintbrush and throw it into a bucket.

He laughs, like I just told him I bought some magic beans that are going to grow into a beanstalk. For him, my fixer-upper is just a fairy tale. But for me, it's the start of something new, the next chapter of my life. I still believe that life can be beautiful even when it's broken.

He shakes his head. "I see you haven't come to reality yet."

"You always said you liked that part of me." I'm hoping by reminding him, he'll remember why he fell for me.

"Nothing's wrong with it. I'm just not sure how realistic it is."

There it is. He thinks I'm holding on to frivolous dreams—the dream of a marriage that can be fixed. A dream of having someone love me despite my imperfections. I might not know how to keep wild animals out of my house or fix my water heater, but I'm learning.

"Give me time, and this will become an amazing home for Violet."

"Maybe you should start by cutting that jungle down." He nods toward my untouched backyard, a mammoth field of overgrown bushes and weeds.

"It's on the list. Plus, I'm going to redecorate Violet's room for her birthday in a few weeks. She wants a big-girl room now that she's in kindergarten. With superheroes."

Dex smiles. "Finally, something I can get into."

"But not the superheroes you're thinking of. She's into the little-kid superheroes—the cartoon ones."

"Oh, shoot." Dex's face drops. "For a second, I got excited."

"You can *still* be excited. If there's something you want to buy her for the room redecoration, let me know."

He shakes his head. "I'm not into decorating. When she comes to my place, she gets the guest room."

I try not to let Dex see my disappointment. If we get back together, there's no way I'm living in his condo.

"Speaking of parties, I almost forgot." He checks the calendar on his phone. "I'm throwing a party next weekend. Adults only. I wondered if you'd like to come?"

I try not to act shocked, but this is great news. I'll finally have a chance to bring Jack along. "Really? You're inviting me?"

"Yeah, and some people from work."

I wonder if he's inviting the coworker he cheated on me with.

"Can I bring a friend to this party?" I ask.

"You have friends?" He laughs at his own joke.

"Yes," I say, trying not to show my annoyance. "A guy friend."

He pauses, like it's the first time he's considered that I could date again. Something sweeps across his eyes, then he shrugs. "I guess."

"Okay, great!" I turn back to the mess on my counter.

He hesitates, his gaze still on me. "Who is the guy?"

"Someone I knew in high school. Jack Oliver."

He frowns, searching his memory. "Didn't you date him before?"

"Our senior year. We were friends before that."

He nods again, like he's trying to remember everything I've told him about Jack.

"I need to put Violet to bed. See you at the party."

I've planted a seed. Now I'll see how Dex responds when I show up with Jack. Which means this whole dating plan will finally begin.

———

Violet runs into my room, waking me from a deep sleep.

"What's going on?" I mumble, sitting up on one elbow.

"I'm scared of the thunder." Violet crawls over my body and covers her head with blankets.

"There's no—" I say as thunder booms, shaking the panes of our old windows.

"Um, Mommy, what was that?"

Outside, a thunderstorm is bearing down on our street. Lightning splits the sky, like a flashbulb popping with light.

"Can I sleep with you?" Violet asks, even though she already has claimed one side of the bed.

I flip on the bedside lamp and cuddle under the covers. A violent crack shakes the house again. Branches hit our roof as the wind swirls against our home.

"Is it a hurricane outside, Mommy?"

"No, just a thunderstorm." A bad one. I grab my phone and see the storm warning along with the threat of damaging winds. Suddenly, the lamp dies, and we're plunged into darkness.

"What just happened?" Violet asks.

"I think we lost power," I say, trying to flick on the lamp. *Don't panic or you'll just freak her out.*

This is the first terrible storm I've been through alone. Even though Dex usually slept through thunderstorms, it was still nice to have someone else there.

Violet starts to sniffle, and I realize I need to do something fast before we descend into full-blown cries.

"How about some ice cream?" I suggest.

With the power out, the ice cream will turn to soup by morning.

Her eyes widen. "Really?"

"Why not?" I say, jumping out of the bed. Call it eating my feelings. Or a terrible coping mechanism. But I'm calling it survival.

Violet races past me to the kitchen. "Can I even put sprinkles on it?"

"Even sprinkles."

I find an old camping lantern to light the kitchen and take out the vanilla ice cream. Violet and I hover around the container, eating it directly from the cardboard tub. Dex always hated when I did that, but who cares what Dex thinks now? He's probably snoring through the storm.

My phone buzzes with a message from Jack.

Jack: Everyone okay at your house?

Maeve: We're eating ice cream. So I'd say we're coping pretty well. You?

Jack: George is freaked out, and there's no emergency ice cream here.

Maeve: I'd invite you over, but you probably shouldn't go outside in this storm.

Jack: Too late.

Someone pounds on the door. Jack stands on our front stoop, his T-shirt soaked and clinging to his skin, his hair tousled and wet. How is it possible he looks even better wet?

"Get in here," I say, pulling him and George inside. "How did you get here so quickly?"

"I was already outside when I called you." George shakes his fur, and the water droplets pelt Violet.

"You were standing in the storm? Have you lost your mind?"

He runs his fingers through his hair. "I can't help you if I'm at my house, and you're here."

"You risked your life for us?" I stand there, trying to understand why he'd do something so dangerous.

"I had to be sure." His expression lightens. "Besides, I couldn't let you eat all the ice cream."

I glance down and realize I'm still holding the container in one hand. I lick the ice cream off the spoon, and his eyes drop to my mouth.

"You wanna join us?"

"I'd love some."

He follows me to the kitchen while peeling off his wet T-shirt. After taking one last bite, I turn around and realize Jack's shirtless. My gaze drops to the hard lines of his chest, and I nearly drop the spoon of ice cream.

"Oh," I gasp.

Jack catches me staring as heat rushes to my face.

Someone needs to spray me with a firehose before I internally combust.

He drapes his wet shirt over a chair. "I guess this will have to do since we don't have power."

I nod, still holding the spoon in my mouth, because I'm afraid of saying something dumb.

He looks up and grins. "I'd borrow some clothes, but I'm pretty sure Violet and I don't wear the same size."

"Oh, I don't mind at all," I blurt, then catch myself. "I meant about drying your shirt, not walking around half-naked." Why do I say whatever my brain vomits out?

Jack grins, like he's enjoying me putting my foot in my mouth.

Violet grabs my spoon, sinking it into the soft tub of ice cream. "Can we watch a movie?"

"No electricity. And Jack's only staying until the storm lets up." The thunder cracks outside like split wood, making it clear it's going to be a long night. George paces the floor nervously, settling under the table.

"George likes to hide when there's a storm. Do you think we could make a blanket fort for him?" Jack suggests.

"Great idea!" she says, running off as I grab Jack a bowl for his ice cream.

"I normally don't eat out of the container. Dex always considered it rude."

"Then don't bother with a bowl for me." He sinks his spoon into the ice cream just like we did and savors his first bite. A wicked smile curls across his lips. "I hope this doesn't shock you, but I always eat ice cream straight from the tub." Then he moves closer, so I'm almost backed against the fridge.

He holds out the ice cream container and we dip our spoons together. They clink as we scoop, and I suddenly realize that I don't feel nervous about the storm any more. That's just the way Jack makes me feel, safe and calm, like he always knows what I need before I realize it.

We get down to the last scoop, and Jack jostles for the final bite.

"Hey," I say, laughing, trying to steal the last bite.

He scoops it in one swift movement and then pauses, holding up the spoon. "For you."

"What?" I frown. "You take it. You won, fair and square."

His eyes darken. "I want you to have it." As Jack's gaze lands on me, my knees almost buckle. Then his mouth hitches into that adorable smile that makes me want him to feed me all the ice cream.

How does he do that to me?

Before I can protest, he slides the spoon into my mouth. His eyes drop to my mouth as the spoon lingers on my lips. Then he slowly slides it out.

I never knew ice cream could set off every spark in my body, lighting my heart up like a sparkler on fire. It's like every nerve ending is ablaze, melting everything inside me like soft ice cream. I'm not sure if we're playing games, or this is another lesson, but it's clear this is no longer about ice cream.

Is this part of his plan to help me through my fears? Or am I just desperate for his attention because I haven't had any for so long?

"Did you leave me some?" Violet asks, coming down the stairs.

I don't want Violet to see us this way, so I quickly step away from Jack and accidentally back into the freezer, hitting the ice dispenser button. Even though the freezer is off due to the storm, some ice cubes lodged in the chute fall out, nailing me in the seat of my pants.

"It's not what it looks like," I say. Because it's exactly what it looks like. Jack is feeding me ice cream, and I'm ready to melt all over him.

Except I can't. That's not part of the plan.

"Looks like what?" Violet asks, frowning. She has no clue what is going on, so why am I so paranoid?

"Like there's a scoop at the bottom." Jack covers for me, handing off a tiny spoonful to Violet while shooting me a knowing grin.

I want to ask him what that moment was about, whether this was another test, and whether I passed. But doing so might reveal feelings I've been trying to deny, and the conflict I'm having about Dex.

"I'm going to get some blankets," I say, fleeing the room.

When I return, Jack is already snuggled on the couch with Violet. She's tucked under his arm, and he's showing her cartoons on his phone as she leans into his arm.

"Don't you want to save your battery in case you need it?"

"What would I need it for?"

The thunder rumbles in the distance as the rain patters outside. I sink into a chair next to Violet and Jack and cover up with a blanket. It's going to be a long night, and I have school in the morning.

Jack looks me over. "Why don't you go to bed? I'll stay here with Violet until she's asleep."

"But she might need me. What if she's scared?"

He touches my arm. "I've got this. I'll carry her up to her room when she's asleep."

I give him a grateful smile as relief washes over me. Rather than trying to be a hero, I drag myself to bed.

As I slide between my sheets, my brain circles back to the ice cream incident, the slow slide of the spoon between my lips, the way he looked at me. And before that, the almost-kiss that happened over a plate of parmesan risotto.

He might have been flirting with me, helping me get over my fear of dating again, or I might have been reading into everything.

It's been so long since I've felt seen, I'm not even sure I can trust my own judgment. All I know is that I can't tell Jack what I felt. Not when he thinks I only have feelings for Dex.

If I stray from the plan now, it could derail everything, setting myself up for future heartbreak. Isn't this exactly what Annie warned me about? Getting hurt by the charade I created?

But I refused to listen, because I thought I could keep it all under control, like I'm some wizard behind the curtain, throwing switches because I can. But the truth is, I'm not in control. Not with Dex and whether he wants me back. Or my feelings for Jack. At this point, there's nothing I can do, except throw myself headlong toward this foolish plan and hope it works. Because if it doesn't, I'll be the one to take the hit, and I'd better brace myself for the fall.

A few hours later, my phone's alarm buzzes, and the hazy memory of ice cream resurfaces. Jack's eyes dropping to my lips. The shock of cold sweetness melting on my tongue. I wake up in a sweat and nearly tumble out of bed.

As soon as I reach the living room, I stop. Jack and Violet are sleeping on the couch, his arm protectively wrapped around her. My breath catches. The way he's cradling her in his arms makes my heart skip a beat.

Jack's dark eyelashes flutter open. "Is it morning?" he mumbles, digging the palm of his hand into his eye.

I touch my lips and point at Violet's sleeping frame, and he slowly scoops her into his arms. She's as limp as a potato sack, still sleeping soundly as he carries her to her room.

When he returns, he runs a hand through his mussed hair. I never knew how attractive a man could look with messy hair and no shirt. I glance away, intent on not staring and making my feelings worse.

"I didn't know I fell asleep." He stretches, reaching his arms overhead like a cat, his stomach tight.

"I probably should head back." He slides on his dry shirt.

I take out some bacon from the fridge. "You could stay for breakfast, if you like bacon." I probably shouldn't be doing this. *Don't give him another reason to stay, stupid girl.*

"Is that even a question?" He straddles a chair and props his arms on the back, watching me cook. "You had me at the word *bacon.*"

As I turn up the heat, the bacon sizzles and cracks, the scent of fried meat filling the air. "By the way, Dex invited me to a party at his house. And I asked if I could bring you."

Jack lifts his face to me, surprised. "What did he say?"

"He said yes. I think he was shocked I might bring a date."

"Did you tell him we're dating?"

"I let him assume as much. Dex loves to have big parties with music and dancing."

"Dancing? Are you comfortable with that?" Jack asks slowly.

I shrug a shoulder and keep my distance. I should definitely not dance with Jack, not if I want to keep my feelings hidden, tucked away for good.

"How about we practice first?" He walks toward me, and I shrink back.

"You want me to dance with you . . . now? In the middle of my kitchen?"

"Why not?" he says. "When's the party?"

"Next weekend."

"Then we'd better get practicing," he says with a mischievous smirk.

He turns on some music, and I recognize the song, "Enchanted" immediately.

"But I thought you hated Taylor Swift . . ."

"Remember when I caught you dancing in your kitchen? I saw the look in your eyes."

"What look?" I say, trying to hide my embarrassment.

He reaches out his hand. "The one that says you love to dance when no one's looking."

I take his hand, and he pulls me close, our bodies meeting and swaying while bacon pops on the stove.

I'm suddenly embarrassed that I'm still in my pajamas, dancing in the kitchen, even though he doesn't seem to care. My body falls into a rhythm with his, so that we're only inches apart, the heat pulsing where his hand wraps around my waist. His other arm snakes up my back, as I let my fingers skate across the hard muscles of his shoulders.

"Are you nervous yet? Any panic?" he asks, measuring my reaction. "Because I'm not going to turn you down, no matter how badly you dance."

"Even if I step on your toes? Because I'm very good at that."

"My toes are all yours." He grins. "What else do you want to learn?"

Everything, I want to say, even though I know he's talking about dancing and nothing more.

He grips my lower back more tightly, pulling me into him so there's no space between us. I'm pressed up against him, my body buzzing with electrical current, the nerves spiraling and bubbling in my chest. I'm only able to keep them under control because it's Jack. *Just Jack.*

"Do you think he'll believe us if we're dancing like this?" I ask.

Suddenly Jack stops, his hands still firmly in place around my waist. "I think this is pretty believable."

His warm breath rushes against my ear, sending waves through my body. His palm drifts to my face where he brushes my cheekbone with the back of his fingers so tenderly, my knees buckle. My defenses feel like they're crumbling through a force I can't even control.

"Are you still feeling okay?" he asks.

Better than okay. I swallow hard as my body flames. It's like someone set me on fire when he pulled me close.

"No panic yet," I say, pretending I'm totally unaffected by him.

Maybe I want what I lost years ago. Or perhaps, after being rejected by Dex, I'm just desperate for someone who wants me in that way again. But I'm clearly not thinking rationally. Because if I were, I'd remember why Jack and I couldn't be together before, and that those same reasons keep us apart now.

FOURTEEN

Jack

"Jack, are you done with the projections for the next quarter?" My father stops in front of my desk while I scroll through my phone. Maeve mentioned she's redoing Violet's room in a superhero theme, and I'm already thinking about how we can incorporate some ideas into the design. I shift my body, hiding my phone, while the incomplete spreadsheet on my computer screen gives me away.

"I'm working on it." Lately, I've been spending so much time at Maeve's house, I've had to pull three a.m. work sessions just to keep up.

Dad frowns. "This is the second weekend in a row you've missed your deadline. What's going on?"

I ignore his glare and focus on my computer screen. "I've been busy," I answer vaguely. It's not like Dad would understand why I'm helping Maeve. Even in high school, they didn't consider her good enough for the Oliver family and made sure we both knew it. It's what broke us up in the end. I couldn't let them sink their talons into her soft heart and reject her like Mom and me.

"How long until it's in my inbox?" he asks.

"As soon as it's done." I glance at the clock. Only thirty more minutes until the end of the workday, and then I'm planning on heading to Maeve's house. Which means there's no chance I'm going to finish this soon.

My stepbrother, Craig, saunters toward my desk, the top button on his shirt open, shirtsleeves rolled up. "Does Jack have plans? I wouldn't believe it except I haven't seen you at the gym lately either."

"I'm taking a break."

He crosses his arms. "You never miss your workouts. Which means you must have something pretty important going on."

His smug look makes me suspect he knows something, although I don't know why he'd care.

"I'll get it done." I have no idea *how*. Especially since I've been staring at this blinking cursor for at least thirty minutes. I've been completely distracted by thoughts of Maeve and what happened a few days ago.

"I'd like the report tonight," Dad says.

"I can't tonight. I have plans." I promised Maeve I'd assemble a new swing set for Violet.

"Something's up," Craig says, looking me over. "Are you seeing someone?"

The last thing Craig wants is for me to become his competition and take away his coveted role as the *responsible son*, destined to become CEO. A title that's laughable for someone like Craig, because he's anything but responsible. Especially with his notorious flirting among the office staff.

"What if it is a woman?" I challenge.

Craig looks surprised. "So I'm right?"

"Sorry to disappoint you, but it's not a girlfriend." I return his smug smile. That's part of the reason I agreed to this fake dating plan. Because my stepbrother can't interfere with a relationship that's not real.

"Bring her to the company party," Dad suggests, ignoring the tension between Craig and me. "I'm sure Elizabeth would love to meet her."

I'm sure my stepmother would *not* agree, though she'd never say this to my father. There's nothing she wants more than for Craig to take over Oliver Financial so that her son beats me. If I get in the way of that, she'll do whatever it takes to stop it. She doesn't care that I want the position so I can take care of my mom's medical needs. It's all about her.

"I need to head out for a meeting," Dad says, checking his watch. "But I need those financial projections ASAP."

"I'll have them to you tonight," I say, wishing I didn't have to, but knowing there's no other way. I'm the one putting out fires at work, making sure Mom's needs are met, and cleaning up the messes others leave behind.

Craig waits until Dad leaves and leans toward me, his eyes gleaming.

"You're afraid to bring her."

"The only one who's afraid is *you*," I shoot back.

He laughs in disbelief. "Why would I be afraid of that?"

"Because you think you have an advantage when it comes to the future of the company. But everything could change, couldn't it?"

Craig lets out a humorless laugh, but behind it, he cracks just a little. "You'd have to really put on a show to convince anyone you're ready to take over the company."

Something twists inside me. What Maeve and I are attempting, this whole dating game, *is* a show. Maeve doesn't care for me the way I want her to, even if everything she's sending tells me otherwise. I'm just her temporary fix, the one she's trying on for size until things work out with Dex. At least, that's what I'm telling myself, because letting myself believe there could be a happy ending for us is more painful than this make-believe relationship we're role-playing. And now that I'm in deep with her, there's too much at stake to turn back now.

When I arrive at Maeve's, she and Violet sit cross-legged in the newly mown backyard, surrounded by metal pieces of a new swing set. They both wave as a sprinkler lazily spins in the yard for Violet.

Mom always told me that when you care for someone, they will fill you up from the inside, and I never understood that until now. Every time I see Maeve and Violet, something expands inside me, a light-as-air feeling so that I nearly float.

Maeve stands and wipes her hands on her faded Daisy Dukes, her cutoff T-shirt the color of lemon chiffon pie. Maeve holds a large pole as I strip off my shoes and walk across the grass. "If you're here to rescue me from this job," she says, "I'll pay you in cookies."

"Good thing I accept cookies," I say, grinning. She holds up the instructions, and I pretend to read them over her bare shoulder, distracted by the scent of lavender and vanilla mingling with freshly cut grass.

"Jack?" she says, glancing up at me.

"What?"

"Did you hear what I said?"

"Um, no." I drag my eyes away from her shoulder and skim the directions.

"I'm missing a part," she says, pointing at one piece on the chart.

"I'll look for it." I take the paper from her as a red car pulls up slowly behind mine. "Are you expecting someone?"

"Jaz and Mia are coming over to do a practice makeover on me. For the party."

"A makeover?" I try to hide the surprise in my voice.

"Jaz said it will give me a confidence boost." She shoves her hands in her pockets and watches Violet as she jumps through the sprinkler. "If I'm going to get Dex's attention, I need to do something. Even though he probably won't notice . . ."

"He'll notice," I say quickly. *Unless he's blind.* What she doesn't realize is that she'll catch my eye, and I'm the one who shouldn't notice.

"Dex doesn't pay attention to details," she says. "He doesn't know what sandwich I order at Frank's. Or that risotto is my favorite. Unlike you, he doesn't have a spreadsheet in his brain."

She turns to glance at me, one side of her mouth curled.

"It's a curse sometimes," I say, still watching Violet. I'm not trying to memorize everything about Maeve. It's just the combination of my brain's wiring and what happens when you care for someone. I finally turn to her. "You don't need to change anything for him."

"I know," she says, thinking it over. "But if I want to make this work, I have to step up my game. Be someone he can't resist."

But you already are. And if Dex doesn't see that, he's not worth her time. But that's not for me to decide—at least, not for Maeve.

Jaz rounds the corner of the house, carrying a large tote overflowing with hair tools that look like torture devices. She looks over Maeve's limp ponytail and frowns.

"What do we have here?" She pulls out some grass clippings from Maeve's hair. "Dirty hair? Have you been rolling in the yard?" She shakes her head in disapproval.

"Mowing," Maeve admits. "And weed whacking."

"Well, this is not going to work." She tries to fluff Maeve's ponytail, but it falls flat. "Before I can work my magic, you need a shower. Do you have a place where I can plug these in?" She motions toward her bag.

"Why does it take four tools to fix my hair?" Then she looks at me. "And I thought chemistry was complicated."

"Mommy, can I watch?" Violet asks.

Maeve looks at Jaz. "Do you mind?"

"Of course not." Then Jaz gets down on Violet's level. "If you wanna call me Auntie Jaz, I'll show you how fun makeup is!"

"You might regret saying that when she uses your lipstick as blush," Maeve says.

"Makeup education comes with risks," Jaz replies. "Mainly to your bank account when she's sixteen."

Jaz holds out her hand for Violet, and they disappear into the house with Mia.

Maeve turns to me before following. "You need anything for the swing set?"

I shake my head. "I've got this. Have fun with the girls."

"I'm not sure I'd call it *fun*. I'm reconsidering whether going to the party is a good idea at all."

"You're ready," I tell her. "Dex isn't going to be able to keep his eyes off you."

"You think so?" she asks.

"I know so," I say.

She gives me a relieved smile. "I don't know what I'd do without you." Then she turns and heads inside.

I hold my smile until she's gone.

I don't know what I'm going to do without you, either.

———

A few hours and one partially assembled swing set later, the patio door swings open.

"I hate to bother you," Mia says. "But I've been sent to announce our upcoming show."

"Show?" I ask, putting a final twist on a screw.

"That's what Violet calls it. She's currently dressed up with a ghastly amount of makeup. While we were busy, she applied her Halloween face paint. So whatever you do, pretend she doesn't look like a deranged clown."

"How bad can it be?"

Mia tosses me a strained look. "See for yourself."

Then she disappears for a moment, before Violet prances out in a cotton candy-pink dress that looks like someone exploded a glitter bomb on her.

I clap loudly, even though she's wearing florescent pink lipstick that extends unnaturally over her lip line.

Violet beams, then runs back into the house as I pick up the last two screws. I hold one between my lips while I insert the other in the correct spot. As I twist the screwdriver, the door opens behind me.

My head flicks toward the house as Maeve steps outside and I . . . I immediately lose my ability to think straight—*or to think at all.*

She smiles across the lawn, and I can't even breathe, because she's sucked all the oxygen out of my world.

Her hair falls in soft waves around her shoulder, and her face glows with a shimmery look that brings out the mossy green in her eyes. She wears a light blue silky dress that floats over her body. Even though she always looks good, I wasn't ready for this totally different woman standing before me.

"Wow," I say, forgetting that I'm still holding a screw between my lips. It tumbles out, and I fumble for it, missing completely.

"Um, I . . ." *Can I stop making a complete idiot out of myself?* Because that's what I'm good at around her. Being an idiot for her. "Wow. Just . . . wow." It's amazing I can even form words at all.

"Do I look okay?" she asks, glancing down at her dress. She's barefoot like me, except with her dress on, she reminds me of a bride on a beach, wearing a wedding gown with no shoes.

"Are my multiple wows not enough?" I ask. "You're way above okay, Maeve. I'm having trouble . . ." *Controlling my involuntary reaction to you right now.* "Finding the right words," I say instead.

"Oh?" She frowns. "Is that bad?"

I shake my head and smile. "Not at all."

As she draws closer, my heart hammers in my chest. Looking at her is like staring at the sun. She's blinding, but I want her warmth on me, filling me from within.

"I think you dropped this." She bends over and plucks something out of the grass. She holds up the screw I lost. "Please don't turn this into another pickup line," she says with a wry smile.

I laugh. "Believe me, if I was trying to get your attention, I wouldn't use any line at all. I'd tell you the truth. No pickup line needed."

"Really?" she asks. "Do you think Dex will like me?"

"Maeve, there's no way he could *not* like you right now."

She beams, and the pain of that statement drills into me. Because no matter how much I'd like to have her to myself at that party, I already made a promise.

When you care about someone, you want to give them the world. You want to make them happy more than anything, even at the expense of your own.

I swallow down the knot in my throat, knowing the crash course we're on is about to come to a head.

FIFTEEN

Maeve

"You have a few seconds?" I lean around Annie's classroom door, where she's grading pencil sketches after school. Her room smells like oil paint and soap, and there are stacks of wet paintbrushes drying in the sink behind her.

"What's up?" she says.

I scan the classroom to make sure it's empty, and sink onto an art stool across from her. "I'm afraid you were right."

"About?" she asks, frowning.

"I'm having second thoughts about this dating arrangement with Jack. I think I've made a terrible mistake by agreeing to go to Dex's party tonight. Because . . ." I can't say it. I drop my head into my hands and cover my face.

She circles around her desk. "Oh, sweetie, what is it?"

I'm not sure if I can tell her, but ever since I almost gave in to my feelings and asked Jack to kiss me, I've been dying to confess to someone.

"I . . . almost kissed Jack," I say, my voice wobbly with emotion. "I don't know how it happened. We were eating together, and the whole time, all I could think about was why we have always gotten along so well. Then, I started thinking about how kind Jack is and how comfortable I am with him. And now,

I'm scared . . . because I think I really wanted him, even though I'm not supposed to." My hands are shaking badly, and I don't know how I'm going to apply my eyeliner tonight without it looking like I have a tremor.

"Hold on a second. You almost kissed him?" she nearly exclaims. "Like, on purpose?"

"That's the thing. I'm not sure. We were role-playing a date, and I guess I got into my part too much, because I wanted to kiss him. But I don't know if it was the real me or just the role-playing me." I lift my face to Annie. "You warned me this would happen. You said I might develop feelings for Jack. And I insisted that would *never* happen. But at that moment, I wanted him to kiss me more than anything. And I started questioning all my life choices." I drop my head back into my hands and groan. "Please don't tell me *I told you so.*"

She rubs my back. "Sweetie, I'm not going to say that. I'm your friend, remember?" Then she pulls up another stool beside mine. "Tell me, *why* is this a bad thing?"

"Because tonight I'm supposed to go to Dex's party, and all I can think about is kissing Jack. Which is kind of a problem, don't you think?"

"That's what I don't understand," she says, frowning. "Has Dex told you he wants you back? I'm no love expert, but building a relationship on jealousy isn't exactly a good thing. Has Dex hinted there's a future with him?"

I shake my head, sadly. "But there *could be.* That's what I can't give up—hope. I grew up with parents who stayed together even when they didn't agree. And I feel like I failed because Dex didn't stay with me. He broke his promise, and this is my chance to fix the past."

Annie's face softens. "Maeve, listen to me. You're not a failure because your husband left you for another woman. Do you hear me?"

"I know that," I whisper, even though I'm not sure I believe it.

"No, you don't. Because you believe getting back with Dex means you haven't failed. And now, you're confused because your heart is telling you to take a chance on Jack. If you need to believe anything, it's this: Your marriage falling apart was *not* your fault."

"Then why doesn't it feel that way?" When Dex cheated on me, it felt like my whole world collapsed around me. It knocked the breath from me, and I've blamed myself for it ever since.

"Because you won't let yourself accept the truth," she says. "You've always tried to do the right thing, Maeve. And you did the right thing, when you tried *everything* to save your marriage. Let's face it, Dex didn't want to be married anymore, and there was nothing you could do to change his mind."

"Which is why I need to go tonight and focus on the plan. I need to see if Dex will give me a second chance. And I can't let go until it's clear there's no future for us."

"But what about your feelings for Jack?" she asks. "You can't just pretend those don't exist."

"But I'm not sure they're real, or if I'm just enjoying living in a fantasy world where Jack is my boyfriend, and I don't have any problems."

The truth is, I've never been happier than in these past few weeks with Jack. But that's the problem with fantasy worlds. It's not a reality I can exist in forever.

I turn to Annie. "If I tell him, and he doesn't feel the same, it will ruin our friendship. That's why I don't know what to do. I feel like I'm walking into a situation tonight where I could lose everything."

"Then don't go," Annie pleads.

"I have to," I say. "Because if I don't, I might not get another chance with Dex. This might be the only time I'm brave enough to try."

An invisible weight presses against my chest. I need to stick with the plan, or I'll never forgive myself for letting this opportunity slip through my fingers. *One more shot.*

"Maeve, I know you want what your parents have, and you

believe getting back together with Dex is the solution. But what if the right thing is not going to this party? What if stopping this charade is the best thing for you?"

"I can't do that," I say.

"Why not? Do you really have feelings for Dex?"

I look down at my knotted fingers and shake my head. "The ones that are still left from before. But there's also the hurt and the mistrust. Maybe that will change. I have to try one last time, and if it doesn't work, I'll know it's over."

"Then will you tell Jack the truth?"

I rub my forehead, wishing I hadn't let myself get emotionally involved with Jack. "I don't know if I can. If I admit my feelings, he'll think I've been lying to him all along, using him for a stupid crush. And Jack hates lying. Especially since his stepfamily is so good at it."

"But you didn't lie to him. You *thought* Dex was what you wanted." Annie takes my hand and squeezes it. "It's not too late to back out of going to the party tonight."

But I know what I have to do. I've already come this far, and I can't turn back now.

———

When Jack picks me up for the party, his eyes sweep over the dress Jaz loaned me. It's deep blue with tiny straps that show off my shoulders without being too revealing.

"You look fabulous," he says with a smile. He drinks me in, and it feels good to have someone look at me this way, like I'm not invisible.

"I did my makeup and hair myself this time," I say, feeling like I deserve a gold star for my efforts. "No huge mistakes, except for this angry burn mark on my neck that looks like a hickey."

Jack bursts out laughing. "It just makes our relationship look more legit. And I didn't even have to kiss you."

Too bad.

"What?" he asks, looking at me with a funny expression.

Did I actually say that out loud? "I would have enjoyed it more than the burn."

His lips quirk and his finger brushes the red mark, sending a wave of pleasure snaking down my spine. Jack is dressed in an immaculate white linen dress shirt and jeans, and it's unfair how good he looks without even trying.

"Should we go over our game plan?" I ask, trying to get my mind off how good he looks. Tonight is all about going through with the plan, and I'm determined to focus on that.

"Game plan?" He tilts his head.

"You should know me by now. There's always a plan. Maybe it's because I'm a mom and I can't leave the house without emergency snacks and wet wipes, but I plan for everything."

"What kind of emergency snacks do you have?" Jack smirks. "Just in case."

I search through my clutch, which is smaller than my usual purse. "Fruit snacks and a half-eaten granola bar that Violet didn't finish, which I wouldn't recommend."

"And if things don't go according to plan?"

"That's why I call you MacGyver," I say. Jack's always been good at figuring things out on the fly. And I fully trust him to use that skill at this party. I hold up a sticky note from my purse with scribbles on it. "I even wrote down some ideas. First, we show up at the party with me on your arm, because that's usually enough to let everyone know we're together. Then we'll smile and flirt, and you'll hold my hand. And if that doesn't work, I might throw myself at you."

"You mean, I have to catch you before you hit the floor?"

"Just don't miss," I say, smirking.

"What about going off script?"

I'm not sure what he means by *off script*, but I trust Jack. "I give you full permission to deviate from the plan, especially in an emergency."

He smiles, then takes my hand, and his touch sends little shooting sparks through my body.

Annie's warning echoes in my head.

But right now, I can't go back. Because more than anything, I need to follow through with the plan and see what happens. For once, I finally feel hope tingling inside me, like something big is about to happen.

SIXTEEN

Maeve

When we arrive at Dex's, I'm greeted by an unfamiliar woman dressed in a low-cut tank top and a lovely floral skirt. She's tall and beautiful and makes me feel like I showed up at the wrong house.

"Welcome to the party!" she says. "And you are?"

I frown, trying not to feel irked that a strange woman is answering Dex's door. "I'm Maeve. Who are you?"

"I'm Jenny. Are you Dex's neighbor, by chance?"

"No, I'm . . ." I almost say *ex-wife* but I stop. "An old friend. And this is Jack."

She gives Jack a big welcoming smile, which is the reaction he gets from most women. He places his hand on my lower back, and I love that he can make me feel special and wanted, even when other women are trying to flirt with him.

"How do you know Dex?" I ask.

"We're friends," she says with a brightness to her voice, and I wonder why I've never met this woman before. "Drinks are on the counter in the kitchen. Help yourself."

When we walk into the crowded condo, unfamiliar faces line the rooms, and I suddenly feel like I don't belong. Considering we were married not so long ago, I thought I'd know more guests.

137

The only ones I recognize are his parents, who don't bother acknowledging me. Even in the best-case scenario, divorce is so weird. I still can't get over the strange feeling that I'm not welcome, even though Dex personally invited me.

Jack leans toward me as we make our way through the crowded, open-concept room. Except for the bedrooms, the whole condo is one large space. "Do you want something to eat?" he asks, his crisp fresh scent washing over me, making me dizzy. Whether it's because Jack has that effect on me, or because I didn't eat anything all day, I'm not sure.

"Maybe later," I say, anxiety swirling in my stomach. "Do I look nervous?" I ask, running a hand across my stomach, trying to suck it in instead of my usual tired-mom slouch. I don't want Dex to sense my awkwardness, but to appear confident and self-assured. All the things I don't feel at the moment.

His eyes hold mine, easing the nerves bubbling inside me. "You look beautiful. But the way you're holding me right now—it's like a death grip."

I glance at my hand, digging into his arm. I didn't even realize how hard I was clinging to him until now.

"Oh, sorry." I release his arm and feel like a boat unmoored in the water. Right now, I have this vague sense of dread, probably because my heart and mind are in raging conflict about this entire night, yet I refuse to consider an alternate plan.

"Do you think this was a bad idea?" I whisper to Jack. Maybe Annie was right, and I shouldn't have come tonight.

Jack faces me, giving me a stern look. "You're not leaving now. You've worked so hard for this. The least we can do is stay long enough to talk to Dex."

"Then I'm going to need some of that punch," I say, nodding toward a large serving bowl in the corner containing a pink drink.

"Do you even know what that is?" he asks.

"Right now, I don't care. I just need something in my stomach before I throw up from nerves."

"Consider it done." He winks and immediately beelines to the punch while I stand in the corner, feeling invisible.

Everyone here seems to know each other, and I still haven't spotted Dex. Why would Dex invite me to this party if he knew I'd be a stranger? What happened to the friends we used to hang out with? It's an incredibly odd feeling to realize that your ex-husband has moved on without you and is living a life you hardly recognize.

Jack returns with my punch, and my stomach rumbles and protests at the same time.

"To the most beautiful woman here," he says, holding up his drink for a toast, then he winks, trying to loosen me up. And because he's so cute, it works like magic.

We clink red plastic cups, and just as I'm about to take a sip, Dex enters the room. As he strolls through, he doesn't see me at first, a fact that sends my already shaky self-esteem spiraling even though I know it doesn't make sense. Why doesn't he look over? I worked really hard for tonight. I even burned myself for him.

Even as I think it, I hate that I need his attention to feel seen. Because that's what rejection has done to me. It's made me dependent on someone else for approval, something I'd thought I was long over.

I grab Jack's free hand and force it around my waist.

"What are you doing?" Jack asks.

I tip my head toward Dex, and Jack's eyes slide over to him.

"Time to improvise, MacGyver." Then I down the punch in one swallow, barely registering the taste. It burns as it goes down, but I figure that's just my nerves. "Pretend to whisper in my ear."

"Um, what about the plan?"

"What plan?" I say, still tracking Dex across the room.

"The one on the sticky note in your purse. I thought we were holding hands first."

"We need to do something bigger, more attention-grabbing. He hasn't even looked at us."

Jack's face pales, and I wonder if he's the one who's nervous now.

"Just do it," I insist, suddenly emboldened by my desperation. "Tell me your deepest secret. Make it up if you have to."

Jack dutifully obeys, tipping his mouth close to my cheek, as he pulls me into his tight grip. His breath brushes my ear, a move which proves temporarily distracting.

Then he whispers, "*You* are my deepest secret, Maeve."

My eyelids flutter, and for a moment I close them, completely caught up in what Jack is doing to my insides, which are melting like hot wax.

"Is this . . . working?" he whispers, and I don't know if he's talking about whether it's working on Dex or me. Because right now, I'm going to die from happiness. I don't care if I end up a wax puddle on the floor.

"Like a charm." I swallow hard, referring to my own weak state. "That is really . . . um, *nice*." I don't want to make it obvious that I'm basically putty in his hands.

"Nice, huh?" Then he lets out a low chuckle, dark and gravelly. "I can do so much better than *nice*."

I'd like to see you try.

Someone turns on music, and the middle of the open room becomes an impromptu dance floor.

"As long as we don't have to . . ." Before I even finish my sentence, Jack suddenly grabs my hand and pulls me toward the other dancers. His hands snake around my waist, skating across my lower back, sending jolts of electricity up my spine. Our bodies press close, every cell buzzing with energy, every place he's touching me like hot stones against my skin. His cheek rests against my hair, his breath brushing the top of my ear, making it easy to melt into him.

"Is this just for practice?" I ask. Right now, I don't even care whether it's real. I just don't want it to stop.

"You know what they say about practice," he teases, my body tensing with anticipation.

"What?" I know he's trying to make Dex jealous, but right now, I'll take any excuse to have Jack this close.

"Practice makes perfect," he says.

"If that's the case, I need you to take the lead tonight. It's time to see if our experiment works. And for me, to get over my nerves." I can't tell him my brain is dizzy with pleasure, and I can't think straight.

"As long as you tell me how this experiment works on *you*." As he says it, he gives me an intense look, his dark, inky eyes roving over my face. Then he drags his hand across the curve of my waist, so that my whole body turns to liquid. His arms are the only things propping me up now. Otherwise, I'd fall on the floor. I know this game is all for Dex's sake, but it's working like magic on me. Jack has the attraction formula down to a science.

I slide my hands onto his chest and feel the wall of hard muscle under my palms, and all my thoughts about "the plan" evaporate like smoke in the wind.

"If this practice is for research, then I'm a willing participant. Especially if it makes us look more convincing as a couple. Because that's what we're here for, right? To make everyone believe us."

"That would require us to experiment with some things that might make you nervous. Are you up for the challenge?" he asks with a wolfish grin.

I meet his gaze. "You know how competitive I am. But with my fear issues, the results might not be reliable."

"I'm not looking for reliable," he says. "I'm looking for results. There's a difference." He sounds like he's enjoying this as much as I am.

He wheels me around so that we move into an empty hall, to our own private corner. Currently, I'm so into this game, I don't even know where Dex went or whether he'll find us. And somehow, I don't care. Annie would probably remind me this is slightly problematic, given that I'm playing with fire, but at least I'm learning what I need to know about the attraction formula.

"How does this experiment begin?"

He thinks for a second. "It'll be more fun if we make it a game. I'll try out one thing at a time, and you rate it on a scale of one to ten. One being low and ten being extremely satisfying. We'll start with something easy and work up from there."

"I like a challenge," I say, too confident for my own good.

His lips quirk as his gaze darkens. "Challenge accepted."

He lifts his hand, and traces his fingers down the back of my neck, barely grazing the skin, then skates his fingers across my collarbone.

My knees turn to jelly, and I hope he has fast reflexes before I hit the floor. "I thought you said you're going to start easy?"

He gives a low *huh*, like he knows exactly what he's doing. "What's your score?"

"Can I score them all ten?" I ask, closing my eyes. "Because I have a feeling I'm going to like them all."

"That's not very scientific," he teases. "I need accurate data."

"Fine," I say. "I give it a six."

"So, not bad?" he asks.

"Um, not at all. What's next?" I ask, trying not to seem too eager even though I am.

He pauses a few seconds, ramping up my anticipation. Then he moves closer and grazes his lips across my cheekbone, tracing a line to my ear, and finally ending at the curve of my jaw.

"That feels . . ." I almost whimper, my head spinning slightly. "*Really* good."

"I need a number, Maeve," he says with a grin.

"A nine, for sure. Maybe a nine point five because you made the room spin."

"Ready for another?" he asks, a little impatiently.

You have no idea.

I nod, and he gently pulls the hair back from my neck, leans close, and finds the hollow spot between my earlobe and neck and presses his lips there. The warmth of his mouth on my neck causes my breath to catch and my knees to buckle.

"That is . . ." I murmur, breathlessly. "Just, wow."

"All I want is a number," he whispers between kisses.

"Then I'd say that's like a twenty."

He gives a low laugh. "There is no twenty."

"There should be," I say, my eyelids closed, my body heavy with want. "I just don't want you to stop doing this. Like, *ever*."

He pulls away and his expression twists, like he's wrestling with this experiment. "Maeve . . ." His breath catches as the teasing light dims from his gaze. "I don't know what kind of self-control you think I have, but I'm not sure I can do this . . ."

I pull away, suddenly feeling this odd sense of being in the wrong place at the wrong time, but with the right person.

Before I can answer, Dex walks in on us, his gaze flicking from me to Jack, his face struck with surprise. It's subtle, but enough to wrench me away from Jack, and I feel yanked back to reality, hard. *Just breathe. Just breathe. Just breathe.*

"Dex?" I choke out as my chest tightens.

"Hi, Maeve," he says with no emotion on his face. No flicker of what used to be between us. Where is the jealousy I thought I might catch in his eyes? The unspoken warning under that gaze that says, *She's mine?*

"Um, this is Jack," I say, trying to steady the unease swirling inside.

Jack steps forward and offers his hand, but keeps one hand on my back, a reminder that he's silently supporting me.

Dex shakes his hand, but totally ignores a greeting. "Maeve, can I have a word?"

I nod, then follow Dex, glancing at Jack one last time.

A conflicted look passes over his face, then a flicker of something *like* envy. But Jack couldn't be jealous of my ex. That's Dex's role in this game, and I'm wondering whether I read his face right. My stomach twists violently, and I suddenly don't want to leave him.

But isn't this what I want? What we both want?

As I reluctantly follow Dex into the kitchen, he hands me a

punch cup and grabs one for himself. "Have you tried this? It's good stuff."

I take the punch and clutch the cup, so it'll steady my nerves. I need to get my head in the game, so I don't mess up this chance with Dex. But I can't stop thinking about Jack. The way he traced his fingers across my neck, how he rattled my senses and sent me spiraling.

Dex glances around, like he's checking to see who can hear us. I have the feeling I don't have his full attention, though I don't know why. "I was hoping you would come tonight."

"Really? I didn't know if you wanted me here." Maybe seeing Jack and me together actually worked.

"I wouldn't have invited you if I didn't want you to come," he replies, then pauses. "Can I tell you something?"

A surge of hope rises inside me. *Oh my goodness. It's really happening. He's going to admit he misses me.*

Dex sips his punch and glances over my shoulder, like he's waiting for something. This seems weird in the moment, because doesn't he want me?

"I wanted to tell you my news in person," he says.

"What news?" I say, a little confused. Isn't this his big confessional moment when he finally reveals how much he's missed me? I shake my head. "I don't understand."

"I found someone," he says. "She's here tonight, and we've been seeing each other the last few weeks."

For a split second, I think I've misheard him. *Found someone? You mean, found me.*

The party is loud, and the room tilts, like I've been gut-punched, knocking the wind out of me.

"What did you say?" I take a swig of the punch, hoping to settle the rising panic in my stomach, but it seems to only make it worse.

"I'm in a new relationship," he says. "Her name's Jenny."

The words feel like another swift punch. The girl who answered the door. How could I be so blind?

"You're . . . dating?" I repeat, even though I'm sure I heard him loud and clear this time.

"It's pretty serious." He pauses. "Even though we haven't been together long, last night, I asked her to marry me."

"You what?" I nearly drop my punch. "Are you *crazy?*"

He nods. "Never been more sure."

"But . . . but . . ." *What about us?* I can't even get the words out, I'm so blindsided by his news.

When Dex cheated on me, I reasoned it was a temporary distraction. *A short fling.* But marriage is something totally different, a commitment to have and to hold, until death do us part.

"But do you love her?" I ask, like the answer isn't already clear. Maybe it's because there's still a part of me that hopes I'm the only one he's ever loved.

"I've never met anyone like her," he says with a goofy, love-struck grin that makes me want to slap that smile right off his face.

There's an agonizing pause as I frantically look around for Jack. When I don't see him, I blink back tears. "I . . . I hope you're both happy," I stammer before chugging the punch like it's liquid courage, searching for an escape route.

Even though the room is still spinning from his news, I pinwheel through the crowd, and it takes all my focus to cross the floor. I frantically search for Jack, but he's disappeared, and all I know is that I don't want to be here when Dex makes his announcement.

Before tonight, I tried to imagine every possible outcome, but I never saw this coming. Why wasn't I more prepared? How could this happen? I feel dumb for even believing I could get Dex back. *Stupid girl.*

Suddenly, an ear-piercing whistle slices the air, and everyone turns toward Dex. With my heart battering my chest, I try to claw my way out, but there are too many people blocking the way.

"I have a very special announcement to make!" Dex says, and everyone in the room quiets.

I glance over my shoulder and see Jenny next to him. *Tall, slender, perfect Jenny.*

Dex beams as he wraps his arm around her waist, pulling her close, just like they're posing for an impromptu engagement photo. "I'd like to announce that Jenny and I are getting married. I asked her to be my wife, and she said yes!"

Everyone cheers while I want to sink into the floor, to disappear completely, to erase this night from my memory. My stomach churns violently, and I think I'm going to be sick. The only option now is escaping down the hall since I can't reach the door. I push past a stranger and bump into another, and finally, flee to the bathroom where I lock myself inside. As I put my hands against the door, I lean my forehead on the cool wood and silently crumble.

Dex is getting married, and Violet's going to have a stepmom. A woman I don't even know.

Then I turn, cover my face, and slide down the door, crumbling on the tile floor.

SEVENTEEN

Jack

My first mistake was losing sight of Maeve. If it wasn't for this strange woman in overalls and a butch cut who trapped me in the corner and told me her life story, I wouldn't have lost Maeve.

I hurry upstairs and check two bedrooms that are empty, and that's when I hear it: an aching sob from the bathroom.

I stop outside the door and hesitate, putting my ear closer to listen. "Maeve?" I whisper. "Are you there?"

There's a moment of silence, and then a sniffle.

"No, I'm not here," she says in a wobbly voice.

"It sounds like you're there," I say, trying to lighten the mood. "Open the door."

"Go away, Jack."

"I'm here to take you home. And I'm not leaving unless you're with me."

"Well, I'm not coming out," she announces. "Not until everyone leaves."

"Then it's going to be a long night." I wait, and when she doesn't respond, I sit outside the bathroom. "Especially if I'm guarding the door."

"You're guarding the bathroom?" she asks.

"So no one bothers you."

"Just go. Don't worry about me. I'm locking myself in here."

"You want to sleep in your ex-husband's bathroom?" I hope she realizes how ridiculous she sounds. "You think Dex is going to let you?"

"I don't care what he thinks *now*," she says, her voice cracking. "I'm staying here *forever*."

"That's not an option," I say as gently as I can. The problem with Maeve is that when she's highly emotional, reasoning becomes a losing battle.

"Why not?" she says, sharply.

"You can't live in a bathroom forever. At some point, you're going to have to eat."

"Eat . . ." Her voice fades. "I forgot about that," she mumbles, like it finally occurred to her that her unofficial bathroom stay must end for practical reasons. "That's why I'm feeling nauseous. I forgot to eat today."

"You didn't eat?" Of course, she's *hangry*. Bad news on an empty stomach only makes things worse. "Can you at least let me in? I've got food."

There's a pause. Then the lock clicks open.

Maeve cracks the door and peeks around it. Dark mascara stains her cheeks, like black river trails.

"Where's the food?" she says, her words slightly slurred. This is much worse than I thought.

I pull out a pack of peanut M&M's from my pocket.

"You brought me M&M's? Why?" Her face nearly crumples, like she's about to cry.

"I thought it might help with your nerves."

"Spreadsheet brain," she says. "You remembered, didn't you?"

"You didn't tell me you haven't eaten."

She takes the candy and opens the door, so I can slip inside. There's a mound of tissue paper on the floor from blowing her nose, even though the trash can sits close by. "There are a lot of things I don't tell you, Jack."

She slides down the wall and pats the white tile next to her. "Wanna join me on the grimy tile? Actually, it's not grimy. It's bleach-clean, which infuriates me even more."

"I think that would be preferable to dirty," I say, joining her.

"When we were married"—she tears open the bag with her teeth—"he never bothered to clean. Tell me, who is cleaning this bathroom? It's probably *that woman*. What's her name? Bev? Liv?"

Not even close. "Jenny," I correct.

"Whatever." She waves a hand. "*Perfect Jenny* is cleaning his bathroom so much better than I ever did. It's like he's rubbing it in." She rests her head against the wall as her eyes fill with tears. "I'm such an idiot. Thinking I could win him over with a bit of flirting and a really hot pretend boyfriend." She drops her face into her hands and moans, and I wonder if now is a bad time to bring up the fact she just called me hot.

"You're not an idiot," I tell her. "And bleaching the bathroom does not make someone a better person."

"That's good, because I hate cleaning the bathroom." She wipes her eyes and glances at the black smudges on her fingers. "Did I mess up my makeup too?"

She can't see herself in the mirror, and I'm not going to tell her she's sporting raccoon eyes. "It's a little off, but no one will notice."

"I worked so hard on my makeup, and for what?" Her lips quiver, like she's about to burst into tears.

"I still think you look beautiful," I say, and I mean it. Raccoon eyes and all.

"You think I'm beautiful?" She stares up at me with big, watery eyes, and I want so badly to make all her hurt disappear.

"Absolutely," I whisper, wiping a mascara smudge from her cheek.

"But, Jack, I'm a mess!" Her face crumples into an ugly cry.

"You're not a mess," I tell her, even though she's clearly in no state to make any decisions. I see an empty punch cup sitting on the vanity, and it hits me.

"Maeve, how many cups of punch did you have?"

She squints at me, like she's trying to focus. "I dunno . . . two, I think? Dex handed me one, and I was so nervous and hungry, I didn't even care." Then she hiccups, confirming what I suspect. "Why?"

"Because the punch was spiked. I didn't realize it until some lady cornered me and told me. I'm so sorry. But then we got interrupted, and I lost you." If I'd had any idea that Maeve hadn't eaten, I would have forbidden her to have punch.

She blinks, like this news is still sinking in. "No wonder it burned going down. Alcohol even on my best day is bad." Then she looks at me in horror. "Oh, no, Jack. Am I . . ."

"It was an accident," I say, trying to make her feel better. She didn't mean to consume spiked punch on an empty stomach, and it didn't help that people kept handing it to her.

"But no one knows it was an accident, and everyone is going to think I drank too much because of Dex's announcement." She throws her hands in the air. "Now I'm a sad drunk, which is the worst kind of drunk to be." She drops her head in her hands and starts sobbing again.

"You are *not* a sad drunk." Even if she is.

She looks up at me in dazed wonder. "That's the nicest thing anyone has ever said to me." Then she bursts into tears again.

I desperately need to get her home before Dex sees her this way. "Don't you think we should leave? The sooner we get away from here, the better."

"But I need to talk about this. And I know you won't judge me because I'm paf . . . pas . . ." She stops, like she's thinking hard about how to work her lips.

"Pathetic?" I ask.

"Yes, that." She points at me. "Prophetic."

"Pathetic," I repeat, correcting her.

"Whatever." Then her lips quiver, and she sniffles some more.

"No wonder Dex doesn't want me. I'm a ruined woman!" She breaks into a giant sob, so loud it sounds like a wailing sea lion.

"Maeve, you are not a ruined woman. We don't live in the eighteen hundreds." I rub circles on her back, trying to talk some sense into her, which is impossible because the combination of alcohol and Dex's terrible news is impairing her ability to think rationally.

"Then why does it feel that way?" She wails again, then leans her head against my shirtsleeve and wipes her snotty nose on it. Under normal conditions, I wouldn't allow her to do this, but given our situation, I'm desperate to help.

I grab some tissue and dab the wet spot on my sleeve. "Again, the punch is not doing you any favors. It's making you feel like it's your fault when it's not."

"Is that why I'm so angry?"

"You have every right to be. What happened tonight isn't your fault. Not the punch, which should have been labeled. Or Dex's new girlfriend. You don't deserve any of this." I'm fuming at Dex for having invited Maeve to the party where he announced his engagement.

"I'm just so livid, I could punch someone," she says through gritted teeth.

"You wanna punch me?" I offer, opening my arms wide. "I'll be your punching bag."

She pulls away, her cheeks rosy, her forehead crumpled with lines. "You? No! I could never ruin that handsome face."

"What?"

"You even have a perfect nose," she complains. "It's a rare man who has a nose proportionally balanced with the rest of his face."

"I get told that a lot," I say, teasing.

"You should. You're the perfect male specimen. So perfect, it's annoying." She pops another candy in her mouth.

"Well, it helps that I don't use my sleeve as a handkerchief."

"Ew, please don't." She's already forgotten about the giant wet mark she left on my arm.

"But we still need to get you out of here before you embarrass yourself," I suggest, hoping I can get her away without further humiliation.

"I'll walk home," she says, trying to stand and nearly toppling over.

I grab her arm, catching her before she falls. "I'm pretty sure you'll end up in a ditch if you do that. I'll drive you."

"But we don't have to pretend, Jack. I'm not your date anymore. The plan failed. You can go home with whomever you want. You're free." She waves me away, like she's resigned to her fate. A life of failed happily ever afters.

"I don't want to go home with anyone else." She looks at me in disbelief, so I tuck my fingers under her chin, and tip it up, so she'll look at me. "I want to go home with *you*."

Her glazed eyes crinkle at the edges as her mouth curls into a broken smile. "That's the most romantic thing anyone has ever said to me. Even if I'm a sad loser." Just when I think we are making progress, her face crumples into tears again.

"Oh, Maeve." I pull her into my chest, and she buckles in my arms, limp from too many drinks and the effects of a broken heart. "First, you are *not* a loser. Your ex and that woman win that prize. Second, you wouldn't think I'm romantic if you could see yourself right now." Her raccoon eyes and black-streaked cheeks are proof of that. "I meant what I said. But let's fix you before we leave."

Tearing off some tissue paper, I cup her chin and gently erase the black streaks. She doesn't argue but slumps onto the toilet seat, silently enduring the cleanup. Then she takes the tissue and loudly blows her nose, tossing it onto the pile.

She's still a mess of faded mascara and rosy cheeks, but it looks like an intentionally smoky eye now. Mostly passable. "When we leave, you'll hold on to me, and I'll walk us out the door." As long as no one stops us and she leaves the talking to me, it's the best plan I can think of.

She wobbles when she rises, and her shoulders sink inward as she slumps against me. "You are the nicest person, Jack. Even though you told me not to say that, because *nice* is what grandmas say before they pinch your cheeks."

"Are you going to pinch my cheeks too?"

"No," she says, rubbing my beard instead. I have a feeling she's been wanting to do that for awhile. "It makes me cry how kind you are." Then she starts to weep again, and I wonder if we're ever going to get out of here.

"Hey," I say, grabbing her by the shoulders and turning her toward me. "The last thing we need is more raccoon eyes." I cup her face and gently wipe the tears with my thumbs, catching every one.

"I can't help it," she stammers. "I wear my heart on my sleeve. It's a problem because there's no hiding how I feel."

"I know." My voice is soft, and I stop wiping to tip up her chin. "I love that about you."

"You love something about me?" Her voice breaks on the last word, right before she blinks back more tears.

I point at her. "Don't you dare sob. But yes, I do."

"Jack?" she says, trying to keep her emotions in check. Then she tackles me with a bear hug that nearly knocks me down. It's the kind of embrace that has zero restraint, probably due to the punch, but I adore how unrestrained it is, like there were no second thoughts.

I steady myself against the vanity, then bundle her in my arms, slipping my palms around her lower back, everything in me wanting to shelter her.

"I'm so glad you're my friend," she says, sniffling into my shoulder. "Even if you're so hot scientists should study you in a chemistry lab."

I laugh. "You're clearly not sober yet."

"I mean it. You are. All the women stare at you. Which I probably shouldn't admit right now."

"That's okay. You probably won't remember this tomorrow."

"What a relief," she says, then starts for the door. "Wait." She turns to face me. "What if we see Dex on the way out?"

"Hopefully we won't," I say. "But if we do, I'll think of something. Just hold your head high. You have every right to leave unashamed."

She stops for a minute, like she's trying to think of a plan. "Whatever happens, I trust you, Jack. I know you'll take care of me."

"I'll do whatever it takes," I promise, lightly brushing my hand across her cheekbone. So much harm has already been done. More than anything, I want to show her what it's like to treat a woman well, like something priceless. Not like a piece of trash you toss out the window.

I offer her my arm. "Shall we?" She links her arm through mine, still slumping against me.

"What am I supposed to do if someone talks to me?"

"Let me take care of it," I tell her as we descend the stairs. "Don't say a word." My heart races as I scan the room for an escape route. As we push through the crowd, she trips over the edge of a throw rug and stumbles before I catch her arm. I grip her palm and pull her forward, eager to escape the nagging feeling that we need to move faster. The front door is across the room, but it's light-years away at this point.

"Leaving so soon?" A voice booms behind us, and I already know who it is.

"Come on," I mutter under my breath, ignoring Dex, while tightening my grip on Maeve's hand.

"Dex?" she says slowly, finally realizing who's behind us.

Whatever happens, I need to stop Maeve before she publicly humiliates herself. In her highly unpredictable state, I don't know if she'll fall at his feet sobbing or slap him silly. I quicken my stride as she tries to keep up, but with the state she's in, it's difficult.

"What are we going to do?" she whispers.

"You said you trust me, right?" I say under my breath, still pulling her toward the door.

"Yes," she whispers. "I do trust you. But we're not going to make it to the door, Jack."

"Then we'll have to pull a MacGyver," I say. "And improvise."

I wheel around before I can think too much about what I'm about to do. Dex is only a few feet away, his eyes locked on her.

I sweep her into my arms and crash into her lips hard, our bodies meeting in what I hope looks like a passionate display of affection. As my hands climb her back, she falls into me, nearly limp, and then kisses me so hard I'm taken aback. I tangle one hand in her hair, and stroke the other across her neck like we practiced earlier, our bodies so close, there's no space between us.

With every frantic press of my lips, I'm surprised to feel her body respond, deepening the pressure, drinking it in, like we're racing to devour each other. If there ever was an Academy Award for Best Kiss, this would win, hands down.

With one last move, I scrape my hands down her sides until I reach the top of her waist, pressing her body to mine, so that there's no space between us. Then I tear myself away, chest heaving, breath ragged.

I glance over at a frowning Dex, whose face sags with disgust and embarrassment.

"Sorry to run, but we can't keep our hands off each other." I offer a smug smile. "I'm sure you understand why we need to go."

A muscle in his jaw leaps, but he doesn't say a word as we slam the door behind us.

EIGHTEEN

Maeve

I don't remember the car ride home or if I said anything after
Jack pressed his mouth to mine like I was a dying woman in
need of CPR. The only thing I know, in my less than ideal state,
is that I enjoyed the kiss way more than a rational person
should.

And I know where that leaves me—*alone, again.*

Jack parks in my drive, startling me awake.

"That was a fast trip," I say. "Did you drive the speed limit?"
Even though I really don't want this night to end, I can hardly ask
him to stay after everything he's done for me.

"I think you were dozing," he says.

"No, I wasn't," I insist.

"Your mouth was hanging open, and there's drool on your
chin." He reaches to wipe it away, but I pull back.

"There is not . . ." I begin before I feel it—a line of warm
liquid right below my mouth. I quickly brush it away and wonder
how much more humiliation I can endure in one night.

Why do I manage to embarrass myself so thoroughly in front
of Jack? It's the same reason I chase melons across grocery store
floors. Because the threat of a man's attention frightens me. Love
is dangerous. *Once bitten, twice shy.*

He climbs out of the car and circles around to open my door, holding out his hand.

"I don't need help," I insist as I try to stand but then realize that was a terrible mistake. In the dark, everything seems soupy, like a thick fog has descended over my brain.

"And that's why I'm helping you to the door." Jack grabs my arm, steadying me. "You're still under the influence of some very deceptive punch."

"That's where you're wrong," I say, pointing at him. "I'm a klutz even when I haven't accidentally punch drunk."

"You mean, *drunk punch*," he corrects.

"Isn't that what I said?" I can't even remember now. "Anyhoo, I'm okay. And I'll sleep off the punch."

"Do you have your keys?"

"I hope so, because I really need to pee." I search through my bag and come up empty. "There's no key. I've lost all hope."

"Let me try." He takes my purse and immediately plucks the key. "Winner winner, chicken dinner!"

"I'm not trying to cut short your victory, but could you hurry, please?" I beg.

As he unlocks the door, the moonlight catches the sharp outline of his cheekbones, the gentle slope of his nose, the way his lips are just slightly crooked.

"What are you staring at?" he asks, his eyes flicking to mine as the door swings open.

"Your face is so . . ." I search for the right words, but my mind is blank.

"So what?" he says, an amused smile playing on his lips.

"Symmetrically balanced. Except for your lips. They're just *slightly* crooked. But that's what makes you so endearing. You're not *too* perfect." It's the reason all the women think he's attractive. Jack could have anyone he wanted.

"Not anyone," he says.

"What?" That's when I realize my mistake.

I really need to stop sharing my internal monologue with Jack.

"There are some women who aren't interested," he comments without emotion.

"Like who? And don't say Beyoncé, because she's not available."

"Beyoncé?" He laughs. "I meant you."

I frown. "Me?" Clearly, he has no idea how my sensory neurons spark like firecrackers whenever he's near. That's what frustrates me most. Every time he gives me a crooked smile or that inky gaze, I slip and turn into a dumb squirrel.

"Because you were hoping things would work out with Dex," he says.

"Dex? Please." I crinkle my nose. "There's no question now." Getting back together with Dex is impossible. Even if he begged me, I know in my heart he wouldn't stay faithful. It's something I've known for a long time, even if I couldn't admit it.

I step into the house and realize how dark and sad and lonely the place is. Violet is at her grandparents' for the night, and I don't want to be alone right now. Since I'm making so many great life choices, I might as well continue. "Do you want to come in?"

He pauses for a second and studies me, like he's trying to decide whether this is a good idea. I'm in no state to have company, but I hate coming home to an empty house. Besides, Jack's looking so yummy, I'd like to feed him ice cream with my bare fingers. Which I should definitely *not* do.

"Stay right there while you decide," I say, then yell over my shoulder. "And no sneaking off."

I sprint to the bathroom and hope Jack doesn't disappear, even though it would probably be better if he left and let me sleep off the punch. He looks so conflicted, like he wants to make sure I'm okay, but he's afraid of the state I'm in and what stupid thing I might do.

Until now, our relationship has been based on an entirely fictional plot, and he played along because we both believed I wanted Dex. But now, our role-playing is over, and a sudden desperation is clawing at my heart, warning me I'll end up alone. *The show is over.*

Guilt curls around me like a vine. Am I using Jack to fill the empty hole in my heart? I wouldn't purposefully do that to him, but I'm also not in a good place to decide. *Especially* after that kiss.

I splash some cold water on my face, hoping it will help me think more clearly. Do I *really* want Jack, or is this the punch talking?

When I return, Jack is leaning against the wall, hands stuck in his pockets, that same heaviness bearing down on his shoulders. That's when it sinks in: *I'm another burden for Jack.* As if taking care of his mother wasn't enough.

"You didn't go?" I ask.

"Why would I?" he says, then frowns. "And why are you so wet?"

I glance down and realize I must have dripped water on myself when I was washing my face.

"Were you crying again?" he asks, concern etched into his forehead.

I shake my head. "I'm all out of tears," I say, because I've already cried buckets of them. I probably should just go to bed, but something in me resists. Jack makes me feel less alone. And tonight, I *cannot* be alone. "This is my least favorite part."

"What is?"

"When you leave. Especially since everything went so disastrously tonight."

"Not everything," he murmurs quietly, and I wonder if he's thinking of when his hands slid across my back, his breath on my ear, his lips on mine.

"Would you stay a little longer?" I ask.

Something flickers across Jack's face, a pained, conflicted wrestling, and my stomach drops. *He doesn't want to stay.*

That crushing reality buries me.

"Maeve . . ." he says, rubbing the back of his neck, the struggle evident in his gaze.

"I can't stay here alone," I insist. "I can't, Jack. Not after everything. My ex-husband just rejected me for a second time. I can't stand being here alone."

He studies me, the crease in his forehead deepening, then finally relents with a silent nod. Maybe it's because he feels sorry for me. Or more likely, he's worried I'll do something stupid.

"How about a movie?" he asks. "Since Violet is at your parents'."

"Okay, let me change first." This dress, although stunning, isn't as comfortable as my lost-all-hope sweatpants.

"By the way . . ." he interrupts as his eyes graze over my dress one last time. "You looked lovely tonight. If Dex didn't notice, he's a fool."

Maybe it's the drink, but a hard knot settles in my throat. I press my fingers to my lips, trying to keep myself from going over the edge, and swallow it down. "You're going to make me cry again. And this time it's not the punch."

Before I can finish, he strides over and wraps me in his arms. This hug, unlike the others, is warm and safe and completely innocent. There are no underlying assumptions. Nothing to second-guess. As I lean into him, soaking in his cedar and beach scent, I rest my head on his chest and close my eyes, letting him rock me gently.

"Feel better?" he asks.

"Mm-hmm," I mumble, burying my nose in his shirt, trying to encode his smell in my brain.

He loosens his grip, signaling the hug is over, but I don't release him. I'm clinging to him like a drowning woman clings to a life preserver.

"Uh, Maeve?" he asks.

"Uh-huh?" I respond, my eyes still closed, my hands still wrapped around his waist. I'm soaking up this moment as long as I can.

"I thought you were going to change?" he asks.

"Oh, right," I say, finally peeling myself off of him. "Be right back."

I run upstairs to my bedroom and strip off the dress, feeling a pinch of sadness. This must be how Cinderella felt when the clock struck midnight and she returned to her dreary life. Jack and I have to go back to our *friends only* status, all the magic evaporating like smoke in the breeze.

But can I ever go back? How can I stop thinking of his lips grazing my skin, kissing the hollow of my neck, his fingertips lightly climbing my spine?

I can't return to my pre-Jack life. But I can't move forward either. Because no matter how much I want Jack, I can never have him.

When I come downstairs in black sweatpants and a chemistry club T-shirt, Jack's crooked grin hitches up one side of his mouth. "You look more like yourself."

"Like a sleep-deprived mom? An overworked teacher? All the above?"

"Like my friend Maeve."

"Right," I mutter, the cold pinch of reality twisting my gut. Of course, I could never be *that girl*, the one who's more than a friend, someone he'd sacrifice anything for. To him, I'll always be *his friend Maeve*. While he'll always be Mr. Unattainable.

Like every romance novel I've ever read, he's the book boyfriend I could never have in real life.

I flop down on the couch, pulling a pillow into my arms, and sneak a glance while he's working the remote. My eyes graze the open collar of his shirt, wondering where his weak spot is, the one thing that makes him melt.

"You're staring again," he says. "What are you thinking?"

"You don't want to know," I say, shaking my head.

"Try me," he says, his eyes flicking to mine.

"Okay." I pause, fiddling with a tassel on a pillow. "I was thinking about the attraction formula."

He doesn't look at me, just stares at the screen, his jaw muscle flinching. "What about it?"

I pause, wondering if I should go on or just cut my losses and call it a night. Something flames inside me, a curiosity I can't satisfy. "Why did you kiss me like that?"

"Which time?"

"All of them."

He pauses and holds my gaze, trying to measure his words carefully. I know it's because he doesn't want to crush me, because he knows my heart's as fragile as the brittle wings of a butterfly. But I can see it in his eyes—he doesn't want to be here. He doesn't want *me*.

"I wanted to experiment, to see what worked," he says. "I'm a guy who likes data, and I'll tuck that information away for future use."

Well, that's disappointing. He wants to use those moves on other women. There was nothing about it that meant something to him.

"Oh," I say softly, trying to hide my disappointment.

"What did you think I'd say?" He cocks his head, his eyes searing into me.

"Nothing," I murmur, avoiding his gaze. I can't ever tell him the truth—how he'd made me feel wanted and desirable again. "What about the last one?"

"I didn't know what to do. We were caught in a no-win situation, and I needed to stop Dex from making you look bad since I knew you'd had too much to drink."

"It was out of desperation?" I ask.

He nods. "We made Dex speechless, and no one knew about the punch, so it worked, right?"

"Yes," I say. *In more ways than one.*

He turns to me, and something closes off in his eyes, his usual warmth gone, replaced by a wooden formality. "I hope this doesn't make things awkward between us, because that wasn't my intention."

I shake my head. "I don't feel awkward with you. I just wish . . ." My head swims with jumbled thoughts I can't seem to straighten out. Why are matters of the heart always so complicated?

"You wish what?" Jack asks, his gaze an endless pool of dark waters.

Things were different. That I could kiss you. That you were mine.

Maybe it's the punch—or a stupid, desperate attempt to feel loved—but a sudden boldness rises inside me, an inner urgency to claw my way back to the relationship we used to have.

I put my hands around his neck and pull myself closer, so I'm almost on his lap.

"What are you doing?" Jack asks, his brow creasing.

I don't answer, and let my gaze drop to his lips, moving my body closer to his. As I try to lean in to kiss him, his hands land on my shoulders, stopping me.

"We shouldn't do this," he demands, pushing me off his lap.

I tumble onto the couch. "What? Why not?"

"Because . . ." He looks almost pained to say it.

He doesn't want me.

"What is wrong with you?" I ask. "It would thrill most guys to have a girl throw themselves at him."

"I'm *not* most guys," he says, looking at me darkly. "And you're not thinking straight."

"I am so," I shoot back, trying to stand and nearly falling in the process.

"You just proved my point," Jack says, rising from the couch. "I don't want you to regret this in the morning."

"I won't regret it," I insist, offended he thinks I will. Why was he willing to do this when it was pretend, but now that it's real, he won't even entertain it? Am I that repulsive to him?

Jack hesitates, then shakes his head. "You should sleep it off, Maeve."

He heads for the door and I leap toward him, nearly throwing myself in his way. The punch, along with tonight's devastating rejection, has made me desperate, and that desperation has turned me into something pathetic. The pity is evident all over Jack's face. *Stupid girl.*

"Please, Jack . . ." I beg, stumbling toward him. He catches me but stiffens under my touch, holding me at a distance, like he's keeping me from a decision we'll both regret.

"Maeve," he says. "I can't kiss you. I won't forgive myself for feeling like I'm taking advantage of you when you're . . ." He hesitates. "Like this."

I take a step back, feeling Jack's rejection sink like a stone in my heart. Why did he say that thing about me being his deepest secret? It seemed like something special at the time, like maybe if I tried hard enough, I could believe it, too.

But now, it makes me realize there is no secret. And everything I'd gambled on is slipping away.

NINETEEN

Jack

I wake up to a text on my phone from Maeve: *About last night.* And then an emoji of her shaking her head.

I want to ask her, *What do you remember about last night? Slow dancing at the party? That kiss at the end? Or how you nearly threw yourself at me later?*

I can't tell her how easy it would have been to kiss her goodnight or how much I wanted to. Instead I type, *Forget it.* Even though I never will.

Maeve: I need to say a few words first.

I start to type a reply, then stop and set my phone down, letting the silence answer for me. *We've said everything we could.*

I need to get my mind off Maeve, so I head out for a quick jog, avoiding her house on my way, and then take a shower, refusing to check whether Maeve has sent any more messages.

I'm running my fingers through my wet hair when Maeve shows up at my door, her hair in a messy bun, still wearing the same chemistry shirt and loose black sweats she had on last night. The mascara streaks are gone, but her eyes are puffy and red-rimmed, giving away how little sleep she got.

"Good morning," I say, like there's nothing wrong between us. Like she didn't just humiliate herself last night spectacularly.

"You don't have to ask me in," she says firmly. "But I won't let you ghost me. Just let me say what I need to, and then I'll go."

I lean against the doorframe, the heaviness of last night feeling like a weight I don't want to carry. Maeve glances over her shoulder as a kid on a bicycle passes by.

"I think it's more awkward to have you standing in my doorway, like a salesman. Come inside." I step back to let her enter, and she hesitates.

"I don't want to make you uncomfortable," she says stiffly, folding her hands. "After last night, you have every right to not trust me."

She's trying to hide her shame, but it's rippling under the surface, the way she won't quite look me straight in the eyes.

"Maeve, you don't make me uncomfortable. And you haven't lost my trust. Now please come inside, or I might have to pick you up and carry you," I say with a grin.

Her face softens a little before she enters, her eyes sweeping over my house. That's when I realize she hasn't been inside before. I've been spending so much time at her place, there never was a reason for her to come here.

"Everything is so clean," she says, glancing at the modern lines of my living room, the dining room table I rarely use, the empty counters. "It looks like a model home where no one lives."

"I don't spend much time here." Between work and caring for Mom, this place echoes with reminders of how alone I am.

"How have you stood my messy home?"

"Your house is not a mess."

She shoots me a look of disbelief.

"I'd call it *lived-in*," I add.

"*Very* well lived-in," she repeats. "I should've known your place is perfect. Not a single thing out of order, just like your spreadsheet brain."

I sink my hands into my pockets and lean against the wall,

crossing my ankles. "You're living with a five-year-old in a fixer-upper. You can't compare us."

"I know, but I didn't realize how different we were," she says, the realization dawning on her. We're mismatched in so many ways.

"If it makes you feel better, I like your place," I say. "I like how lively it is. I like the chaos and the messes and the piled shoes in the entry. I like that your couch has stains on it, because I don't have to worry about spilling food on it."

"I'm not sure that's a compliment," she says, frowning.

"I like your place because it feels like a family lives there. There's life and laughter, instead of silence and . . . no one but George. And he's not much of a conversationalist." I nod toward my black Lab, who's lazing around in his dog bed. "Why do you think I avoid spending time here?"

"Because I'm constantly asking you to fix things."

"That's my excuse, Maeve. I like coming over. And it's because I don't like silence. It reminds me I'm alone. When I'm at your place, I'm never alone."

She frowns and studies me for a moment, then her gaze drops to the floor. "I hope you still feel comfortable enough to come over after what happened."

"Maeve," I say, my voice softening. "Last night doesn't change our friendship. Nothing could do that."

She shakes her head and squeezes her eyes shut. "I'm completely ashamed of myself. I feel stupid that I didn't know the punch was spiked. When Dex told me his news, I hit a tipping point and broke. I acted like a complete idiot, and I'm ashamed that I compromised your integrity and lost your trust."

"No," I say, shaking my head, an intensity in my voice. "You didn't lose my trust. You could never do that. Blame it on the punch. Blame it on Dex. But don't you dare blame yourself."

She glances at me, uncertain if what I'm saying is true, like she wants to believe it, but can't forgive herself. "But . . ."

"*No buts,*" I say. "What happened at that party, stays at that party. I won't bring it up again." *Even if I can't forget it.*

She nods, then turns to go, and the tension tightens between us, like a taut guitar string just before it breaks.

"One more thing," she says, the expression on her face pained. "About last night. I'm sorry if I made you uncomfortable. It won't happen again."

Then she flees out the door before I can respond, before I can tell her that the problem wasn't that she made me uncomfortable, but that everything about it was *too* comfortable.

———

My dad stands across the office, talking with Craig, and then looks over at me. I'm still behind on my work, and I have the feeling I'm about to get reprimanded for it.

Ever since the disastrous party at Dex's, I'm not sure where my relationship with Maeve stands, and I'm too afraid to bring it up for fear that I'll just make her more ashamed.

Instead, I've texted her with excuses about why I've been so busy and avoided our usual evenings together. *Can't stop by tonight. Gotta work late. Need to visit Mom.*

Her replies have been cordial but succinct. *No problem.* Like she's afraid to make things more awkward and is intentionally keeping her distance.

"Jack," Dad calls across the office. "I need to talk with you." My father unbuttons his crisp suit coat, signaling that he means business, and my body reacts with a shudder, just like when I was a kid. *What have I done wrong now?*

Craig's eyes follow me across the room. Getting called to Dad's office is a sign of something important, and he's aching to join us.

"What is it?" I say, closing the door behind us.

"You're still behind," he says immediately.

"I've had some other things to take care of."

"Like?" He waits for me to answer.

"Personal stuff."

An awkward pause hangs between us.

"Jack, you've always been my reliable right hand. So whatever's happening in your personal life, you need to get it straightened out. This company will need you when we change to new leadership."

I stare at him to see if he's serious. "Are you retiring?"

"Not immediately. But I'm working on a major restructure for the company when I retire." He shuffles some papers on his desk, ignoring my obvious interest. "I'll make the announcement at the upcoming company party. That's when I'll be sharing information about the transition plan."

The way he says *transition plan* makes it sound like a formality, somehow detached from our relationship as father and son. It might only be a business decision for him, but for me it's personal. I've been trying to prove myself to him my whole life.

"You're announcing who'll replace you?"

The sun streams in, deepening the creases in his face as he folds his hands. I don't remember my father growing old, but somehow he has, right before my eyes. And yet, our relationship remains the same. I'm only worthy of his time when I can do something for him.

"I can't say anything until the big announcement. Until then, it's confidential."

I fold my arms and level my gaze. "I understand why you need to keep things secret for the others. But I'm in leadership under you. I'm your son. And I'd like to prepare for this transition of leadership without being blindsided."

He tilts his head and gives me a smile that looks oddly like Craig's. Maybe that's why he always played favorites. Favorite wife. Favorite son. Everyone else just falls away like chaff.

"Just get your work done on time, Jack. Prove to me you're still reliable."

Reliable, like a used car? Does he know how that sounds? It

feels like he's trying to make me believe there's still a chance, when he's probably already decided on Craig.

I turn to go, frustrated that he still has this control over me.

"Oh, and, Jack?" he says. "The party is a formal affair this year. You can bring a date, if you'd like."

I frown, trying to figure out if this is a game, or if I'm so used to trying to get my dad's attention that I read manipulation into everything.

"Anyone?" I say.

"Yes," he adds. "Might be good to have someone with you that night."

Is that because I'll need the support? Or is this my chance to prove to him I'm finally ready?

If Maeve will attend with me, maybe I can convince Dad I'm ready for a new role, to show him I'm not the only one who's planning for the future.

That is, if Craig hasn't already stolen it from me.

———

I spend the rest of the week buried in financial reports, client work, and eating takeout at my desk, visiting Mom on short breaks, and pushing Maeve out of my mind, even though I can't.

Even if this dating experiment is over, I've grown too close to let her fade back into my past.

On my way home from work, a message from Maeve appears with one word: *Hi.*

I pull into my drive and stare at it, wondering if she misses me the way I've missed her.

Jack: Hey.
Maeve: I have a bad feeling about the squirrels.
Jack: I'll be right over.

When I arrive, I spy Maeve through the screen door, her hair loosely pulled into a ponytail, wearing cutoff overall shorts while precariously balancing on a stepladder. She's painting the entrance a buttery light yellow, the gentle sweep of color like a field of buttercups in bloom.

In the last week, she's made major progress on her fixer-upper, painting the front door a similar shade of creamy yellow and adding a new wreath of white forsythia and coral-pink begonias. The house is slowly changing with each tiny transformation, almost the way a dirt garden plot greens up under spring rain. It's not a dramatic reveal like on the home renovation shows. Real changes—whether in a home or life—are painstakingly slow journeys. With her magic touch, Maeve is turning this place from a badly neglected eyesore to a place that feels homey, like the first slice of warm bread, heavy with butter.

"You called?" I fiddle with George's leash, trying to resist the pull to move closer and catch a whiff of her lavender, vanilla scent.

She turns, and her face melts into a grin at the sight of George. *How I've missed that smile.*

She gives George a scratch under his chin, and he settles next to her feet. "Your house has been dark this week. I almost checked on George, I was so worried."

"So you were more worried about my dog than me?" I ask. "I'm not sure how I feel about that."

"George has thoroughly won me over," she says, giving him a full-body rubdown. George has rolled to his back and looks like he's in heaven.

"Now, if I only could win over people that way."

"Oh, you do," she says, then checks herself. "In your own way."

If she's still thinking of the other night, she doesn't let on. Maybe she doesn't want to revisit the embarrassment, but I won't let one night of spiked punch put a wedge between us. Her text was the only breadcrumb I needed.

Violet rushes in, her face lighting up. "Are you here to help my pet squirrels?"

Maeve passes me a knowing look.

"I'm checking on them, yes." I try to sound unconcerned, hoping I won't be playing squirrel coroner if things haven't gone as planned.

"Why don't you stay with George for awhile?" Maeve leads Violet toward the living room with George and places a stack of colorful books next to her. George willingly flops down on the couch, while Violet cuddles up next to him and reads.

"We probably have fifteen minutes, tops," she whispers as we head up to check on the squirrels.

I stop at the top of the attic steps. "Why don't I look first? Just in case—" I don't complete the sentence, but she already knows. *In case they didn't make it.*

I approach the nest, the chicken wire still neatly intact, and peek over the nest.

"Is it . . . bad?" she asks.

"More like empty," I say.

"What? Where did they go?"

I shrug. "Probably escaped through the same hole their mom discovered. Now they can live in the trees, wild and free." I don't know why this matters so much, but it feels like a small win.

"You can add that to your resume. *Jack Oliver, baby squirrel rescuer.*"

I laugh. "My father doesn't know I help with animal rescues. The only thing he cares about is what I can do for the business."

Never just a son. Our relationship has always been transactional.

Her face softens. "Have you ever considered telling him that?"

I turn away, pulling at the chicken wire so I can tear it down. It's easier than looking directly at her.

"I've tried, but he doesn't see it that way." I jiggle the wire, loosening the staples. "I'm stuck between needing this job to care for my mom and pleasing my father."

She tilts her head. "It's not your job to make everyone happy, Jack."

Even though she's right, I can't let go of this sense of responsibility, the feeling that it *is* my job to please people. Where my dad failed—to stay with Mom, to make things work—is the one place I refuse to fail.

"I'm all my mom has," I add as I pull the last piece of chicken wire down. If only I could find my own escape route, instead of being caged inside a life that feels too small.

"Are you in a hurry to leave? Because I'd at least like to feed you as a way of saying thanks."

"I won't turn down food," I reply. "Is there time to fix this hole first? We'll put an end to this squirrel invasion once and for all."

She nods, and I head off to find some spare wood in the garage and then spend an hour nailing it in place, sealing the hole afterward. It's a temporary fix, but it'll keep out other rodents.

Then I head downstairs and notice George's distinctive snoring coming from Violet's room. When I peek in, George is sacked out next to a sleeping Violet. There's not really room for a large Lab on her tiny bed, but Violet doesn't care. Her arms are wrapped around his neck, and George doesn't bother opening an eye when I leave.

I shut the door and follow a delicious smell to the kitchen, where a cheesy lasagna bubbles in the oven.

If I'm going to get Maeve to attend the company party with me, I need to get things back to how they were.

I search through Maeve's cupboards and finally find the nice china tucked in the back, along with two wineglasses. I'm not sure if Maeve's had a chance to eat, but judging from the single dirty plate in the sink, I'm guessing she hasn't.

I slice two pieces of lasagna onto the plate and then search for a drink to pair with it. Unfortunately, there's nothing but juice and milk in the fridge. I'm pouring juice into wineglasses when the patio door opens.

"Why do you have those out?" Maeve asks, stripping off her gardening gloves. There's a smudge of dirt on her cheek as she lifts her forearm and swipes away the sweat beading on her temple.

"My mom taught me to always use the nice china for celebrating small wins."

"I'm not exactly dressed for a party," she says, glancing at her outfit.

"You're dressed perfectly since we're eating outside."

"Did I mention there's no place to sit? Not even a plastic patio chair."

Even though the backyard has improved, the patio is still vacant, and the landscaping beds aren't finished. It's not exactly a paradise.

"We're not eating there. Follow me."

I hand her a plate and glass, and she follows me to the attic, where I discovered a little hideaway.

"This is an interesting picnic spot," she says.

"Not *inside* the attic," I tell her, setting my dinner on a cardboard box next to the window. "Outside."

As I climb through, Maeve freezes. "You want to eat on the roof? Is that even safe?"

"While I was working up here, I noticed a section of roof that's flat and perfect for watching the sunset. My guess is that it was once a sleeping porch, but now it's a secret balcony."

I climb through the window, then look back at a concerned Maeve.

She bites her lip. "Jack, I can't go out there. What about Violet?"

"Her bedroom window is right below us. And I promise, this is worth it." I hold my hand out. For a second, I think she might turn me down.

"Trust me," I tell her.

She frowns. "That's what you told me at Dex's house right before you kissed me."

"It worked, didn't it?" I say with an amused grin. "We were *very* convincing."

"It's not something I'm proud of," she says, climbing through the window, trying to get her balance. "Or what happened afterward." She avoids my gaze and stays focused on the edge of the roofline. "Do you hang out on rooftops often?" she says, sinking to her knees for our makeshift picnic. I join her, facing the big oak tree where the sunset looks like spilled paint across the sky. The air smells like salty ocean and wood smoke.

"I used to do it at Dad's house. Since it was an enormous home, no one noticed me on the roof, gazing at the stars. It was the only place I could find peace."

I hand Maeve her drink—grape juice in a wineglass—and lean against the cracked wood siding. Balancing plates in our laps, we devour messy lasagna, wiping long strings of cheese from our chins, and drain tart grape juice until Maeve finally leans her head back and stares at the sky.

"When you're up here, it's almost like your problems don't exist," I say.

Maeve tips her face toward me. "As much as I want to erase the memory of Dex's party, I owe you for saving a shred of my self-esteem. It's all I have left after the humiliation of my divorce."

"You don't owe me anything." I turn my face to hers and brush off a shadow of dirt still on her cheek from planting flowers.

"But it's my turn to help you," she urges. "Has your dad said anything about his retirement?"

I set down my fork. "Funny you should ask. He's sharing the future of Oliver Financial next week at a company party."

"Jack, that's great."

I shake my head. "He hasn't said a word about me taking over, and I can't imagine him making plans without his successor knowing."

She sets her empty plate to the side and studies me. "It's not too late, Jack. If anyone can show him they're prepared for the role, it's you. If we don't convince your dad now and he chooses Craig, you'll always wonder what would have happened if we'd tried."

I can tell she won't let me get out of this. "And what if he's already decided?"

"If he doesn't hire you, then you should think about what you'd really like to do. This is your chance to do what you want. Have you ever thought of that?"

I pause, my gaze lingering on the bruised purple clouds. "If money didn't matter and Mom was living independently, I'd start a wildlife nonprofit. With all the beach condos going up in the area, many of our native species are losing their natural habitats. It won't be long until there's no place left for them."

"Jack, I could totally see you doing that. What's stopping you?"

I turn toward the pink-taffy wisps stretched across the sky. "My dad would make my life very unpleasant."

"He'd really do that after choosing Craig over you?"

"Loyalty to the business *is* loyalty to the family. If he introduces Craig at the party as the next CEO, I'm going to have to accept that."

She thinks it over. "Do you need me to show up with you? Prove to your dad how ready you are for this? Unless you have someone else in mind . . ."

I'm not sure if she's saying this because she's hoping I won't take her up on her offer, or if she's still embarrassed about what happened.

I tip my face to her. "You know how my family is. I can't let you get torn apart by the wolves. I promised I'd never let that happen again."

"It won't, since we're not really dating," she says, trying to prove she's ready to face them.

I still remember her hurt expression when my stepmother told Maeve that she would never fit into our family. That she was *too* different, *too* odd, just like her parents.

When I broke up with Maeve before graduation, I told her I needed to focus on my goals, heading to college in California and eventually working in my father's business.

"There's no future for us," I told her then, but that was only half true. What I couldn't bring myself to say is that I couldn't watch my family cut her down in a million little ways. They could reject me, but I wouldn't let them do the same to her.

"I want to be there for you," Maeve says. "No matter what happens."

"Are you sure about this? After everything that's happened?" I ask, feeling like this is the second chance we need after Dex's party. I don't want to mention her dating phobia, but I wonder if Dex's announcement triggered a minor relapse.

She lifts a shoulder. "I told Annie I'm never dating again. But she insists I need to get back in the saddle."

"We can take things slow," I say.

She meets my gaze, keeping her distance. "Speaking of going slow, I have something to show you. A surprise for Violet's room."

She leads me to the garage, which is still packed with boxes. We snake around the stacks until we come to a sheet tossed over some furniture. She strips off the cover to reveal a partially painted headboard and old dresser.

"What do you think? I bought it at a secondhand store, and I'm repainting it to match her favorite superhero colors."

"I like it. When do you need to finish this?"

"End of the month, by Violet's birthday. That's the completion date for all my painting and redecorating, since everyone is coming over. Several rooms need fresh paint, and there are still some bushes left to plant."

I raise an eyebrow. "You're putting a lot of pressure on yourself. You know Violet won't care as long as you buy her a superhero birthday cake with colored frosting."

"I know, but *I* care. Do you think it's a good idea?"

"A magical superhero room renovation? It's fantastic," I say. "When should we start?"

She drapes the sheet back over the secret project. "How about we get through your company party first?" she says. "Truthfully, I can't wait to see your stepmother's face when I show up with you. I kind of feel like I'm Elizabeth Oliver's worst nightmare."

TWENTY

Jack

As I pull into the parking lot of Mom's care facility, I see her gentle outline through the first-floor window. She's holding her well-worn sudoku book, a brightly crocheted blanket on her lap, her lips puckered into intense concentration. This feels like a necessary stop before I pick up Maeve and head to the company party, like I need her blessing to get through tonight.

The last week has been overwhelming, with the tension at work between Craig and me at a breaking point. Every time I see my father, I can't erase a nagging feeling under the surface. I'm the son *who was a mistake*. The one who needs to make up for being *not enough*. Dad's already admitted as much about his marriage to Mom.

I stop at the door to the facility and straighten my tie in the glass door. Not bad for a guy with an emotionally distant father who's about to face the battle-axe of crushed dreams.

I take a deep breath before entering Mom's room, wanting a little encouragement before I face off with my stepfamily.

Her gaze flits over my suit, and she puts her book down. "Jack, you're the epitome of handsome."

"And you're not biased at all."

"I'm completely biased." She smiles. "As every mother should be. I love seeing you in a suit. What's the occasion?"

I haven't told her yet about the company party, mainly because I didn't want her worrying about the outcome. "Dad's making his big announcement tonight."

Mom's face falls. "Did he tell you anything yet?"

I shake my head. "Not yet."

She pauses, thinking this over. "What will you do if he chooses Craig?"

"I'm not sure yet." Working for Craig would be challenging. Mostly because he doesn't do much work.

She tilts her head, considering something. "You've focused on being CEO for so long, I wonder if you've ever stopped to consider anything else?"

"You, of course." I squeeze her hand.

She gives me a look. "There has to be someone other than me."

"There is," I say, trying not to make a big deal about it. "I have a date tonight. Maeve is attending with me."

Mom raises an eyebrow. "Jack Michael, you're just now telling me this?" My mother has a flair for the dramatic, and the stroke didn't lessen that at all. "Well, do you have feelings for her?"

Judging by the way I felt kissing her, no doubt. But those probably aren't the feelings Mom is talking about.

"A better question is whether this could work the second time around," I reply. "And I'm not sure."

I can't tell my mother that even if I wanted to, I couldn't put Maeve through the torture of my stepmother's criticism. And I need this job to provide for Mom's care. Either way, I'm stuck between family obligation and family dysfunction.

"Jack," she says, her tone soft. "If you like this girl, don't push her away. That's always what you do when you're afraid."

Even if she's right, this time I don't have to push Maeve away. She's made her feelings clear. Ever since Dex's party, she's not interested in dating.

I tuck a strand of Mom's hair behind her ear and then kiss her forehead before saying goodbye.

Tonight is my last chance to pretend we could make this work. That she could be mine. Even if I know she never could be.

———

When I get to Maeve's house, Violet answers the door, rushing toward me with a full-body hug. "Uncle Jack!" she squeals.

Jaz and Mia peek around the top of the stairs, minus Maeve. I'm guessing they're giving her another makeover for this date.

"You should know better than to arrive early for a formal event," Jaz says.

I check my watch. "Does five minutes really make a difference?"

Mia and Jaz both turn to glare at me. "Yes," they say in unison.

I sigh and look at Violet. "I guess it's you and me."

"Then let's pretend you're taking me to a ball! I'll get my dress on."

Violet rushes to put on one of her dozen princess gowns and returns with it hastily pulled on. "I'm ready!"

"What do we do at this princess ball?" I ask.

"You ask me to dance, of course," she says.

I get down on one knee and hold out a hand. "Will you dance with me, Princess Violet?"

I take her hands while she stands on my feet, and we sway back and forth.

"I've never danced with anyone this short," I say.

"Well, honestly, you could use some practice," Violet says bluntly.

I pick Violet up. "How about if I spin you around, like this?" We wheel around in circles until she can't stop giggling. "Is this the right way to dance?"

"I'd say you need someone more your size," Maeve says, behind me.

I stop spinning and almost drop Violet when I see Maeve. She props one hand on her hip, looking stunning in a floor-length gold strapless dress. Her hair is swept over to one side and falls down her shoulder in gentle waves.

"Um," I say, swallowing hard, my mind suddenly erased of all coherent thoughts. "You look incredible."

The one thing I haven't calculated for tonight is Maeve's effect on me. I've been so preoccupied with Dad's announcement, I haven't considered how one look from her melts my resolve. The chemistry between us is like a live wire, and I'm about to get burned.

"You don't look bad yourself." She smiles and my heart nearly trips over itself.

"I think you've rendered him speechless," Mia says with a triumphant smile.

"Mission accomplished," Jaz says, before high-fiving Mia.

She gives Violet a quick hug, then turns to me.

I offer her my arm and she wraps her hand around it, her touch sending waves of pleasure through me, the air thick with the heady scent of lavender fields. If only this night were an actual date and not me facing a future I'm not ready for.

As I open the door for her, a text from Craig comes through with five words: *May the best man win.*

I delete the text, suddenly slapped back to reality. Even though tonight is going to determine my future, I need to protect Maeve from my stepmother's cutting remarks while proving to my father I'm worthy of the job, even if he doesn't choose me.

"What's wrong?" Maeve asks, sensing my sudden mood shift.

"Nothing," I say, which is only partially true. Nothing is wrong *yet*. But I sense tonight isn't going to turn out the way I want—and my whole future rides on this.

TWENTY-ONE

Maeve

"Are you sure I'm not overdressed?" I ask Jack as he parks at the venue.

Jack's eyes skim over me with an approving grin. "I think you're perfect. In my family, there is no such thing as overdressing. My stepmother always dresses like she's got her own Vegas stage show."

We step out of the car, and the heat from the blacktop slams into us. While some women glisten, I'm sweating like a sumo wrestler in a sauna.

"Excuse me?" Jack gives me a concerned look.

"Did I say that sumo wrestler comment out loud?"

"You seem to have that problem a lot," Jack muses. "Not that I mind. It's great to have a front-row seat to your inner thoughts."

"You should run away now, Jack. My inner thoughts are terrifying."

"They're not. And you look nothing like a sumo wrestler." He gives me a boyish smile as his eyes graze over me.

I wave my hands, trying to keep the makeup from sliding off my face. "Why is it so humid here?"

"Because it's the South. Every day is humid. We basically breathe water."

"That's a shame after all the work I put into my hair and makeup." I place a palm on my stomach, trying to quell the anxiety.

Jack glances at my hand. "Are you nervous about tonight?"

"Is the Pope Catholic? I'm terrified."

"About what?"

I stop at the ballroom doors. "I'm afraid I'll throw up, or get cornered by your stepmother, or a dozen other things my active imagination concocts . . ."

Jack smiles and brushes his knuckles over my cheek with the lightest touch. "You could *never* embarrass me."

"Then you haven't spent enough time with me. I'm *really* exceptional at humiliating myself. Just ask Annie."

"Oh, I know you, Maeve. More than you realize." His eyes slide over my bare shoulder, and I thrill under his gaze, even though I know he doesn't want me that way.

"Have you prepared your parents for this awkward encounter? Because no matter how much I'd like them to welcome me with open arms, I have a feeling that won't happen."

"I told my dad."

"And your stepmother?" I ask biting my lip. "Tell me you at least mentioned it."

"Maeve, you know there's no preparing when it comes to the Wicked Witch. That's why I'm going to make sure we don't get cornered by her."

"Great. So, basically, I'm dead."

"Not dead. This is your get-back-in-the-saddle moment. You know what Ted Lasso says, right? 'Taking on a challenge is a lot like riding a horse. If you're comfortable while you're doing it, you're probably doing it wrong.'"

"That's why I don't ride horses," I reply.

"Me neither. But if we get bucked off tonight, we're gonna do it together. Oh, and one more thing . . ." He reaches inside his coat pocket and pulls out a yellow package of M&M's. "I brought this for you. It's king-sized, in case you accidentally drink some spiked punch." He's looking at me like Ted Lasso right now, his face radiating buckets of hope.

"I will not be drinking punch tonight," I insist. "We do not need a repeat of Dex's party."

"I know they help you when you're nervous. And I was afraid you didn't eat. Did I guess right?" He raises an eyebrow and I quickly look away.

"I did not," I admit, taking the package and popping them into my purse so I can sneak them later. "And you're right. I am nervous, but it helps that you're with me." Once again, Jack is taking care of me, making sure I'm not walking into this party on an empty stomach.

As we enter a decadent foyer, I quickly assess everyone's clothing and am relieved to discover that I'm definitely not over-dressed and the air-conditioning works fabulously, which is good news for my armpits and what's left of my makeup.

Most of the women are dressed in glittery ballgowns that look like someone raided Dolly Parton's closet. Jack never told me he had so many pretty female coworkers, and my stomach twists uncomfortably at the thought of these women flirting with him daily.

Several people wave at Jack and greet him as we walk by, and it's clear that he's well liked among his staff. Even with him being the boss's son, you can't *not* like Jack. That's what he and Ted Lasso have in common. They're everybody's favorite person.

"I don't see your family." I loop my arm through Jack's, making it clear he's mine for tonight. "Maybe Elizabeth regret-fully got sick with the stomach flu?"

"We couldn't get *that* lucky," he says with a smirk. "Knowing my stepmom's love of making an entrance, she's probably going to show up late intentionally."

"Great! That gives me plenty of time to grab a snack." Since I haven't eaten all day because of my nerves, I'm ecstatic to see a table overflowing with appetizers. I knew if I ate, I'd never close the zipper on this dress. I'd have to jerry-rig it with duct tape, just like they do in those home renovation shows when something breaks.

If there's one thing I've learned from HGTV, it's that duct tape can pretty much fix anything.

In the ballroom, a band playing nineties pop music starts a bouncing bass line, and couples flood the ballroom's dance floor. Jack grabs my arm and pulls me toward the dance floor, gazing at me with a lopsided half-smile that's so cute, I want to plaster my lips to his.

"I'll bring you all the food you want if you'll dance with me first," he says with a dark gaze. "This is my chance to make an impression and show that I'm ready for the next step."

The way he's looking at me right now, his eyes sliding down to my lips, I'm almost lightheaded. He slides his hands around my back, tugging me closer as our bodies press together.

"I'd be happy to dance with you, Jack Oliver."

How could I say no to this man? If he asked me to bear his children right now, I'd say yes, even if it means putting up with his witchy stepmother.

But that doesn't resolve my problematic feelings for Jack. Even though tonight is a temporary arrangement between friends, the chemistry between us is *real*, even if I'm the only one who's feeling it.

I've already accepted that Jack isn't interested in a long-term commitment with me. And I'm still scared and reeling from losing every shred of my self-esteem. Why would Jack want me—a broken-hearted, single mom with a boatload of baggage—when he could have one of these younger and decidedly prettier models?

No matter how much I want someone like Jack, he's off-limits.

Tonight, the only thing Jack needs from me is to pretend I'm totally into him, which shouldn't be hard since I actually am. He's rescued me from Dex's party, fixed half of my house problems, and been an unexpected answer to my prayers for Violet.

The guy is a freaking superhero. And if he's my hero, I need to act like his loyal sidekick, the one who's willing to take one for the team.

Jack pulls me to the corner of the dance floor, his fingers entwined with mine, ignoring everyone else in the room. Then he wraps his arms around my waist, tugging me closer, while I lace my fingers behind his neck. Right now, his hands are shooting sparks through my skin, and I'm hoping I don't start sweating profusely.

"So this is it, huh?" I say, feeling stiff and uncoordinated. "Time to implement what I've learned and put those flirting lessons to good use."

He lifts an eyebrow. "You're ready for the final exam?"

"What final exam? I thought we were just dancing, and I was supposed to fake laugh at your bad pickup lines."

He grins at me. "Maeve Baxter, what kind of man do you take me for?"

"The kind of man who can woo a woman with cheesy pickup lines."

His lips quirk, but he doesn't argue. "Then, baby, you must be a star—"

I cut him off before he can finish. "Because I'm *falling for you.*"

"You've heard it before?"

"I did my research before tonight's big date."

"I've taught you well, young Jedi," he says, grinning.

"Have you used these pickup lines on your dates before?" A twinge of jealousy pricks me inside. I don't want to think about Jack dating other women, but I'd bet he's even dated a few gorgeous women at this party.

"No, just on you," he says.

I let out a soundless laugh.

"Why do you look surprised?" he asks.

"Because I'm sure you've dated lots of women. Why would you need to research anything for me?"

"I have dated many women, but no woman with a dating

phobia. Remember when I told you I was researching techniques to help you get over your fears?"

I nod. "So, Mr. Phobia Expert, what else did your research say?"

He tilts his eyes to the ceiling. "Let me see. That physical touch is important. Did you know hugging someone for twenty seconds makes endorphins flood your body, reducing stress?"

"Now, who's the scientist here? You didn't tell me you were studying neuroscience."

"Only for you. It's the reason I touch you a lot."

"Oh," I say, slightly disappointed. I was hoping the reason he touches me is because he can't keep his hands off me. I should've known there was a reason that wasn't based only on attraction.

"What's wrong?" he asks.

I stop moving. "I suddenly feel like a science experiment. Like you've been testing me to prove a hypothesis."

He frowns slightly. "But isn't that what you wanted? To get over your phobia? Move on from Dex?"

I can't say it, even though everything in me is bleeding this message. *You. It's always been you.*

Instead, I nod weakly. "Of course I want to move on."

He stares at me hard, like he's reading my emotions, filing them away for later.

"You look like you need a hug," he murmurs. Without warning, he erases the gap between us and folds his arms around me. I'm suddenly burrowed into his chest, intoxicated by his musky cedarwood scent, tunneling into the safe blanket of his arms.

"Am I that easy to read?" I say.

"You've always been easy to read. That's because I've been studying you."

"If you weren't my friend, I'd be very creeped out right now."

He lets out a full, glorious laugh that fills my heart. I love his laughter and how it spills over like a glass of champagne.

He loosens his grip, leaving a few inches between us, in case there was any question. I can breathe more easily now, but it's disappointing not to be so close to him.

"You seem more relaxed now," he whispers in my ear.

"You have no idea," I say. "And you're doing a great job being my pretend boyfriend."

"Am I?" he says. "Good to know." He nuzzles his face into my hair, like he's breathing in my scent, and lets the music move us in rhythm. "Since this is the final exam, what else would a pretend boyfriend do?"

"Well." My body tenses with anticipation. "He'd probably gently kiss my head in that sweet way men sometimes do."

"Like this?" he says, his lips brushing against my hair, sending fireworks through my body.

"Then what?" he asks, his crooked mouth quirking up on one side. "Hypothetically, of course."

"Hypothetically, he's going to leave a trail of kisses to my . . ." I'm not sure I want to tell Jack my weak spot, but if we're just pretending, what can it hurt?

"And that is?"

"You have to guess."

He swallows hard, like this might be torturing him, then grazes my cheek, pressing his lips gently to my cheekbone. "How about here?" he asks.

I shake my head. "Getting warmer."

He tries again, moving to my forehead. "Here?"

"Definitely colder," I say.

He shifts back, gently kissing the spot right in front of my earlobe and whispers, "What about here?"

"That's really hot," I say, trying to control my ragged breathing.

"Good thing I'm a quick learner," he teases.

Right now, my knees feel so weak, I might faint if he kisses me again, which is probably going to happen anyway.

"I'm pretty sure you passed," I manage to say. "With flying colors."

A wolfish grin hitches one corner of his mouth. "And you didn't freak out or throw up, which means we're making progress." He looks so proud of me, even though I'm pretty sure he could have this success with any woman. "So scientifically, explain to me what's happening that's different from before?"

"It sets off a chain reaction in my entire body," I say. "Like the Fourth of July fireworks finale. But instead of being scared, it's a different feeling. The kind I'm pretty sure I'm supposed to have."

"And then what happens after all that explosive energy releases?"

"A rush of endorphins floods my system," I whisper, trying to sort through what I remember from my neuroscience studies. "They're the pleasure chemicals. They make us happy without us even being aware of it."

"I love that this can make you happy," he says in a low voice.

I've forgotten about pretending now, or even that I'm not supposed to feel this way about Jack, because my brain is totally present in the moment. I love being with Jack, and if this is my last date with him, I want to make it unforgettable.

"You're so good at this," I murmur.

"I aim to please." He grins, satisfied that he's helping me get over my fears.

"You're definitely getting an A on this exam," I say.

"We haven't even gotten to the extra credit yet."

"What extra credit?"

"An experiment of your own choosing," he says. "But only if you want to . . ."

"I want to," I shoot back, probably too eagerly. "The extra credit might come in handy, given how I'm trying to beat this phobia." If I'm getting into my role tonight, I might as well make it totally believable. "But where might we perform this experiment?"

He lifts an eyebrow, grinning. "In a hurry?"

"I love science," I reply with a smile. "And I need practice. *Lots* of practice."

He takes my hand and pulls me off the dance floor. "No time like the present," he adds, rushing us out of the ballroom. He leads us to a small storage room at the end of an empty hall, far enough from the ballroom where no one will bother us. He jiggles the handle of the door, and like magic, it opens to a room filled with spare stacked tables and chairs puzzled into the tight space. With no windows, the room is off-limits, private—the perfect hiding place.

He shuts the door and then backs me against the doorframe.

"No one will bother us here," he murmurs. He takes my hands and gazes at me, his pupils darkening, the dim light seeping under the door, outlining his sharp cheekbones.

"So what's the experiment?" he says.

I pause, knowing this might be the last time. Because whether Jack gets the job, after tonight, our charade will be over, and I'll go back to my lonely life. And that scares me more than anything. When Jack re-entered my life, I finally had a friend to call in the middle of the night and someone to watch movies with or help me fix my home. Even better, I gained all his friends too, which meant I never was left out. Jack made me feel like I belonged when I needed it most.

"This might seem crazy," I begin, nervously playing with my clutch. "I want to see what happens when I kiss you. Because I don't have fear anymore. Not about kissing you."

He narrows his eyes. "What do you mean?"

"I told you what was happening to me when we were dancing. But now I want the same from you. I want to know if I have an effect on *you*."

For a moment, his gaze darkens, and he looks almost pained. "Remember when I promised I wouldn't break any rules?" He hesitates, his inky eyes skating over my face. "Unless you can give me a really good reason . . ."

Isn't *Shut up and kiss me* a good enough reason? Even though I know what I *should* do—which is think logically and save my heart from more disappointment—I can't think at all.

Should I *really* kiss Jack tonight? What if I end up hurt even more?

Right now, what hurts worse is knowing Jack and I might never have this opportunity again. I'm obviously over my dating phobia, and there's no reason to keep our charade going once tonight is done.

I swallow hard, and say in a shaky voice, "I want to finish what we started on the dance floor." I pause, the air between us shimmering with tension. I feel like I'm about to leap out of an airplane and hope the parachute releases. "I want you to kiss me."

His gaze drops to my mouth, like he's wrestling with this decision.

I close my eyes, waiting for the soft touch of his lips.

"Not yet," he whispers, still resisting.

Everything in me is knotted up, pulled tight, like a rubber band about to snap.

He rests one arm against the doorframe above my head, his gaze suddenly fierce and intense. With his free hand, he brushes his thumb across my hand, tracing the tracks of veins beneath my skin.

"The first thing I notice . . ." he says, his finger following the blue-veined roads along the delicate folds of my wrist. "Is how you feel. How your hands fit perfectly in mine. The smoothness of the skin along the inside of your wrist, like silk." He traces the veins up my arm, and my nerve endings spark. "How does this feel?"

Like I've died and gone to heaven? "Until now, I thought holding hands was boring."

He shakes his head slowly. "Holding a woman's hand is *anything* but boring. It's the warm-up to so much more."

I swallow. "The warm-up?"

"Before the kiss." He continues following the map of my skin, reaching the soft curve of my shoulder with his finger. "Your shoulders are really tempting, because they're usually covered."

"Oh, really?" I say, trying to hold in my ragged breathing but totally distracted by the way his finger follows the path along the hollow of my collarbone, finding sensitive spots I didn't know existed. "I hate to interrupt, but I wonder when we're going to get to the fun part."

He leans close to my ear, his soft breath startling me with its heat. "This *is* the fun part."

As he reaches the base of my neck, my body grows limp, and I lean hard against the doorframe for support. Because unless we're in the Regency era, and he's got smelling salts on hand, I'm going to faint in this closet.

"How are you so good at this?" I ask.

"Remember when I said I'm a guy who likes data, and I tuck away information for future use? Well, I've been studying you for a long time, and now seems like the appropriate time to use my research."

With every touch, my breath hitches, and he can probably see the delirious effect he's having on me. If he doesn't kiss me soon, I'm going to combust internally.

"Are you ever going to kiss me?" I ask, my voice ragged. "Or are you using the attraction formula on me?"

"Remember what I said about the warm-up?" Even in the dark, his crooked grin makes me come undone.

He spiders his hands across the soft curve of my neck, and my head suddenly feels too heavy to hold, the air thick. I tip my head back, letting it rest against the frame.

When he finally reaches the base of my neck, he cups one hand under my ear, his thumb gently stroking the hollow spot behind the lobe, and then traces my jaw.

"Everything leads to this," he murmurs. "The softness of your cheek, your tempting lips." He brushes a thumb over them and whispers, "You are my deepest secret."

With his hand still propped on the frame above me, he dips his head toward mine and I instinctively close my eyes. His lips are a breath away, the air between us heavy with tension as I lift my chin toward him.

"Do you want to know what's happening now?" he teases.

With Jack this close, it's like all the air in the room has disappeared, and I'm nearly breathless with want.

He strokes my lips with his finger, featherlight. "Right now, the pleasure chemicals are flooding my brain, because that's the effect you have on me. I'm not sure I could stop if I tried."

With Jack's head tipped toward mine, if I moved just an inch, our lips would meet instantly.

Instead, he's drawing this moment out, sending every nerve in my body into a tingly mess.

"Then don't," I tell him. "Don't stop."

Without a moment's hesitation, he leans forward, his lips crashing into mine, drinking me in, like we're both dying of thirst. If my nerves were tingling before, now they're shooting rockets into the sky.

I don't know how long it's been since I've kissed someone with reckless abandon, but it's been way too long for a woman my age.

That's the hard thing about this whole charade. I like Jack way more than just a friend, but I'm too scared to let myself take the next step. After all I've been through, rejection has scarred me, its deep ache warning me that if I let myself become vulnerable, this house of cards will come crashing down.

But right now, I'm pushing my fear aside, because all I want is Jack. He's the only person I could completely love and trust after all I've been through.

Suddenly, muffled footsteps sound in the hall, and someone calls Jack's name.

"Jack," I whisper, but he keeps kissing me, which makes it hard to stop because I want it too. "Someone's in the hall."

He lets me go reluctantly, tearing his lips from mine, still breathing hard from our encounter. The last thing either of us needs is to get caught making out in a storage room.

"I probably should go." He rests his hand on the back of my neck and tips his forehead to mine. "But I'll find you later." He kisses my forehead one last time, a small promise before rushing off.

I brush my hands over my hair to make sure I don't look as disheveled as I feel, then find my clutch, which I dropped on the floor while we were kissing. My heart is still beating wildly, and my stomach suddenly rumbles from hunger.

Even though the food isn't nearly as appealing as Jack, I'm a ravenous woman.

I head back to the foyer, where Jack has all but disappeared, and I beeline for the shrimp appetizer and the tray of endless cheeses. I still have my M&M's as emergency candy, in case I need it later.

As I load up my plate, someone joins me at the table.

"Maeve? What are you doing here?"

I glance up to see Elizabeth Oliver, Jack's stepmother, dressed in an audacious black and silver glittery ballgown that looks like something Cruella de Vil would wear.

I nearly choke on my shrimp. "Oh, Mrs. Oliver," I stammer, clutching my plate of food. "I'm here . . . for the party."

I scan the foyer, searching for Jack, but can't find him. He must have gone into another room, but where? He promised not to leave me cornered with his stepmom. And yet, here I am.

"But who did you come with?" She frowns, not hiding her displeasure.

"I'm here with Jack." Maybe I shouldn't have told her, but I figure she's going to find out sometime.

The lines in her forehead deepen. "I see."

There's an awkward pause as she sizes me up.

"I moved back after my divorce to be closer to family," I say. "And Jack lives in my neighborhood."

Something passes over her face, an unpleasant realization that makes her pucker her lips. "You're divorced?"

"Yes," I say weakly, suddenly feeling all the insecurities of my teenage years again. She purses her lips again, something awful brewing behind that look.

"How are your parents? Still living with a zoo full of animals?"

"My dad's retired and still keeps a few pets," I tell her without mentioning how many. Since she lacks any sense of humor, it will only seem like another reason to label me an oddball. "My mom says she'll never retire from teaching botany classes at the university. She loves her students too much."

No matter what she thinks, I'm proud of my parents, of the way they've pursued their passions, without caring what others thought.

"Your mother always was . . . a *different* sort." She says it like a slam, only this time, I'm not going to skitter away in fear.

I set down my plate and level my gaze. "Just because my mom isn't like you does *not* make her odd. It makes her someone to look up to, like Marie Curie or Sally Ride."

Elizabeth grunts. "I'd hardly compare her to those women."

"Well, I would. I'm proud of where I come from, even if you think less of people like me."

She leans toward me so I can see the pores under her heavy makeup. "Well, I can tell you one thing. Jack's never going to fall for someone like you. So you may as well give up that pathetic dream and go back to your trashy fixer-upper."

"My home is not trashy," I say through clenched teeth. Then it hits me. None of this is a surprise. She knows where I live. She's checked out my house. How else would she know I live in a fixer-upper? The fact that I showed up tonight isn't entirely a shock to her.

I'm the only one who's surprised here.

She smiles wickedly, like she's enjoying my shock. "Jack's been missing deadlines at work and absent for family events. It doesn't take a *scientist* to figure out he's been seeing someone. Craig followed him home one night. Except he didn't go home, he went to your house."

Right now, I'm so angry, I'm surprised there aren't flames

shooting from my nostrils. "What if he did? He's a grown man. He can make his own decisions."

She lifts a finger to stop me. "Except when it involves his father's company," she says. "You wouldn't want to ruin that for him, would you?"

She turns back to the food table, and it takes everything in me to shoot Jack a call for help.

Maeve: Your wicked stepmother has arrived.

He responds almost instantly.

Jack: Coming to your rescue.

TWENTY-TWO

Jack

"Elizabeth, I meant to introduce you," I say with a stiff greeting. "You remember Maeve?"

Maeve stands helplessly near the appetizers as my stepmother fills her plate with melon.

Elizabeth glances at me with an annoyed look. "Of course I remember Maeve. We were just chatting."

Maeve has that cornered-animal look, like she's trying to warn me of something.

"Maeve and I reconnected recently," I explain. "I wanted to bring her tonight to introduce her."

"Yes, how lovely," Elizabeth says without an ounce of belief. It's a stock response she uses even when things aren't lovely. "Have you seen your father? He was looking for you."

"We just talked," I say, wishing I had a moment alone with Maeve to tell her the news. "But we didn't finish our conversation. This seemed more important."

I glance at Maeve, who shoots me another pointed stare. I don't know what Elizabeth said to her before I arrived, but it obviously wasn't good.

"By the way, have you found the Oliver table in the dining

room? Your seat is located at the front table next to the podium. For family *only*." Elizabeth pops a melon in her mouth.

I place my hands on Maeve's shoulders. "Maeve will sit next to me tonight. She's my date. And I'm not letting her sit at another table."

Elizabeth doesn't even blink. "Unfortunately, there's no room for anyone else at our table."

"Then I'll sit with Maeve at her table," I say.

She rolls her eyes. "Oh, Jack, don't be ridiculous. It's not my fault our table is full."

"We won't sit at separate tables," I insist. "And I won't let you make her feel like an outsider tonight."

Elizabeth clucks her tongue. "It's not like you actually have feelings for her. You've never dated anyone seriously enough to care about them."

Elizabeth has always excelled at spearing people in public.

Instead of lowering myself to her level, I tighten my grip on Maeve's shoulder. "I do care about her, and that means she sits with *me*."

Elizabeth lifts an eyebrow, somewhat shocked by my admission. "If that's the case, then do whatever you want. But didn't your father make it clear how he feels about the company's future? Think how that's going to affect everyone."

"Nothing's been decided." I need to find my dad, to tell him that I don't want him to announce anything yet.

"Then you'd better decide quickly." Her eyes barely flick to Maeve. "Before everything changes." Then she stalks off.

I spin around, trying to track down my dad, but he's nowhere to be seen.

"Wow, she was nice," Maeve says, popping another shrimp in her mouth.

"Sorry about that. And just so you know, you're not sitting at a table by yourself."

"Jack Oliver is going to snub the Oliver Family table?" Her

mouth drops into a pretend gasp. "It's like you're abdicating the throne."

"It's called beating my stepmother at her own game," I say, watching Elizabeth snake through the room.

"So I'm just a pawn in your dysfunctional family dynamics?"

I shake my head. "Not at all." I brush a hand across her cheek. "It's time for people to see us together. No more hiding in dark closets," I say with a grin.

She holds up a hand, a panicked look on her face. "In case it's not clear, I'm not comfortable making out in front of your parents."

I burst out laughing and her face relaxes. "Me neither."

She moves closer and places her palm on my cheek. "Thanks for not leaving me alone," she murmurs.

I kiss the inside of her palm and then hold it there. "Maeve, there's something I need to tell you before we go into the dining room."

"There's something I need to tell you too," she interrupts before I can tell her about the conversation I just had with my father. "Your stepmom knows."

"What?" I frown.

"About you spending time at my house."

I shake my head. "I was careful *not* to mention it to any of my family."

"She seemed to enjoy dropping that bomb tonight. The good news is she totally bought our dating charade." Maeve flashes a smile that would normally make me soar, but right now, her words flatten me. Does she *still* think this is a charade? Haven't I made my feelings clear? Because there's nothing I want more than to figure out how to make this work.

"That's what I wanted to talk with you about." I swallow hard, trying to steady my nerves.

She gazes up at me with so much hope, it nearly splits my heart. "What is it, Jack?"

"I . . . I don't know how to say this."

Someone taps on my shoulder, and I hold up a hand. "One moment, please," I say without turning around.

Maeve's eyes flick to someone behind me.

"What I'm trying to say . . ."

"Jack," she murmurs. "Craig's behind you."

Seriously? I wheel around. "What is it?"

"Well, hello to you, too," he says with a frown. "Father is requesting that you join him now."

I sigh in frustration. "Tell him I'll be right there—and Maeve is sitting next to me."

"I'm just the messenger," Craig says, backing away. "But we're starting soon."

More like Dad's puppet.

By now, the room is nearly empty. "It looks like we're the last ones," Maeve says. "We probably should join them."

I nod, but there's a tension burrowing through my chest, a missed opportunity slowly fading from my grasp. I wanted to get this out in the open, to let Maeve know what she means to me, but now it's too late.

We zigzag around tables, all eyes on us, and I instinctively grab Maeve's hand for support, needing her touch to bolster my lagging confidence. I've brought other girls to company parties, beautiful women who were usually more caught up in my status and name than building a relationship, and that sealed my decision to stay single. I wanted to live alone, to insulate myself from the pain of what I'd come to believe about most marriages.

And then Maeve came back into my world, shattering all the arguments I'd put up against love. She would choose me for who I am and not what I could do for her.

As we finally reach my family's table, I offer my seat to Maeve as she looks at me uncomfortably. Craig and Elizabeth glare at me, and there's a sudden chill in the air, their icy stares anything but welcoming.

"I thought we were sitting in the back," Maeve whispers, not moving.

"We are sitting here with my family," I say, pointing to her seat.

Maeve sits, and I grab an empty chair from the corner and squeeze in between Maeve and my brother. My father hasn't noticed our appearance because he's reviewing his speech notes, too absorbed in his own announcement.

I clear my throat and wrap my arm around Maeve's shoulder. "Sorry for being late."

My father glances up while Craig and his wife, Charis, exchange looks.

"This is a change," Craig says. "You normally bring bimbos you found on the internet." Craig smiles smugly, while I resist punching him in the face.

"You remember Maeve?" I say. "She and I went to high school together."

Craig nods. "Vaguely." Charis takes a sip of her seltzer water.

Dad knots his fingers together, as if he's trying to place Maeve. I'm not surprised he doesn't remember her since he was barely around for my high school years.

He clears his throat and addresses her directly. "And what do you do?"

"I'm a science teacher at the local high school," she says.

"Sounds like a nightmare," Elizabeth grumbles. "Teenagers are horrid."

"Actually, they can be quite charming," Maeve says.

Everyone stares at her like she's from an alien planet.

"I guess somebody needs to do it," Dad says, like Maeve's job is such a sacrifice, no one would actually want to.

"She teaches chemistry and biology," I add.

"I love it," she says. "Every day is completely different. It's so fun to share my love of science with my students."

Again, complete silence, like my family doesn't know how to talk to normal people.

Luckily, the waiter breaks the silence and begins passing out our dinner plates.

After a meal of awkward pauses and stilted conversations that intentionally leave Maeve out—mostly about country club gossip and golf scores—my dad drops the cloth napkin on his empty plate.

"We should start," he says, rising to head for the podium. "Are you both ready for this?"

He glances at Craig and me, like we actually have a say in what's about to happen. Instead of waiting for a response, he taps the microphone and attempts to say something into it, but the harsh squeal of feedback drowns out his words.

"I've been thinking a lot about the future of Oliver Financial and the legacy I want to leave after I retire," he begins, looking at his notes. "Recently I signed a contract to buy out our competitor, Stronghold Investments." There's a hush in the room as Dad continues. "The contract was signed this week, which means we'll take over their offices, including their headquarters in California, where many of you will move. Some of you will continue here locally, but this merger will require flexibility and, perhaps, a big sacrifice from some of you." He pauses and looks over at our table, pinning me down with his gaze.

"We're currently restructuring our leadership, and I'm proposing we have co-leaders running our different locations. Craig will stay on as the leader here in South Carolina, while the new team in California will be led by Jack, who will move there as soon as he can. When I retire in six months, he will officially take over as CEO after I step down."

A rush of applause fills the room as all eyes fall on me. I know I should be happy—even gleeful about beating Craig. Instead, it feels like the air has been sucked from my lungs. Victory never felt so much like defeat.

"Congratulations, Jack," Maeve whispers in my ear. Even though she's happy for me, something swirls in her eyes.

"I found out tonight when you were talking with Elizabeth. Dad took me aside and told me he'd finally made a decision."

"California?" She puts on a brave face, but I've known Maeve long enough to read her like a book. "It's just . . ." Her smile wavers. "So far away."

Elizabeth leans across the table toward us. "Isn't this wonderful? Craig and Charis get to stay in town! And Jack is moving to California." Then she tilts her head and looks at Maeve. "Or didn't Jack tell you?"

She already knows the answer, and she can't help but rub salt in Maeve's wound.

"I didn't have the chance," I say quickly. "Dad told me tonight. I wish he'd mentioned it earlier."

Was there a reason he delayed telling me? What role did my stepmother have in this decision?

"He didn't sign the papers until this week," Elizabeth says before shifting her gaze toward Maeve again. "I'm sure Jack will be extremely busy cleaning up the dumpster fire that Stronghold Investments has left for us. I doubt he'll have time to visit much." Then she smiles, as if this is satisfying news.

That's when I realize why she's so happy. I'll be out of the picture, far away where I can't interfere, while she'll still have Craig nearby. Moving away means I won't see Maeve much either, and I'll have to relocate Mom to a long-term care facility in California.

"I'm sorry," Maeve says, pushing back her chair from the table. "I'm not feeling well. If you'll excuse me . . ." Then she rushes from our table, weaving through the room to escape the crowd.

I shoot my stepmother a sharp look. "Why do you always have to say things like that?"

"I didn't say anything but the truth," she says. "You're the one who wanted to lead the company. And you got what you wanted."

But did I? Not when it means leaving behind everything I really want.

I hurry after Maeve, rushing past the rest of our employees to catch Maeve before she leaves.

"Maeve!" I call when I reach the foyer, but she won't turn around. I grab her arm before she flees out the door.

"Hey, are you okay? Where are you going? You don't even have a ride."

Her face is flushed as she slowly wheels around. "The news—you moving—like my world wasn't just turned upside down? I naively believed if you led the company, you'd stay here. We could still be . . . *something*."

It's not that I tried to keep this information from her, but right now that's how she sees it, even though I was given little notice.

"My dad asked me tonight if I wanted to run the company. I agreed to it but told him to wait to announce it because I wanted to tell you first."

She frowns. "So either way, you'd decided to go . . . without even mentioning it to me?" She shakes her head, holding back something under the surface. "Jack, I can't talk about this right now."

"Maeve, this doesn't have to change things between us."

She stops and throws up her arms. "How's that possible? Of course, it changes things. It changes everything."

"Jack!" I turn to see Craig behind me, waving me toward him. "Dad wants you up at the podium, now."

I don't want to have to choose between Maeve and my father, but I'm stuck in a position I never dreamed I'd be in—deciding between her and my father.

I glance at Maeve and give her an apologetic look. "I'm sorry, I have to go."

Her face closes off before she turns and leaves.

How is it possible that I got what I wanted and lost everything on the same night?

TWENTY-THREE

Maeve

"I'm not sure why you feel so much pressure to finish house projects when it's just a birthday party," Mom says, examining the new curtain panels I picked out for the living room. "When you were a kid, I bought a generic white cake from the store and powdered lemonade."

"Because if I don't do something, I'll binge-watch home renovation shows and then sulk in misery. I need something to get me out of this funk."

"I'm not sure curtains will do anything for a funk," Mom says, trying to slide the geometric print onto a rod.

As a woman with a broken heart, I'm throwing myself into finishing house projects like it's the grand finale of a home renovation show. Tomorrow is Violet's birthday party, and I promised myself I'd have this house looking like a *Fixer Upper* special, even if it takes a massive amount of duct tape, superglue, and last-minute home decor purchases.

Distraction is not a cure, but it's the needed motivation to prep for this party and avoid the ache in my gut left there by Jack. In the last week since the company party, I've finished painting Violet's superhero furniture, applied the special decals, and painted her room. I even scored a cute vintage wicker set for the patio, and finished the landscaping bed in the back with pale blue hydrangeas, purple coneflower, and pink climbing roses, which Mom helped me plant after amending my soil to the correct pH. (One of the advantages of having a botanist in the family.)

"Mom, I'm not ready to hang those curtains yet. Didn't you notice the creases?"

Mom looks over her teal-blue glasses at me. "You know I don't iron."

I climb down from a stepladder. "I can't stand looking at wrinkles either." I peek into the kitchen where Dad is installing a new farmhouse sink I picked up at a scratch-and-dent sale.

Mom gives me a look. "Your dad is spending all day on that new sink. I don't think he'll have time for anything except a nap."

Violet takes a curtain panel and wraps it around herself like a cape.

I feel bad that I've asked my parents to help me finish these projects when I know their energy is limited, and they already do so much. At the same time, it's been impossible to keep Violet entertained while I try to accomplish everything, and I've been letting her spend too much time in front of screens as a substitute.

"What about calling Jack?" Mom asks, peering over her cat-eye glasses. "Or some of your friends? I bet they'd help."

"I can't call Jack," I say, heading into the kitchen and opening a strawberry-flavored water. "He's packing up to move to California soon. And Jaz and Mia already came over yesterday. The only person left to ask is Annie, and she's decorating for the school dance today. Which means it's just us."

I can't tell Mom the real reason I can't invite Jack over—that seeing him just makes things worse. Despite my determination not to fall in love, Jack has slowly woven through my heart like an endless thread. When I have to cut ties with him, everything is going to unravel.

"You and Jack are good friends," Mom says with a knowing look.

"Jack is moving away for a job," I add, taking a sip of water.

When I settled here after my divorce, this was where I wanted to grow old. I knew if I found someone who wanted to spend his life with me, he would have to follow my rules. I'd already sacrificed too much for a man who left me for another woman. I wasn't going to let that happen again.

"I'm not suggesting anything, except that Jack is a good man who cares for you and Violet."

I put down my drink. "But it's California, Mom. That's not even a weekend road trip."

Mom shakes her head. "Happiness starts with the right person. Not a perfect life. That's what your father taught me, and look how long we've been together."

What Mom doesn't see is that their success partially stemmed from my father accepting that Mom would never turn into a traditional wife. He accepted her dedication to academia as much as she accepted his commitment to veterinary care. They made a family around their dreams and forged life their own way. But they're the exception, not the rule—and I'm only seeing that in hindsight now.

"It's not that simple," I say. "Relationships never are."

I thought my marriage to Dex would last forever, and now I just need to accept I might never find that kind of love again. If it wasn't for Jack, I could accept it. I used to believe in happily ever after, but I don't believe it anymore.

"As your parents"—she glances at Dad—"we know you better than anyone. If you're still holding out for the perfect relationship . . ."

"I've already given up on that." My gaze flicks between them. "But Jack's leaving, and I'm staying here. That's not exactly the recipe for an ideal relationship." I lean against the counter, grasping the edge for support, like it's the only thing that can prop up my weary body. Even if Jack was staying, he hasn't revealed his feelings for me, other than kissing me in a closet. It doesn't take a rocket scientist to know that isn't true love.

"It's okay to find someone else," she says. "To give up what you and Dex had. It's time to try again with someone new."

I've told myself that dating Jack would be irresponsible. Too risky. Even if Jack asked me to have a long-distance relationship, I would turn him down. How do I know Jack wouldn't do the same as Dex? The thought of getting stuck in this exact situation in California with no support system terrifies me.

"Don't call Jack for your sake," Mom says, peering over her glasses. "Call him to help your dad. I'm not sure he can even get up off the floor."

Dad *does* look exhausted. But calling Jack might give the wrong impression—that I still want something from him—and that's the last thing I need.

"I can't call Jack. I'm sorry," I tell my parents.

"I want to see Uncle Jack," Violet complains.

"Listen, I'm not inviting Jack over. Did you hear me?"

"Loud and clear," a voice says behind me.

I spin around, where Jack stands in the foyer.

"What are you doing here?" I ask, bewildered by Jack's appearance. "I didn't even hear the door open."

"That's because I fixed the squeak in your door when you were putting Violet to bed as a surprise. Didn't you notice?" he asks.

I shake my head. *That little sneak.* No wonder this house has been so peaceful and quiet.

"I'm fantastic at fixing things when you're not looking," he brags, like it's a superpower. Jack has a lot of superpowers, and I'm not immune to any of them.

"I didn't invite you over today."

He lifts a shoulder. "What if someone else did?"

I glance around, trying to guess who the guilty party is.

"It wasn't me!" Violet says.

"Mom and Dad?" I ask.

Mom shakes her head.

"I'd ask you first," Dad says. "But I can't say I'm disappointed."

I cross my arms. "Well, someone invited you over." I cross the room, narrowing my eyes. "Who was it?"

He pauses, then grins. "You."

"Impossible," I insist. "I didn't call you."

"You butt-dialed me," he says, trying to hold back his laughter.

I pull my phone from my back pocket and discover an outgoing call from me. "It must have happened by accident."

"When I answered, I heard a garbled conversation about needing help. I figured this was like calling for backup with the superhero league."

"What exactly did you hear?" I ask, my face growing hot. I'm trying to recall everything I said about Jack and whether I gave away any incriminating evidence.

"Your dad needs help with the sink." He glances at me warily. "Don't worry, I'll stay out of your way."

Dad shimmies out from the sink cabinet. "I'll let the young gun fix the plumbing while I take a break."

I give Dad a pleading look. "Earlier you told me you enjoy learning new tricks."

"I didn't want you to feel bad," he says, leaving.

I watch as Jack slides under the sink more easily than my father. As he does so, his shirt hitches up to reveal a glimpse of his abs.

I quickly turn away and pretend to color-coordinate the rows of plates in the cabinet. Right now, the best thing I can do is keep my distance. Forget I ever cared for him.

Mom puts her hands on her hips. "Now that Jack's taking over, why don't you and I iron these curtains, Violet?"

I shoot Mom a look. I know what she's trying to do. Leave me alone with Jack. "I thought you were morally opposed to ironing?"

"Ironing is morally neutral, my dear," she says. "And it's about time Violet and I learn a new skill."

"Good luck finding the ironing board."

"Oh, I know where it is," Mom says with a mischievous grin. "I hid it in the garage so you wouldn't ask me to find it."

As Violet skips across the kitchen, still dragging one curtain panel, she stops next to Jack.

"Are you coming to my birthday party?"

Jack slides out from inside the cupboard, his face softening. "Am I invited?" He's so tender with Violet, giving her one hundred percent of his attention.

"Honey, Jack is busy," I tell her, trying to discourage him. I haven't told Violet yet that Jack's moving away because I know it's going to hurt her feelings, and right now, I can barely contain my own. *He didn't choose us.* Why should I care if he comes to her birthday party?

"I'm not too busy," he shoots back. "Never too busy for your birthday."

"Yay!" She spins in a circle with the curtain flying behind her. "Don't forget to dress up like your favorite hero."

"That's for the kids," I say.

"Well, it shouldn't be," he says. "I think everyone should dress up."

"Okay!" she says, skipping off to the garage with my mom.

I shoot Jack a look. "Great. Now I have to find a costume."

I turn back to the cupboard and clench my jaw. I didn't want to ask Jack to the party because I don't want to face him any more than I have to. The last thing I need is to give Violet false hope.

He didn't choose to stay.

Maybe there was a time when I could have picked up and followed Jack anywhere, back before I was a mom and my future was as bright and shiny as this brand-new sink. But over time, hurt has changed me, made me realize how vulnerable I am, and I'm never taking that risk again.

"Anything interesting in that cabinet?" Jack slides out from under the sink, watching me as I stare at a stack of plates.

"Not particularly," I say, closing the cupboard doors. I clear my throat and take a sip of water. I don't want to talk about his company party a week ago, even though it's dangling between us.

"How are things going with the party planning?" He sits on the floor, elbows on knees, his T-shirt stretched across his arms, showing off his biceps.

"The plans in my head are magical," I say. "I just wish I had more time to finish my house. I haven't completed Violet's room, but I have to admit that sink is *chef's-kiss* good." I mime a big chef's kiss from across the room, and he laughs, making my stomach turn in circles, reminding me why I liked his laugh so much in the first place.

"Once I finish this sink, I can work on Violet's room. Just call me your personal handyman."

I'd like to call Jack many things, including *mine*, but at this point I need to get used to the fact that he isn't going to stay forever. He doesn't *really* want me. I grip the counter and study him for a moment, trying not to let myself feel anything for him.

"I have to learn to do things on my own," I say.

He opens his arms. "But for today, I'm all yours. I can clean so your place is spotless for tomorrow."

I let out a humorless laugh. "My place will *never* look like yours. I've already given that up. It's why we're so different."

He looks at me, surprised. "I wasn't saying it should look like mine. I told you before that I like your place better. It feels lived-in and comfortable. It feels like *you*."

"So you're saying I'm like my messy fixer-upper? I'm pretty sure that's *not* a compliment."

He gives me a look, like he just realized this conversation has turned into an argument. "I was trying to say I like your house, and I like you and Violet. So if you're looking for an argument, or something else I refuse to give you, then you'll have to look else-where. Because I obviously can't make you happy." His face snaps shut as he slides his body under the cabinet, making it clear this argument's over.

I swallow hard, the truth piercing my heart. Jack can't give me what I need—not the future I wanted for us—and he's telling me to look for my happiness elsewhere. That it's not him. It never was.

"I'm sorry," I say. "Could you please help me finish Violet's room—at least for her?"

He looks at me warily. "I'll do it for both of you, on one condition."

"What's that?"

He leans on one elbow. "No matter what doesn't get done today, you'll be proud of what you've accomplished in this house. You'll see this fixer-upper as something beautiful, and stop looking at the imperfections."

I glance away, realizing how difficult it is for me to not focus on the imperfections. "For Violet, I'll try."

"By the way, plumbing's done."

"Don't tell Dad, but you're faster than he is. After today, I'm not sure he's ever going to do any plumbing again."

"That's why you should learn this."

"You think I could?"

He nods. "But not from there." He waves me toward the sink, and I lower myself to the floor, keeping my distance.

I duck my head inside and lean back against the hard edge of the cabinet. Jack squeezes in next to me. The space is small, forcing our bodies closer than I'd like. His knee pushes against mine, the heat growing where our bodies meet.

He points at the connections above. "Do you see this piece here? It can sometimes come loose."

"What do I do then?"

"Make sure the connection is tight, because any of them can loosen over time."

Even though I'm trying to pay attention to what Jack is

saying, I'm distracted by how close he is—and that this birthday party is the last time we'll spend together.

Stupid girl. You really have fallen for Jack.

"Why are you looking at me like that?" Jack asks, snapping me back to attention.

"What?" I ask, searching for an answer. "I don't know what you're talking about."

"You were zoning out on me."

"I never knew plumbing could be so . . . *interesting*."

He laughs. "That was *not* what you were thinking."

"How do you know?"

"Because you're a terrible liar," he says, poking my side. "Tell the truth."

I try to pull away, but this time his hand holds me firmly in place, growing warm where he touches my side. I'm going to miss him—*and this.*

Suddenly, my gaze catches his, and something dark swirls in his eyes. *You. It's always been you.*

I'm back to that comfortable place of being with Jack, feeling the pull of attraction and letting it take me away like the current of a river.

The garage door suddenly opens. "We finished the curtains!" Mom's voice chirps as she steps into the kitchen.

"Mom!" I yell, trying to sit up too quickly. I smack my head on the cabinet's edge, and pain radiates across my skull. "Ow!" I yell, rubbing my throbbing forehead.

"What were you guys doing?" Violet asks.

"Plumbing," I say, guilt winding up my spine like an ugly vine.

Mom raises an eyebrow. "Is *that* what they call it these days?" Then she turns to Violet. "Let's go upstairs and find your costume for tomorrow."

As they head upstairs, an awkward silence fills the room. What Mom doesn't know is that I'm planning on avoiding Jack the entire weekend.

I wheel around to face Jack. "Just so you know. *That* can't happen again."

"What can't happen again?" he says, a faint smile playing on his lips.

"Plumbing lessons," I say firmly. "I have too much to do." I start up the stairs, trying to put distance between us, making it clear there's no time for whatever *that* was. Now that he's made his choice to move, I can't pretend anymore with him. And I can't let my stupid heart believe that Jack would choose me. I've already given everything I had to a man who walked away from it all. I can't do it again.

"I missed you this week, Maeve," he says in a low voice.

My stomach bottoms out. *Don't fall for it, stupid girl.*

I turn around, and see him leaning against the sink in that way only Jack can, his taut body relaxed, hair gently tousled, his gaze an almost dangerous invitation.

I will not fall for it. Not this time.

I can't change the fact that once again, no one is choosing me. From the time we met in high school until now, Jack is still choosing something *better* over me.

Once bitten.

Then I run up the stairs, putting space between us, letting every spark between us die out.

TWENTY-FOUR

Jack

A doorbell interrupts my sleep as sunlight pours through the cracks in my blinds.

I stayed late at Maeve's last night, hoping I could get her to talk to me, but her list of tasks conveniently kept me busy—and out of her way—the entire time.

When the doorbell rings for the third time, I finally roll out of bed and see Brendan waiting outside.

"Aren't we running today?" he says with a frown, looking over my boxers.

"I forgot," I mutter, running my fingers through my hair. "Late night."

"With Maeve?"

"It's not what you think," I say. "And you're not going to let me get out of this, are you?"

As a former Marine, Brendan is religious about our Saturday runs. "Of course not."

I head upstairs to change into running shorts and a tank top. As we start down the street at a brisk pace, my chest tightens, like someone's tied a rope around it.

"You're quiet today," Brendan comments.

"Your pace is wicked," I say between deep breaths.

"So what happens between you and Maeve after you leave?" he asks as he settles into a more relaxed pace.

"I don't know. It's the one puzzle piece I haven't solved. I still want to be more than friends, if that's what you're asking."

"But you're going to California, so that's tricky. A long-distance relationship would be hard for a single mom. She can't just leave to chase after you for the weekend."

"So what if it's temporary until I get the company in good shape?" I say, weighing options, trying to figure out if there's any way to make this work.

"How long will that take? A year or two? Maybe more? In the meantime, you're making her wait for her happiness. I'm not saying she wouldn't do it, but is it fair to her?"

Our feet fall into rhythm together as I consider this. Is it fair to her to ask her to wait, when she could meet someone here who could make her happy *now?* Someone who could help her finish the house. Someone who could push Violet on the swing on lazy summer days, and have rooftop picnics with grape juice in wine-glasses. Thinking of her with anyone else wrenches something inside me.

"What about your mom?" Brendan asks.

"Mom is staying here until I can find a long-term care facility in California. After the party tonight, I'm flying out on a red-eye to California to look at housing and options for Mom."

"She wants to go?"

"Not really, but I can't leave her here alone. I'm not like you. I don't have a big Puerto Rican family behind me who's got my back when I'm not around."

"You know there is another option," Brendan says, glancing at me, his head bobbing with every step.

"I know what you're thinking, and I can't consider it. My dad doesn't compromise."

If I could ignore my obligation to family, life would be dramatically easier. But I can't abandon Mom when she's the only family I have. It's my one non-negotiable.

He doesn't look at me, just keeps his pace steady. "Sounds like your mind is made up, then."

"But that's what I can't accept. I'm leaving Maeve out of the whole decision, like she doesn't even matter."

He glances at me. "Is she worth giving up this new job for?"

"Of course she is, but it's not that simple. What would you do if you were me?" I say, the rope around my chest pulling tighter with every breath. Choosing one good thing over another leaves too many people in a lurch.

"I don't know," Brendan says, keeping his eyes on the road. "That's the thing about life. Sometimes, there are no good options."

"Thank you, Mr. Encouragement."

"Sometimes, you have to make a decision that leaves someone unhappy. My advice? Just make sure it isn't you."

"But I don't know how Maeve feels about any of this," I grumble. "She won't even talk to me. And I haven't been completely honest with her either."

Brendan shoots me a surprised look. "Why not? You need to let her make her own decisions. And that starts with telling her the truth. Talk to her before you leave tonight."

I slow to a walk, trying to catch my ragged breath. "What if I tell her, and her answer is *it'll never work*?"

Brendan turns around while running backwards. "That's the chance you take, Jack."

———

I can't believe I'm about to do this. My stomach twists uncomfortably as I slide the mask over my face and check myself once more in the car's mirror.

I'm wearing a black mask with bat ears and a fitted black suit and cape for Violet's party, and I'm pretty sure I'm the only brave adult who's going to show up in a Bruce Wayne costume. I also turned my car into what I hope looks like a modified version of the Batmobile for Violet, complete with LED lights and a super-hero soundtrack.

On my run with Brendan, this whole birthday party plan seemed like a good idea. Tell Maeve the truth. Take care of things before I head to California. Don't leave our relationship half-finished, like before.

As I wait in my car, wondering through whether I'm brave enough to follow through with my plan, I see a common thread running through every chapter of our story—the way our paths cross, then diverge, never quite intersecting long enough to become one.

How do you make a life with someone whose version of happiness is different from yours? What if the journey you imagined isn't the one you're supposed to pursue?

Someone knocks on my car window. "Uh, Jack?"

I look up to see Dex outside my car, holding a gift for Violet. I'd totally forgotten he would be here today, even though he's Violet's father.

"Are you planning on going in?" he asks, frowning at me like I'm an idiot. "Or just sitting there talking to yourself?"

I open the car door and step out, and his eyes flit over my costume. He's dressed in a navy-blue polo and khaki pants, and we couldn't look more different.

"Nice costume," Dex mutters, and I know he doesn't mean it as a compliment.

The temptation to say something snarky rises in my chest, but I clamp my lips together instead. I'm doing this for Violet, and I don't care what Dex thinks.

As soon as we both get to the door, we stand there elbow to elbow in complete silence and listen to the doorbell echo inside the house. When Maeve opens the door, her mouth falls open.

"Dex and . . . Jack?" She's wearing a shiny black catsuit that fits her like a glove. My eyes slide down it briefly before snapping back to her face. *Whoa.* It's going to take superhero strength to keep my eyes off her for this party.

She glances at me with a puzzled look. "You came . . . together?"

"Arrived at the same time," I say.

She looks over Dex's clothes. "Violet has requested that everyone dress up in one superhero item. I have a few spare masks and capes if you need one."

"I don't really dress up," he interrupts. He doesn't look at me, but it's an obvious jab to my costume.

"I'm not asking you to do this for me," she says.

He shrugs. "She's a kid. She'll get over it."

What a jerk face.

"By the way," he says, glancing over his shoulder at me. "Can we talk for a minute—alone?"

Maeve crosses her arms. "I'm kind of busy now."

A muscle in his jaw pulses, then relaxes. "Later?" I don't know what he wants to corner Maeve about, but it seems urgent.

She barely nods, and he glances at me once more before leaving to join the rest of the party in the backyard.

Maeve pulls in a deep breath, and I can see how one conversation with Dex messes with her. I reach out to touch her arm, and she takes a quick step back, like she's afraid of my touch.

"Would it help if I surprise Violet?" I offer. "I don't want to get in the way."

She gives me a tight smile, her face still guarded. "I'm sure she'll be thrilled to see you."

"I even have a surprise for Violet in the car. But it will require taking her out for a spin."

She glances toward my car and lifts an eyebrow. "You didn't."

"I did," I say. "She's getting a ride in a superhero's car today."

"Jack, when you leave, she's going to miss this."

I know she didn't say it to make me feel guilty, but a dull ache twists inside me. *When you leave . . .*

Like it's forever.

"Wait until her next birthday. I'm going to think of something bigger. By the way, how did Violet convince you to put on a catsuit?"

She glances down at her costume, shifting uncomfortably under my gaze. "I realized I was being stupid about the whole costume deal. I just needed to get over myself."

She starts toward the backyard, and I grab her arm before she leaves.

"My first thought when you opened the door was that you looked incredible. And I wanted so badly to tell you in front of Dex."

Even under the half-mask, her cheeks flush. "You don't have to say that to make me feel better," she says, like it's just another pickup line from the internet.

"I'm not. I'm saying it because it's true."

I pause, wanting so badly to fold her into my arms, knowing I can't when everyone is here, and she seems determined to keep me at arm's length.

Right then, Violet bursts into the house, her cape flying behind her.

"Uncle Jack!" she squeals and wraps her arms around my legs.

"I'm not Jack," I attempt in my best ultra-low superhero voice. "I'm . . ."

"I know your name." She frowns, clearly not impressed by my fake voice. "That doesn't even sound like a superhero."

I shrug, as Maeve stifles a smile. Then Violet takes my gloved hand and drags me to the backyard where everyone is gathered, including Maeve's parents and our friends.

In only a week, Maeve has transformed the backyard into an adorable postage-stamp suburban lawn with colorful flower beds and a white wicker set on the patio. All the guests, except Dex, are playing along with the superhero theme, wearing brightly colored masks and shiny capes with superhero logos. Even Maeve's parents are donning matching superhero T-shirts.

Brendan meanders over with a plate of tiny hot dogs, wearing a ridiculous blond Thor wig and carrying a large hammer. He glances over my skintight pants and nearly chokes on his hot dog. "Wow, that costume is . . ."

"Tight. I know. It's all they had at the costume shop last minute," I mutter.

Dex stands by the door, watching Maeve's every move. Something feels off about him today, and I can't put my finger on what. Maybe it's because he's out of his element here, but his normal arrogance has fizzled, only to be replaced by a sulky stare.

"Did you talk to Maeve yet?" Brendan asks, shoving another miniature hot dog in his mouth.

"I just arrived."

"That's no excuse," he says, between bites.

"Dex was standing there. It totally ruined my plan. And then I only had a few seconds to tell her she looked amazing before we came outside."

"You're going to have to find time to talk to her *alone*," he insists. "Even if you're still wearing that skintight costume."

"That's funny coming from a man who looks like Fabio's twin brother."

He runs his fingers through his fake wig, which shifts crookedly on his head. Then he nods toward Dex. "You've got to make a move before that dumbhead does."

"Why would he make a move when he's engaged?"

"That's the thing," Brendan says. "He no longer is."

"What?" I ask, shocked.

"Before you came out with Maeve, I overheard him telling Grant that he broke up with her this week."

No wonder he wants to talk to Maeve alone. It all makes sense now. The sulky stare. The way his eyes follow her around, like he's an animal waiting to pounce.

"Maeve's an easy target," Brendan says. "She's the only one who'd take him back."

I shake my head. "She's not going to fall for him after what he put her through."

Brendan lifts an eyebrow. "Are you sure about that? She fell for him once before. And now that you're leaving, she's fair game. The question is, will you get to her before he does?"

"He still thinks we're dating."

Brendan rolls his eyes. "You think he cares about that? He cheated on her before, Jack. Why would he respect your relationship any more?" He glances at Dex. "I don't trust the guy. At least tell her how you feel before he makes a move."

"It's a birthday party, Brendan. I can't spoil Violet's special day. When the party's over, I'll talk to her."

"I'm warning you," he says, watching Violet spin circles on a swing. "Don't wait. Do it before you leave tonight."

"It's hard to take you seriously in that wig," I say, not looking at him.

"I could say the same about your tight pants," he shoots back.

"Just in case you were wondering," I say. "I can't bend over. Which means I'm going to stand here like a statue the entire night."

Jaz and Mia wander over in capes and masks. "We're having a discussion with Ella and Grant. Who do you think will be next to get hitched in our group?" Jaz asks, then turns to me. "I'm placing bets on you."

Brendan can't hide his smile. "See why you need to talk to Maeve as soon as possible?"

"Who do you think, Brendan?" Jaz asks.

His eyes skirt around the party and then land on Mia. "I'm going to say her."

Mia shoots him a surprised look. "Why me?"

"Because you're the quietest and the least likely to fall in love quickly." He crosses his arms. "Especially now that you're heading up north to work on that holiday concert. I bet you'll fall in love with some dude in a flannel jacket. Maybe a lumberjack."

"How did I not know about this?" I ask.

She frowns. "It just happened. And I'm not going to fall in love with anyone. It's a temporary work gig my mom begged me to accept. The last thing I need is a distraction like dating."

"Uncle Jack!" Violet calls across the yard. "Will you play superhero tag with us?"

"Good luck with not ripping your costume," Brendan mutters, slapping me on the back.

I reluctantly agree as Brendan watches me stiffly jog toward Violet. Somehow, I manage to chase Violet and not rip a hole in my suit, followed by a game of superhero balloon volleyball.

The rest of the afternoon is a blur of hot dogs and party games, followed by gift opening and goodbyes. The longer I wait to talk with Maeve, a growing restlessness churns inside me. After I leave tonight, I won't be around to keep an eye on Maeve and Violet.

What if Dex shows up at her door? What if he convinces her he's ready to try again?

As Maeve cleans up the gift wrap blowing like a tumbleweed over the yard, I remember my last surprise for the evening.

"Hey, Violet. I have one more birthday surprise."

"What is it?" she asks, her eyes widening.

"Come see."

I notice Dex hovering nearby, like he's waiting for me to leave.

"Is it okay if I take Violet out for a spin around the block?" I ask Maeve.

"Sure. When you come back, we can show her the new bedroom." She smiles, and I suddenly feel like everything's going to be okay. She wants me in on this surprise, not Dex, and I feel special for being chosen.

I take Violet's hand and look back once more at Dex. Our eyes meet for a second, and something flickers below the surface. Not exactly a warning, but it leaves me unsettled.

"Why are you stopping?" Violet tugs at my hand. "Let's go."

I promised Violet one quick ride. We won't be gone that long.

Before she climbs in, I turn on the special LED lights that are attached on the underside of the car, as well as inside to make it glow.

She gasps and then giggles.

"It's your special superhero car," I say. "Whatever theme song you want to hear, I can play it. Whatever superhero color you want, I can change the lights at your command."

Her eyes widen in delight. "I want all of them!"

"Your wish is my command," I say, starting the superhero playlist.

When the first song booms across the speaker, she lowers her window so the wind catches her hair in a frantic tangle.

With the lights dancing in an otherworldly glow, it looks like we're floating across the dusky road.

"Are you ready for this?" I ask, adjusting my mirror so I can see Violet's enormous smile as she pulls down her mask.

"Yes!" she exclaims, then giggles. Even with my uncomfortable costume, seeing the happiness on her face makes this end-of-the-party surprise totally worth it.

But under the surface, there's something pulsing behind my chest, a tightness buckling under my rib cage.

I'm part of Violet's life now. But for how much longer?

Because no matter how I want to change things, I'm still leaving.

Who will be there for Violet and Maeve when I'm gone?

———

When we return from our drive, I inwardly cringe seeing Dex's car still parked outside the garage. *Will that guy ever leave?*

Violet jumps out of the car as I check my phone. It's almost seven, and I've got a red-eye to catch to California and a message from Mom with the cryptic words: *Call me before you leave.*

My responsibilities are piling up at once, but my conversation with Maeve is first priority.

I strip off my mask, run my fingers through my hair, and search for Maeve inside.

Violet has joined her grandparents in the backyard, where

they're still cleaning up red plastic cups and discarded plates from the party.

When I head upstairs, muffled voices come from Violet's newly decorated room. I stop outside the door and listen, frozen in the falling light.

"I want you to think about what I've asked," Dex says, and the tightness in my chest clamps harder, so I can hardly breathe.

I didn't mean to stumble on to this conversation, but right now, I can't seem to turn away. Surely, after everything that's happened between them, she won't go back to him.

"Maeve? What do you think about trying again?" Dex asks again. "At least consider it for Violet's sake."

There's a pause on the other side, and I don't understand why Maeve would even need to think about this.

Say no, Maeve.

My body tenses, and I'm torn between leaving now and busting down the door to stop her from making a huge mistake.

But no matter how much I want Maeve, the thing she wanted most was to reconcile with Dex and have a marriage like her parents'.

Am I going to ruin that for her? Walk in and demand she say no? Insist she follow me to California, where she'd be unhappy her entire life?

Maybe this *is* what she wants.

It all comes back to the question Brendan asked me earlier.

Is it fair to make Maeve wait for her happiness? Who am I to question what makes her happy?

Only she can decide that.

Because no matter how much I want to change things, I can't stay here and become the CEO of Oliver Financial or take care of Mom. My life has become a tug-of-war of family obligations, and my decisions aren't made in isolation.

Sometimes, we choose our own path in life. But sometimes, we're forced down a road we never wanted.

I can't ask Maeve to leave everything for me, because I know her life is here. If I ask her to make a life with me, I'm stealing the happiness she deserves.

I clench my hands into fists, squeezing hard. I want to bust down this door and stop her from making the biggest mistake of her life.

But what if I'm the biggest mistake of her life?

What if I'm the reason she isn't giving Dex an answer?

Maybe sacrificing my happiness is the best thing I can give Maeve. More than anything, she deserves a second chance at love.

I slowly turn away and head down the stairs silently, almost reaching the door when I hear a voice behind me.

"Are you leaving?" Violet asks.

I give her a soft smile. "Yes."

She stops in front of me. "Why do you look so sad?"

I bend down so that my gaze is level with hers and take her small hands in mine. "Because I'm going to California to find my new home."

"Can I come?" she asks, hopefully.

I shake my head. "Your mom needs you. But will you tell her something for me? Tell her goodbye and that . . ." I stop before I say it. *I wanted this family more than you know. I wanted us.*

She wraps her arms around my neck, her little face pressed into my shoulder. "I miss you already."

I put on what I hope is a confident smile, even though she's chipping away at the mask I'm using to cover my feelings.

"When I come back, I promise to play tea party, okay?" I say.

Her face lights up. "With dresses and crowns and a big ball, too?"

"With everything you could ever want," I say, tapping her nose gently. "By the way, your mom has one last surprise for you in your bedroom."

She smiles as I kiss her on the crown of her head before watching her run upstairs, my heart wrung out and full at the same time.

They say history repeats itself. But maybe it has to, when two people aren't meant to be together.

TWENTY-FIVE

Maeve

I cross my arms, wanting this conversation to be over, once and for all.

"At least consider my proposition," Dex pleads. "Over the weekend."

"It won't take that long," I shoot back. "My answer still stands." I turn to leave, but he catches my shoulder.

I made the mistake of showing Dex Violet's new superhero-themed room, and he turned it into an opportunity to confess his undying love to me, a fact I find ironic since he's had several *undying loves* this year.

After his fiancée left him (supposedly for another guy—an appropriate *reap what you sow* full-circle moment), Dex has been reduced to emotional groveling.

Right now, I'm annoyed by his cheap promises, but I'm also proud of my firm resistance. Because a few months ago, I would have been ecstatic to take him up on his offer. I would have leapt at the chance for another happily ever after, not seeing his repeated patterns of infidelity or how his love was *always* conditional.

I once believed a good wife should let her husband walk all

over her, because that's how you keep him in your life. In my case, I was a doormat that Dex used and discarded at his convenience.

But then Jack swept into my life and helped me trust again. He taught me that some men keep their promises. The difference between these two men couldn't be more stark.

But Dex refuses to accept defeat. He doesn't see that I'm no longer the woman he married. I've changed for the better, and I no longer need him to act as my hero, because I see him for who he really is.

"I'm not going until you consider my offer." Dex crosses his arms, daring me to leave.

I narrow my eyes. "Your offer? What is this—a used car deal? You never even apologized to me."

"Okay." He clears his throat. "I'm sorry?" He says it like a question, making me doubt that it's genuine.

"I'm working on forgiving you," I say. "It hasn't been easy, but I'm trying. But the answer to your offer is still no."

"But we could be a family again."

I roll my eyes, trying to push past him. "Until you find my next replacement."

"What? No!" he exclaims, grabbing my shoulder again.

I level my gaze. "Dex, it's over. I'm not the same person. And I definitely am not falling for this."

"What are you guys talking about?" Violet bursts into the bedroom, her eyes landing on the new decor. All week, I had her camping out in my bedroom so that I could surprise her with a new bedroom for her birthday.

"Is this my last birthday surprise?" she exclaims.

"How did you know?" I ask.

"Jack told me to ask you."

I slap my forehead. I totally forgot about Jack and the superhero-bedroom reveal. "Where is he? He should be here for this."

"You can't invite him," she says as she climbs onto her red-and-blue superhero comforter.

"Why not?"

"Because he left," she says while jumping on her bed. "For California."

He wouldn't leave without saying goodbye. Not Jack. I thought he was more excited about showing her this than anyone.

"Are you sure?"

"Yep," she says between jumps. "He told me to tell you goodbye."

But why didn't he tell me himself? That doesn't sound like Jack. A funny niggling feeling rises inside my stomach.

"How about your dad takes you downstairs to Grandma and Grandpa, and I'll be right back?"

I hand Violet off to a confused Dex and storm outside toward Jack's house. Even though I'm still wearing a catsuit, this conversation can't wait.

I rap on Jack's door and wait, ready to walk in if he doesn't answer. There's a long pause before Jack cracks the door, his eyes skirting over me. He's changed into joggers and a T-shirt, and his hair is messed up, like he's dragged his hand through it too many times.

Without fail, seeing Jack is like getting the wind knocked out of me. It always leaves me feeling out of breath.

"Hey," I say.

He averts his eyes and rubs the back of his neck. "I have a plane to catch."

Jack has always been the friendly golden retriever type. But now he's closed off, like a lid that's been snapped shut. It makes me want to knot my fists into his shirt to get his attention.

"You didn't even bother saying goodbye to me?" I ask.

His gaze darts somewhere distant. "It seemed like you were busy. And I have to go." A sharp edge to his voice splits the air. He leans down and slings a backpack over his shoulder. A rolling suitcase sits behind him. All signs of a quick departure.

Where's the superhero I just saw, the one playing tag in my

backyard and decorating his car for my birthday girl? He's been replaced by a cardboard cutout, a stiff replica of someone I used to know.

"I'm not too busy for goodbye, Jack."

He brushes by me toward his car. I look around for some way of keeping him here a few minutes longer. "Do you need help with George while you're gone?"

"Brendan's stopping by," he says over his shoulder.

"Any plants you need watered while you're gone? Want me to check anything? Baby squirrels nesting in the attic?" My attempt at humor falls flat.

"No," he says, loading bags into the car.

He doesn't even offer a crooked smile, and I suddenly feel desperate, like I've done something I don't know how to apologize for.

He circles the car, keys in his hand, avoiding me again.

"Jack, would you stop for a second?" I follow him, trying to hit pause on this moment that's rushing by me. "What's wrong? Is it the catsuit?"

"It's *not* the catsuit." He avoids looking at me as he swings open the door. Maybe he's trying to get used to how things will be once he leaves, when we go back to being distant acquaintances and we're no longer forced together by circumstances.

I block his way, planting my feet. "Jack, can I at least give you a hug before you go?"

He doesn't answer, his eyes darting away. "I need to go."

"Well, I'm doing it anyway." I wrap my arms around him, expecting our bodies to fall together the way they always do, like two puzzle pieces fitting together with a snap.

Instead, he stiffens under my touch, before he reluctantly skims the top of my hips with his palms, but only briefly, like he's afraid of holding on to me.

Maybe he's afraid of holding on to a future that doesn't exist, and this is the only way to let go.

I release him and step back.

"Why are you acting so weird?"

"There's nothing different," he says, meeting my eyes briefly before glancing away. "Except you in a catsuit."

I rip my mask off, hoping he can see it's me, the same old Maeve, the one who slow danced with him at a party and kissed him in a closet.

"I can tell. Something's off."

He lifts a shoulder. "I'm not good at saying goodbye." As if this explains his strange behavior.

Nobody is good at saying goodbye, I want to yell at him, *it breaks your heart, no matter how you try to protect yourself.*

I try not to think about what I'll do without Jack, but my brain circles over the problem relentlessly, even though I know he's already decided. *He wants this job more than he wants me.*

"It's not forever," I say more to myself than to him, and something shifts in his eyes.

A pained expression passes over his face, before he smiles weakly and brushes my cheek so tenderly, his thumb traces an imaginary line across my cheekbone, setting off sparks through my body.

Then he climbs into his car and holds up his hand, a final goodbye before he's gone.

It's only for a few days, but the niggling in my stomach isn't fading, and I'm worried that something isn't right.

We still haven't talked about what this means for us—whether there is any *us* left.

Is it selfish to want him to stay so we can spend more dinners on the roof and feed each other ice cream on hot nights? Is it wrong to wish I could see him spinning Violet in circles as her laughter echoes through our home?

Our home. The word spills out before I can stop it, rolling through my thoughts, like it's the most natural thing in the world.

But how could it be *our* home—a family with Jack, me, and Violet—without asking him to give up everything he's wanted? Without another thought, I shoot him a text.

Maeve: Violet's not the only one who's going to miss you.

Before I even reach home, he sends a reply, an answer I don't want to accept.

Jack: Don't wait for me.

But that's the thing, Jack. I'll always wait for you.

TWENTY-SIX

Maeve

I check my phone every few minutes to see if Jack has responded yet, and the screen mocks me with silence. I finally break down and text Brendan, even though it feels like I'm going behind Jack's back. Since they were hanging out during the party, maybe he can tell me what's going on with his friend.

Maeve: Was everything okay with Jack today?
Brendan: He didn't talk to you?
Maeve: About???

There's a long pause. Too long for my impatient mood.

Maeve: Brendan, what do you know?
Brendan: You need to talk to Jack.

Those cryptic words will keep me up all night if I don't get an answer. Because right now, my intuition tells me something's wrong, and I can't focus on anything else until I know what.

I glance at my watch. There's almost enough time to get to the airport, but I need Brendan to clue me into what's going on before I jump to conclusions.

I call Brendan, and it rings incessantly until it finally goes to voicemail. "I know you're there, Brendan. Pick up, please," I beg.

Then I call again and leave another voicemail. "Hey! I'm going to keep calling until you answer. So you might as well give up now."

After a third attempt, Brendan finally answers. "Please tell me you talked to Jack first, because it's not my place to say something."

"Jack is refusing to even acknowledge my existence," I say, sweeping my palm across my forehead.

"Why do you think I can help?"

"Because you know something I don't. And don't try to deny it."

"I really can't help you, Maeve."

"*Brendan,*" I say through gritted teeth. "Are you Jack's friend or not?"

He lets out a grunt. "If I tell you, promise me you won't tell Jack."

"I promise."

"Jack was planning on telling you . . ." He pauses, and I'm about to die inside, because every wasted second is a second I might lose if I have to chase down Jack.

"He wants a future with you," he says. "He was supposed to tell you today before this flight. But then Dex showed up, and I warned him he'd better get to you first."

"What does Dex have to do with this?" There's no way Jack would see Dex as a threat. Not anymore.

"Come on, Maeve, *think* about it. For months, you've been plotting to get Dex back and creating an elaborate dating scheme with Jack to do it."

"He wouldn't believe I'd go back to Dex. Not after Dex proved I can't trust him. It's over between us."

"Maeve, if he had any doubts, he'd be the last guy to stop you. That's how much he loves you. He'd give you up if he thought that was what you wanted, so you could be happy."

The words snip at my heart, tiny scissor cuts that gut me. He wanted my happiness over his. That's why he's avoiding me, acting like he doesn't care, so he can let go.

"No," I say, shaking my head, because I don't want to believe it. "Dex can't make me happy. Only Jack."

"But did you tell him that?"

As my brain flips through a mental replay of the last few weeks, I realize that every time I've tried to, I've fled from it, like my body was stuck in panic mode, running from the one thing that would make me happy because I was scared. *Afraid of not being chosen.* Just like before.

When I found out Jack was moving, I cut him off, convinced that he didn't want me because he chose a job over me.

I've literally paralyzed myself from doing *the* one thing that would've solved everything.

"I'm just scared, Brendan. When I found out he was moving to California, it triggered all my stupid fears. I was afraid of ending up alone."

Everything falls into place, the reasons I've been pushing Jack away, hoping these feelings will fade.

"Then you need to tell him that," Brendan says. "The sooner, the better."

"But if I tell him, it still doesn't change the fact that he's moving across the country."

"I know, but at least he'll know that Dex isn't the reason."

I swallow down the knot forming in my throat. "Okay," I say. "I'll have this conversation with him when he gets back."

"That's the other problem," Brendan says hesitantly. "Jack's not really coming back."

"I thought this was a quick trip." I knew my time with him was short, but I thought he'd be around for another month or two before moving.

"His dad said the company they bought was in such a mess, he should stay in California, and the company will move his stuff there. He's only coming back to sign papers for the sale of his home and pick up George. He told me this morning he already has an interested buyer."

"He's selling his home?" I can't believe he was going to sell his home without even warning me.

"Please understand, he did this for *you*. More than anything, he wants you to be happy. And he was willing to sacrifice his happiness by staying out of the way."

"What am I going to do?" I groan.

"There's only one thing you can do," he says. "Get to the airport as quickly as possible."

I roll my eyes. "I can't just run to the airport. I've got a kid at home and a party to clean up . . ." I glance out the window to the backyard, where Violet is playing with her birthday balloons as my parents clean up. It's not surprising that Dex seems to have mysteriously disappeared. Then I remember what Mom told me in the kitchen yesterday. Happiness starts with the right person.

My fear of being rejected and ending up alone has kept me from trying again. But even if I know there is no happily ever after the way I once believed, I can't give up my one shot at telling Jack the truth.

"Maeve, are you still there?" Brendan asks.

"I need to go. I'm heading to the airport to talk to Jack before he leaves. If I'm not too late."

I hang up, grab my purse, and ask my parents to watch Violet. They both look at each other in confusion as I kiss Violet's tousled hair.

"I'll be back soon, baby girl. I promise."

I don't even know what I'm going to say when I reach him. But if I think too hard, I'll destroy any confidence I had. I can't let him leave without talking to him, without taking a chance on *us*, and letting the cards fall as they may.

Violet wraps her arms around one leg. "Are you going to ask him to stay? Because I don't want him to go."

"I'll try."

She looks up at me, expectantly. "He can't say no to Catwoman."

I catch my reflection in the sliding glass door, the sharp outline of shiny black vinyl surprising me. Under normal circumstances, I'd change back into regular clothes, but now there's no time.

Maybe Violet's right. If it requires wearing this costume, then I'll do it.

As I head out the door, I frantically text Annie, explaining the whole misunderstanding with Jack.

Maeve: What should I do?

Her reply is almost instant: *Don't let him go a second time.*

TWENTY-SEVEN

Maeve

I run to my car and pray it starts. Unlike most superhero vehicles—which are sleek futuristic contraptions—my ancient family sedan sounds like a grumpy old man wheezing to catch his last breath.

"Don't fail me now," I beg, screeching out of the driveway, narrowly missing the mailbox, *again*.

When I finally reach the airport, I jam the car into park, and sprint toward the airport terminal, thankful I mistakenly put on running shoes instead of heels. A few travelers glance at me oddly while others stare, but I don't care that I look like I'm headed to a cosplay convention. All I care about now is finding Jack.

As I hustle into the terminal, I suddenly realize I don't know anything about Jack's flight details, including the airline he was flying with, which means I'll have to check all of them.

I dash past each airline counter, searching for Jack and coming up empty.

"You headed to Comic-Con?" one guy asks. I shake my head, but don't stop running. A little boy points at me and shouts, "Look, Mom, can I get my picture with her?"

As I reach the end of the airport desks, I realize Jack is probably already in line for security. Once he's cleared that point, my search is over. Because I can't get past TSA without having a ticket.

I swing around and sprint toward the security line. "Please let it be insanely long," I mutter, in what's probably the only time I'll ever wish for a long TSA wait.

I sprint to the security line and am met with an answered prayer: a huge line snakes around a maze of retractable belts. The queue is so deep that it's hard to see the people toward the front, and there's no way of reaching the front of the line.

I text Jack that I'm at the airport and need to talk to him, and an automated response immediately flashes on my screen: *Notifications are silenced.*

He's turned his phone on *do not disturb*, probably because he's determined to leave, thinking he's doing what's best for everyone.

I skirt the outside of the line, my gaze searching for Jack, knowing this is my last shot. Then I circle around the side, hoping to catch the sharp cut of his jaw or the clingy white T-shirt and joggers he's wearing. In this crowd, there are dozens of guys dressed like him, and it seems like half of them have beards. I strain to catch him, running along the queue as people glance my way.

"Jack, where are you?" I mumble under my breath, my stomach clenching as I reach the end of the line. Something hollow presses inside my chest.

Jack's gone.

I grasp the dividing belt at the end of the line, hoping it can prop me up.

Then something familiar catches my eye, the tousled hair I know so well, and I rise on my tiptoes to confirm it's him. Even from here, the sharp outline of his beard reminds me of how it feels to run my fingers across his jawline.

He's on the farthest side of the queue from me. If I run

around to the other side, he might see me before he makes the next turn, but only if I hurry.

That's the thing about airport lines. It's an efficient method for herding travelers, but I feel like I'm stuck in a version of the *Maze Runner*.

I sprint along the outskirts of the line, my feet throbbing, trying to catch Jack before he makes the next turn in the queue.

"Jack!" I yell. Several people in line shoot me curious looks, except for the person I want to turn around. Just as I reach the closest spot, he shifts around the rope's curve and heads the other way. I groan, pivoting quickly and run in the opposite direction.

"Jack! Over here!" I say louder, waving my hands like an idiot. Why didn't I bring a giant sign with his name? An obnoxious noisemaker? Anything that would catch his attention—and possibly get me arrested.

Instead, I get annoyed looks from strangers. Meanwhile, Jack continues staring at his phone, entranced by whatever is on the screen.

"Jack!" I yell, again, even though it's hopeless.

He trudges ahead through the line, oblivious to me, and then I see why. His earbuds are in, and he's listening to something other than the din of the airport. There's no way he'll hear me unless I'm practically next to him, tapping on his shoulder.

"Who are you trying to reach?" an older man in line asks.

I point toward Jack. "He's wearing a white T-shirt, toward the front of the line." Which is the least helpful answer I could give, since dozens of guys are wearing white T-shirts and are in the first half of the line. "He's a thirty-year-old guy with a beard and head-phones." Dozens of guys fit that description too, but at least it's more specific than my earlier comment.

"How about him?" He points to the wrong guy, and I shake my head. "That guy?" *Wrong again.* The woman next to him joins in the search, but I'm still having no luck.

It's like playing *Where's Waldo?* without the singular red-and-white hat. Jack blends in like a chameleon. And with this many people, it's too hard to point him out quickly.

I finally shake my head, realizing I'm getting nowhere.

"I need a different tactic. Like a louder voice," I say.

"Would this help?" A college girl behind the old man pulls out a small megaphone from her carry-on.

I frown. "It's weird you have that, but okay."

"I'm a college cheerleader," she says. "Headed to a game. But you can borrow it."

"Thanks!" I say, taking the megaphone and praying it works. At the very least, let's hope I don't get arrested before Jack sees me.

"What's it for?" she asks, while we both scoot along the moving line.

For once, I decide not to hide behind a vague answer. If I'm going to be brave in this new chapter of my life, I might as well start now.

"I'm stopping the man I love from leaving," I reply with a shy grin. "If I can get to him in time." Even though I'm twelve years too late, I won't forgive myself if I don't try.

Her face breaks into a wide smile as she places a hand on her heart. "That's beautiful. And so brave."

"Or stupid," I counter.

"Not at all," she says, shaking her head. "I wish I were as brave as you."

Her eyes catch mine, and I realize I'm looking at a mirror image of myself twelve years ago, seeing all the things I missed because I was afraid of fighting for Jack then. "Even when you're not brave, sometimes life gives you second chances." Then I touch her arm.

"Good luck!" she calls, moving away as the line snakes forward. "I hope it all works out!"

"Me too," I whisper under my breath.

During our brief conversation, I took my eyes off Jack, and now he's almost to the front of the line, where the TSA agent checks your ticket. Even if he hears me calling, I'm too short for him to see over this crowd.

I glance around and notice a small construction scaffold blocking a newly painted wall. There's yellow caution tape roped around it to keep people off, but since I'm about to get kicked out of the airport anyway, I might as well make it epic.

Looking around for any security guards, I duck under the yellow tape and step one foot on the first rung of the scaffold.

I'm about to do something that's either very stupid or going to change my life.

I monkey-climb up the scaffold, holding a megaphone while trying not to fall. It won't take long for someone to report me, so I climb faster, looking over my shoulder at Jack, who's almost reached the TSA agent.

When I finally reach the top, I climb onto the platform, then slowly rise to standing.

One shot is all I get. Better make it count.

"Jack Oliver," I call through the megaphone. Everyone beneath me slowly turns to find my voice. "If you leave now, I will never let you eat ice cream at my place again." Jack lifts his head, slowly wheeling around like he's in a slow-motion sequence.

A strange surge of confidence pushes through me. "And I definitely won't kiss you again in any closets. Because we both know how that experiment ended."

Jack drags his gaze to where I'm standing and his mouth falls open slightly. I can't tell if he's shocked or embarrassed, but I've got only seconds to complete this grand gesture.

"Whatever you do, please don't leave," I say. "At least give me the chance to talk to you."

Blasting my confession over a megaphone wasn't quite the romantic scenario I originally imagined, but since I've already fallen down the black hole of ridiculous choices, I might as well finish. "I'm not letting you leave without saying that I love you. I mean, I'm standing on a scaffold in a catsuit, probably about to get hauled out of here by airport security. If that doesn't prove how crazy in love I am with you, I don't know what will."

He shakes his head as his lips curl into a crooked smile, like he's amused by my insane gesture.

"Excuse me, sir," the TSA agent next to him says. "I need you to move through the line. Or step out and address this woman."

The agent's words break the spell Jack's been under, and he pushes his way through the line, moving backward against the sea of people until he reaches the end of the line and climbs under the belt between us.

Then he walks toward me, not even watching where he's going because he's staring up at me.

As he reaches the edge of the scaffolding where I'm standing twenty feet above him, he says, "This had better be good, because I'm going to miss my flight."

"I know, Jack. But it's better than missing what could have been." Then I smile, and my heart swells like it's about to burst, because I'm not afraid anymore. Not afraid of rejection. Or of getting kicked out of here. Or even confessing my love in front of hundreds of strangers.

"By the way, you're still talking through the megaphone," Jack says with a smirk.

I put the megaphone to my mouth one last time. "I wanted to make sure you heard me LOUD AND CLEAR. I love you, Jack."

Jack laughs, and I'm grinning like a fool, because I've already made myself one for love.

He drops his bag to the floor. "Are you going to make me climb up there and kiss you?"

"Let me think about that," I say, not having to think at all. I drop the megaphone and nod. Without missing a beat, he scales the scaffolding in a few seconds. When he reaches me, he wraps his arms around my waist and pulls me close, just like every superhero rescue I've ever seen. Then he dips his head and kisses me gently, but passionately, like there aren't hundreds of spectators watching us.

For a moment, the world dissolves; there's only him and me and a murky but hopeful future.

It's not until he pulls away, leaving me wanting more—so much more—that I realize there's a softness in his face, a confession unfolding in his eyes. "I want you, Maeve. I want *us*."

A crooked grin hitches up the corner of his mouth, right before airport security arrives.

TWENTY-EIGHT

Jack

After Maeve and I got hauled out of the airport by security, where we received a stern warning to take our public displays of affection outside, we headed to the beach to talk over the details, and kiss, and talk about our future, and kiss some more.

You might say we kissed more than talked (and that would be true), but it all seemed necessary—the kissing and the talking. Which means I now have sand in my hair and sore lips, because that's what happens when you have serious discussions at the beach.

Even though Dex is no longer an issue, we still haven't figured out what to do about my move to California with Maeve staying here. Because now that we're together, I don't want to wait more than twenty-four hours between kisses.

So we stuck our toes in the sand, held hands, and hashed out a very scary, but absolutely necessary, exit plan from my new job. Since it was already late, we decided to tell everyone first thing in the morning, starting with my mom.

Of the many conversations I'm going to have today, this will be the easiest, because of Mom's unwavering support. I know the news will delight Mom, but that doesn't erase the uncertainty she'll have about her future.

Only after that can I face my dad. Because it's not going to be long before he figures out that I never made it to California last night.

"It might be best if you wait here," I tell Maeve as we enter Mom's long-term care facility. Maeve sits on a loveseat in the foyer as I make the trek down to Mom's room.

When I enter, bright sunlight fills her room, highlighting a vase of daisies in the window. "I thought you were going to California," she says.

"My plans changed."

Talk about the understatement of the year.

I slide into the chair next to her bed. "I have some big news to share." I pause, wondering the best way to explain this and decide to get to the point. "I'm not moving to California anymore. I've decided to stay here."

Her eyes widen. "Stay? Why?"

"Maeve and I want to make our relationship work. But she doesn't want to move to California—her family's here. You're here. And I know you weren't thrilled about moving."

Mom pauses, considering this change of plans. "I wasn't, but I thought you wanted to lead the company. I was willing to make the sacrifice for you."

"But you've always made the sacrifice. And truthfully, this is where I belong. I want to build a life here with Maeve."

"How did your father take the news?" she asks, visibly concerned.

"I haven't told him yet. But I'm going to be honest with him. I thought getting the CEO position would earn his approval, that somehow, this would make me the better son. But getting this job doesn't change anything between us. If Dad can't accept me for who I am, taking the job won't fix that. Nothing will."

Mom nods slowly, taking in this news. "He won't be happy

about this. But I'm proud of you, Jack." She reaches for me, taking my hand in hers and giving it a gentle squeeze. "I always wanted you to discover who you could be on your own. What happens if he gives Craig the CEO position?"

"I'm still figuring that out. I don't want to work for Craig—that's already been decided. Maeve has encouraged me to start my own business."

"In finance?"

"I'm ready to take a break from spreadsheets and financial projections. My dream has always been to start a wildlife nonprofit for local animal rescues, but I never had time to do it while working for Dad. Since it's going to take a while to build up the donor base, I'll do financial consulting privately on the side. And Maeve has her teaching job. So once we make this official—"

"Do you mean what I think you mean?" she interjects, and I realize I'm getting ahead of myself.

"Maeve and I will figure it out, even though it's financially risky. I don't want you to worry about your future. We'll take care of you, no matter what."

Mom gives me a soft grin. "Oh, Jack, I'm not worried. That's why I tried to contact you yesterday."

In the craziness of the party and everything that happened after, I forgot about Mom's message to call her.

She grabs a paper from her side table and holds it out to me. "I got this in the mail."

I take the letter and scan the information. "The appeal from the insurance company?"

She nods.

Buried in the first paragraph is the insurance company's decision to approve our appeal. "They accepted it?" I say, a weight rising from my chest.

"Yes," Mom says. "It won't pay for everything, but it will help."

It means I don't have to worry about how to scrape together

the needed funds for Mom's care, and it gives me confidence to face Dad later today.

"And Maeve? What does she think of all this?" Mom asks.

"Why don't you ask her yourself?" I say, then I step out into the hall, waving for her to join me.

As she enters, I grab her hand, and we walk in together. This time, we're not putting on a show. It's just us. The same *us* we were in high school—friends first, then something more, but always friends.

As we spend the morning talking, Maeve is every bit as thoughtful and loving with my mom as I expected. And it's not until this conversation that I see how alike they are—two determined women who've forged their way as single moms. When the subject of Maeve's fixer-upper comes up, Maeve shows Mom pictures from the birthday party—the new landscaping and swing set in the backyard, the freshly painted walls and secondhand decor finally making it feel like home, and Violet's superhero room—all proof that with a little work, even a fixer-upper can be something beautiful.

"It's a work in progress," Maeve says about her home, showing off the last picture of the superhero room.

"Kind of like me," I say.

Maeve shoots me a look. "Not just you. *Me.* All of us." She pauses, looking at the picture once more. "Relationships are a work in progress. We learn to fall in love with each version of the person we're with because that's what love is about. Learning to love someone as they change."

Then she glances at me with a soft smile, and I know that no matter what happens, Maeve will stand by me.

As we drive over to Dad's house, Maeve looks at me anxiously. "Are you sure you don't want me to come inside with you? I'm not afraid of your family. I'm pretty sure I could take your stepmom in a wrestling match."

I laugh. "Now, I'd pay to see *that.*"

"But seriously, I'll go with you. Even for moral support."

I shake my head. "I need to do this myself. But I'll call for backup if I need you. Deal?"

She nods, then reaches over and kisses me on the cheek.

As I walk into my family's home, I know exactly where my father will be. Even though it's the weekend, he'll be in his office, finishing up a few details for work during his off hours.

As I turn down the hall toward his home office, Craig walks into the hall, and his eyebrows lift, like they're about to fly off his face. "I thought you were out west. Plane get canceled?"

"Nope," I say, striding past him. I don't even ask why he's there, but it's probably because Dad asked him to help. "Is Dad in?"

"What do you want to talk to Dad about?" Craig asks, frowning.

"None of your business." I give him a tight smile as I reach for the door.

Craig rushes between me and the door, barring the way. "You can't go in. He's busy."

"Watch me." I push him out of the way and barge into Dad's home office.

Dad looks up from behind his computer, surprised. "Jack? What are you doing here? I thought you were in California?"

"I'm here to give you my official resignation," I say without waiting. "I don't want to move to California. I'm staying here with Maeve and Mom, and unless there's a way to do that in this town, then I'm out."

He pauses, absorbing this precipitous change of plans I've just lobbed at him like a live grenade. "I thought you *wanted* to be CEO? That means sacrificing for the job. California *is* that sacrifice."

I let out a humorless laugh. "Who are we kidding, Dad? I've always made sacrifices. You want me to be the guy to clean up that other company's mess. Because I'm good at being *that* guy, the one who fixes things for you. But I will not clean up your messes any more. Craig can do that."

He tightens his lips before responding. "What do you want from me? More money? A bigger house?"

"You're asking me what I want—after thirty years with you?" I ask in wonder. "When I was little, I wanted you to play ball in the backyard with me. I wanted your attention when I had a bad day at school. I wanted you to laugh with Mom, to live like an actual family, instead of treating us like a burden. And when I graduated, I wanted to hear you say three words: *Good job, son.* Instead, I spent my entire life trying to earn them and feeling like I never had. I thought getting the job as CEO would finally mean I'd earned something from you. That you'd finally say those words. But now, I realize I haven't earned anything."

I pause, taking in his shocked face, the realization of everything he's lost over the years. "Is that everything you want to tell me?" he finally says.

"No," I say, the emotion ballooning inside me. "I want, more than anything, to be a great dad and husband. And I will become that man, because I've decided there are more important things than being CEO."

I turn to go.

"But you can't quit," he says. "You're still my son."

I wheel around to face him. "You're right. I can't quit being your son. But I'm not sure you ever treated me as one."

As I turn to leave, he stands. I pause, unsure if he's attempting to make one final offer, even though I've already decided.

"Just so you know . . ." he says, uncomfortably. "I am proud of you. I'm just not good at saying it."

"I know," I murmur. I probably always have, but I needed to hear it.

I pass Craig on the way out and give him a wave. "Enjoy California," I tell him, realizing how much my stepmom is going to hate this.

He frowns. "But I'm not going to California."

I smile. "You are now," I mutter under my breath.

When I reach the car, Maeve pauses, waiting for an explanation. "How'd it go?" she finally asks.

I smile, then take her face in my hands and kiss her lips.

It's the only answer I know how to give.

Epilogue

MAEVE

A year later

I open the oven door and take out the hot chocolate chip cookies from the oven. The chocolate is pooling into brown lava puddles, and Violet leans in close for a whiff. "Can I have one?"

"You know these are for Grandpa and Grandma as payment for babysitting you tonight so I can go out with Jack."

She frowns. "But I watch Grandpa more than he watches me. Last time, he fell asleep in the armchair, and that's after I helped him find everything for my peanut butter sandwich."

Sounds like Dad.

"Then Grandma told me I was big enough to make my own sandwich, so Grandpa handed me the knife and I scooped on extra jelly and it squished out the sides when I ate it."

No wonder I believed I could fix up my house like all the home renovation shows. Blazing your own path seems to be what my family excels at.

"Why isn't Jack here yet?" Mom says, coming inside with a watering can. Ever since I turned my backyard jungle into an actual yard with bushes and plants, she's kept my flowers alive.

I check my watch. "It's for a good reason. He's got a meeting with a new donor for his nonprofit."

The nonprofit has turned out to be Jack's *thing*—something that lights him up more than investments and spreadsheets ever did. While he's building the nonprofit, he's gained dozens of new clients for his financial consulting business, all of them disgruntled former clients of Oliver Financial.

It turns out, Oliver Financial is the one struggling under Craig's new leadership.

After Jack backed out last year, Craig was forced to move to California, which made Jack's stepmother livid. She couldn't accept that Craig was so far away, since she was the one who originally orchestrated the arrangement to have Craig stay in Sully's Beach and move Jack out of town. When Jack ruined her plan, she took it out on his dad and demanded he move the entire company back or she'd leave him.

When he refused, and their relationship imploded, Elizabeth left Donald, moving to California to join Craig and Charis.

I can't say I'm too sorry about this.

But for Jack's dad, the results have been shocking. On more than one occasion, Donald has accepted my invitation for dinner and seems surprisingly content to hang out with us in my fixer-upper. Maybe it's because he's no longer pressured by his ex-wife. Or perhaps he's finally taking Jack's accusation seriously and trying to make up for lost time. For once, he's trying to be a father to Jack with no expectations tied to it. They don't mention the business anymore. And Jack's dad has even pushed Violet on the swing set—something that surprised even me.

Though Jack has every reason not to give his dad a second chance, he's letting him be part of his life again, and this is a shock to Jack more than anyone.

Violet comes around the corner, her eyes bright.

"Mom, come look outside!"

"In a minute. I want to run upstairs and change before Jack gets here."

"No, you can't wait. There isn't time."

She drags me to the screen door where I see Jack parking his shiny black car. He's got the superhero lights on again and the windows are down, with the *Batman* theme song playing. He's even wearing the mask and cape.

"The meeting must have gone well," I say to myself with a smile.

Dad walks up behind me. "Don't keep your superhero waiting."

I head outside and lean in through the open window. "You didn't tell me this was a cosplay date."

"I figured since you showed up at the airport in a catsuit, the least I could do was become your favorite hero for tonight."

"You remembered?" Until now, I'd forgotten I told Jack I wanted a man who could be the hero for the woman he loves. I hadn't actually meant in a costume, but I should have guessed Jack would put his own spin on it.

He smiles. "When it comes to you, *I don't forget.*"

"Where are we headed?"

"Oh, you'll see," he says mysteriously, then opens the car door for me.

As he blasts his superhero playlist, we drive to the beach by Ella and Grant's house, where we had the Twister party last year. As he parks in Grant's drive, I glance around, expecting to see some of Jack's friends waiting for us, but it's strangely quiet.

"Are we going to the beach?" I ask. "I didn't dress for swimming."

He looks down at his black costume. "This costume isn't waterproof, but I hope you won't be too disappointed, because I'm headed inside to change and pick up a few things."

He rushes off, and after a few minutes, comes out with a picnic basket and a blanket slung over one arm. Offering his hand, he leads me down a path toward the beach, the same path we walked the night of Grant's party.

"Does this look familiar?" he asks.

"Grant's party last year. How could I forget?"

"Yes, but before that," he says.

I tilt my head. "Wait . . . this isn't where we lay under the stars in high school and had our first kiss?"

Jack's crooked smile answers for me. "I kept waiting for you to bring it up on the night of Grant's party. When you didn't, I thought you didn't remember."

I shake my head and give him a look. "I wouldn't forget that." Even thinking about it now—his lips finding mine so tenderly that first time, the way he made me feel, my body heats like a lit match.

"The reason I brought you here in high school was because I was friends with Grant. His granny and gramps owned the place back then. I knew she wouldn't kick us off the beach after night-fall. If anything, she was probably placing bets on whether I kissed you." He chuckles, shaking his head at the memory as he stretches a blanket on the sand. "I've thought about that kiss so many times since. That's why the night of the Twister party was difficult. Here we were pretending to date, and all I could think about was how I wanted to replay the kiss from that night."

"You wanted to kiss me then?"

"More than anything. Remember the bet I won from Twister? I almost asked you that night. But it was too soon. You'd gone through too much, and I didn't want to risk it."

"Thanks for being so patient with me."

"You were worth the wait," he says, kneeling down next to me, his gaze roving over my face.

The wind, whipping my hair into tangles, smells like salty earth. Jack nudges me to move between his legs, our bodies folding together as we watch the waves. From behind, he wraps his arms around my waist and rests his chin on my shoulder. "After high school, I wanted so badly to call you again, to see if there was some hope of us being friends . . . and eventually, something more. But I was afraid of too many things—what my dad would say, you getting hurt by my family because I was too selfish to let you go. But after all this time, I couldn't stop thinking of you." He pauses, snuggling me closer as he thinks about the past. "When I found out you were married, I thought I'd lost my one chance. I let you slip through my fingers, and now I was going to have to accept that."

I lean back into his chest, his hands circling my body, folding me into him. "Sometimes we get a second chance at happiness, Jack. We might not understand the timing or why we had to go through so much, but in the end, you were worth the wait."

He kisses the side of my cheek, his lips brushing my ear, sending hot waves down my neck. "Does this mean I get a second chance at cashing in my winning bet from Twister?"

"Depends on what you're asking for," I say.

He reaches inside the picnic basket, and for a moment, I'm confused about why he's suddenly hungry for dinner instead of stealing a kiss, which I'm only too glad to give him.

But when he turns, I discover he hasn't grabbed a sandwich at all. He's holding a small velvet box as he moves to get on one knee.

"I'm asking you to be my wife," he says. "If you'll have me."

I cover my mouth with my hand, too overwhelmed to speak, before realizing he's waiting for my answer. I nod, trying to hold the tears back before they spill out over everything.

"Yes," I say, barely able to find my voice. "I'd love to be your wife."

He pulls out the ring, a simple circular diamond that glitters in the light, before he slips it on my finger. That's when I hear the cheering behind me. I turn suddenly to find that Grant, Ella, Mia, Jaz, and Brendan are all standing on Grant's deck, watching this moment, waiting to celebrate with us. Even Annie is here.

"They were in on it too?" I say, waving to them, realizing they were hiding the whole time.

Jack laughs. "You think the girls would miss this for the world? They helped me plan the whole thing. They even packed the picnic basket and made sure I had the ring. They love you,

Maeve. And they can't wait to plan your wedding shower, your baby showers, and every shower for the rest of your life."

I lift an eyebrow. "You're getting ahead of yourself, Mr. Oliver. We're not ready to talk about siblings for Violet until *after* the wedding."

"I look forward to that," he says, nuzzling my ear, his hands sliding down the curve of my waist, even though our friends are all watching.

"We can discuss this . . . later," I murmur, my body melting like hot caramel under his touch.

"But I'm not interested in *discussing* it," he says, kissing the weak spot by my earlobe. "I'm more of a hands-on guy."

"You know what that means, right? We're going to have a houseful of kids."

He bursts out laughing, a wildly exuberant sound that fills me with so much joy.

"That sounds good," he agrees. "If it's what you want. I can't imagine my life without Violet. And I always wanted a full house."

I blush, feeling a flutter in my stomach at the thought. "In our little fixer-upper?"

"Maeve, I want to give you everything." Then he takes my hand and kisses the back of it, featherlight. "White picket fence and all. I can't promise a perfect life. We both know there is no such thing as happily ever after. But you make me happier than anyone. And that is enough for me."

As he wraps me in his arms, I finally realize it. Love never leaves us how we once were.

Life may not have given me a happy ending the first time, but it gave me a second chance with Jack. And that's so much better than I ever could have imagined.

THE END

———

GET THE NEXT BOOK IN THE SERIES!

The Mistletoe Makeover
A Christmas romcom with Mia and Jace

He's a country rock star. She's an out-of-work event planner. A town mistletoe festival brings them together... but their secret crushes might make this a Christmas they'll never forget.

Order The Mistletoe Makeover on Amazon!

Not ready for Christmas yet?
Get Jaz and Brax's story in *The Roommate Remodel*.
A hockey romance that introduces you to the Carolina Crushers hockey team
Get The Roommate Remodel on Amazon.

FREE BONUS EPILOGUE
Don't miss this bonus epilogue for *The Second Chance Fixer Upper* featuring Maeve and Jack and their unexpected baby news!

Sign up at graceworthington.com

The Mistletoe Makeover

Sneak Peek
Book 3 in the Renovation Romance Series

He's the hottest country rock star in the country whose reputation needs repaired.

I'm an unemployed event planner who's desperate for a job.

When I'm forced to team up with Mr. Smolder for the most ambitious Christmas event around, it might be my biggest mistake yet...

For me, Christmas has never been the most wonderful time of year. It's a painful reminder of my father walking out and my whole family's world crashing down. After that, I never really believed in a happily ever after.

Right now, I've got my hands full giving my hometown Christmas festival a much-needed makeover, while trying to convince Jace Knight (aka: Mr. Smolder) to headline a concert for the event.

It's an uphill battle to wrangle the festival committee and turn the town into quaint Christmas village, while I ignore these feelings that involve mistletoe kisses with the famous music star.

The last time someone tried to kiss me under the mistletoe, it was a total disaster.

Which is why I'm not about to let Jace Knight work his mistletoe magic on me now...especially since I'm hiding a secret: *I've never been kissed before.*

JACE

I moved to Maplewood with one thing in mind: to escape a very ugly public breakup. I don't care if people think I'm a grumpy recluse, I just want to be alone after the year I've had.

Yet, when circumstances force me to agree to a concert for the Maplewood Mistletoe Festival, I'm surprised to find an unexpected connection with Mia MacPherson...and offer her a job as my personal assistant.

It's a win-win situation for us both...until we get stranded together during a freak snow storm.

Now we're forced to navigate our differences, while pulling off the biggest Christmas festival ever. Oh, and figure out how to hide our intense chemistry for each other.

No problem, right?

Not when there's mistletoe everywhere....and every logical reason why we shouldn't fall in love.

But whoever said love is logical, especially at Christmas?

This closed door rom com has all of the holiday fun and none of the spice.

Tropes:

• celebrity romance

• never been kissed

• forced proximity

• grumpy/sunshine vibes

• snowed in with one bed

Perfect for those who love closed door Christmas romance books!

Get The Mistletoe Makeover on Amazon!

Acknowledgments

I want to express my enormous gratitude to you for reading this book! Your support, encouragement, and unwavering belief in the power of love and laughter have been the driving force behind why I write.

Just like Jack and Maeve's story, I believe that life is a journey filled with ups and downs. We all wish we could set up in Camp Best of Times, rather than Camp Worst of Times for obvious reasons. Yet, it is in Camp Worst of Times where we discover our true selves and the capacity for growth.

I like writing characters who stumble, make mistakes, and face hardships. They are flawed and imperfect, just like each of us. Yet, they also embody the resilience and hope that comes with second chances. It is my wish that their journeys inspire you to believe in the power of redemption and second chances.

I hope these pages have reminded you that love is a beautiful adventure worth embarking on, no matter which camp you're living in right now.

———

It takes a village to publish a book and I would be remiss if I didn't thank my fabulous team. An enormous thanks goes to my editor, Emily Poole and my proofreader, Judy Zweifel, as well as Claire Taylor and her amazing feedback on this story.

Joy and Heidi—I'm so grateful for your help reading the early draft of this book! Your insights are always spot on.

Thank you to Alt 19 Creative for the incredible cover design and illustrations.

Huge hugs to my two kids and especially my husband, Sam. Life with you in our fixer upper has been the sweetest love story. Thanks for always being the first reader of my books and my biggest fan.

Also by Grace Worthington

All books are standalone novels with interconnected characters.
You can read these in any order that makes you happy!

THE RENOVATION ROMANCE ROMCOMS

The Neighbor Renovation

The Second Chance Fixer Upper

The Mistletoe Makeover

The Roommate Remodel (Start here for hockey romance!)

PERFECT CRUSH HOCKEY ROMANCE

Perfectly Wedded

Perfectly Faked

Perfectly Grumpy

THE WILD HARBOR BEACH SERIES

Love at Wild Harbor

Summer Nights in Wild Harbor

Christmas Wishes in Wild Harbor

The Inn at Wild Harbor

A Wedding in Wild Harbor

BOXSET COLLECTIONS

The Wild Harbor Beach Collection

Check out Grace's entire backlist here.

Grace Worthington is a three-time award-winning author who lives and breathes sweet romcoms.

A former musical theatre gal and playwright, she brings that same energy, heart, and comedic timing to her stories, crafting witty banter and lovable characters you can't help but root for.

She holds a master's degree in psychology and human development and has also completed graduate studies in creative writing. Her inspiration comes from charming coastal towns and classic romcoms from the '80s and '90s.

When she's not writing, she enjoys spending time with her husband and two kids.

Follow Grace on Amazon to be notified of future releases or follow Grace on Instagram.

———

FREE ROMCOM NOVELLA

Get a free novella or bonus epilogues at graceworthing-
ton.com

www.ingramcontent.com/pod-product-compliance
Lightning Source LLC
Chambersburg PA
CBHW070452300726
48975CB00007B/2144